Critical Praise

"*Spindle Lane* is an ingenious time travel machine. The imagery is so vivid and the narrative so realistic that they instantly transported me into the story's world. I was right there with the characters, experiencing their terror and desperation as if it were my own. A writer's job is to make the story so compelling that the words disappear, and Reefe has done that job magnificently. *Spindle Lane* devoured me mind, heart, and soul, plopping me back into the days of my youth with a delicious demonic twist I'll savor for years to come. Ray Bradbury would be proud indeed. Kudos and bravo. Highly recommended."

— Kerry Alan Denney, multiple award-winning author of *Soulsnatcher* and *Jagannath*

"With *Spindle Lane*, Mark Reefe has gifted us with Chris, a teenage boy of the best and geekiest possible variety. Chris's summer begins promisingly enough, but nose dives into a morass of soul-threatening evil once he realizes the true nature of his friendly, pipe-smoking neighbor.

Given the choice between sacrificing his soul to an old, powerful demon, or watching his brother and sister and friends die horrible, grisly deaths one after the other, Chris chooses to risk everything. Armed with the very best of friends, and all the cleverness and ten-foot-tall-and-(secretly terrified but)-bulletproof courage that teenaged boyhood is uniquely endowed, Chris and his band of brothers attempt to upset the Goatman's applecart for good.

But old demons are cunning and treacherous, and temptation has felled older and wiser warriors than Chris. For all his friends and their bravery, he may be his own worst enemy. Reefe's portrayal of Chris and his brother rings absolutely true, and little sister Katie is glorious and cringeworthily hilarious, especially when she's borrowed by a minor demon to be a part time spy. Reefe's flashback to the 70's is spot on, and once again, his characters are doing battle for their souls.

Don't miss *Spindle Lane*, it's a hoot, a delight and as always, a soul-affirming read."

—Sarah Dale, author of *Something Wicked* and *Something Haunted*

"Reefe never fails to bring the characters to life."

— S.L. Kerns, author of *The Rut*

Spindle Lane

Spindle Lane

Mark Reefe

Apprentice
House Press
Loyola University Maryland

First Edition

Casebound ISBN: 978-1-62720-304-3
Paperback ISBN: 978-1-62720-305-0
Ebook ISBN: 978-1-62720-306-7

Printed in the United States of America

Design by Isabella De Palma
Editorial development by Isabella De Palma
Promotion plan by Justus Croyle

Apprentice
House Press
Loyola University Maryland

Apprentice House Press
Loyola University Maryland
4501 N. Charles Street
Baltimore, MD 21210
410.617.5265
www.ApprenticeHouse.com
info@ApprenticeHouse.com

This book is dedicated to the S-Section Crew.
No one would believe the real story,
so I had to make this one up.

"A dreamer is one who can only find his way by moonlight, and his punishment is that he sees the dawn before the rest of the world."

- Oscar Wilde

Chapter 1

June 2, 1978

It was a risky move, but the sun was almost touching the horizon, and I was less than thirty minutes away from being grounded for the rest of my sorry excuse for a life. I exhaled and with one bold gulp downed what remained of my Slurpee. Icy claws tickled my temples as a cherry flavored avalanche rushed down my throat. Raising a hand to my head, I grimaced in anticipation of the brain freeze sure to follow. A couple of seconds passed before I started counting off in my head. At ten elephant I stopped. Nothing. Nada. No ice pick through the eye or alien hatchling bursting out of my forehead. Guess I dodged a bullet on that one.

Tossing the empty cup in the trash can outside the 7-Eleven, I planted a foot on the pedal of my silver and blue Team Murray BMX—or the Blue Beast as I cleverly dubbed it—and pushed off. I weaved and whizzed between rows of parked cars and shopping carts, negotiating the Hilltop Plaza parking lot with the skill of an F-15 fighter pilot. School had only been out for a day, but the taste of newfound freedom was oh-so-sweet, and I had tons of stuff planned for the summer. Crashing at Paul's house was numero uno on the list. We'd kick off the night's festivities with an Atari marathon fueled by a steady diet of Devil Dogs and root beer, and then maybe, just maybe, I'd sneak in a little *Dungeons and Dragons* action—if I could convince my friend he wasn't too cool to give it a try. Of course, none of that was going to happen if I got grounded for staying out too late. The rules of the Dwyer household were few, but they were enforced without mercy. Rule number one: home before the streetlights came on unless you were dead, dying, or over at a friend's house. Unfortunately, I was none of those.

I slowed for a second to get my timing right before pushing it hard across 450. Once on the other side, I stopped at the entrance to the White Marsh Bike Trail and weighed my options. The path was beyond a doubt the quickest way home and most likely my only shot at avoiding Mom's wrath given the time. The trees standing guard at its entrance stretched wiry branches out and away from the forest toward the open air and sun. Like giant, gnarled fingers they reached forward as if trying to lure me into their grasp so they could tear my body limb from limb. I'd have to be faster than greased lightning. No way in hell I was going to be stuck on the trail when darkness fell.

Taking a deep breath, I plunged beneath a blanket of oak and maple and steered my bike down the paved lane at speeds that pushed the limits of my reflexes. Drinking in the cool, musty air, I looked at the shaded world surrounding me and shivered. I began humming *Shout It Out Loud* to keep my imagination from getting the better of me, as it often did in the presence of twisting shadows and smothering gloom. Whenever I got a bit twitchy, *Kiss* always calmed the nerves and steadied my hands— plus the song had a bitchin' beat. Down the winding, leaf-covered path I cruised, keeping a constant lookout for bikers, pedestrians, stray wolves, goblins, and hungry trolls.

A little more than halfway through my shortcut, movement caught the corner of my eye. To my left something large dove behind a cluster of ferns and poplars. Out of instinct, I slammed on the brakes and skidded to a halt. I listened. After a few seconds of eerie silence, the bushes stirred.

"Who's there?"

Nothing.

I'd been skittish enough when I first entered the forest. Now I was one boo away from dropping a brownie in my shorts. "I know you're out there! I can hear you, dude! If that's you, Steve, it's not funny!"

Still zip.

My eyes dropped to the layer of dead leaves and twigs littering the forest floor. In the rapidly fading twilight, I noticed a path cleared in the dirt. Starting near a shallow puddle at my feet, it ran a half dozen yards and ended where the noise had come from. I imagined some hapless hiker ambushed and dragged off into the darkness by a hidden thing, a furred and twisted horror with razor-sharp claws and bloody fangs. A sudden stillness descended, drowning out all the sounds of nature. In the deafening quiet of this sinister landscape, a low-pitched huffing emerged. Something was breathing—no, panting—in the soggy underbrush in front of me. With greedy eyes it stared at me. The hairs standing on the back of my neck told me so.

Time to split.

Making full use of the measly hundred and twenty pounds God gave me, I spurred the Blue Beast into action. A snapping of sticks and thrashing of leaves erupted from behind as something large crashed through the greenery. Hugging each curve and twist of the trail, I hauled my scrawny butt out of there like the Devil himself was chasing me. The bush monster's thumping and grunting grew louder as my would-be assassin quickly narrowed the distance between us to just a few feet. Twice I almost wiped out while skidding around sharp bends. A stuttered screech came from close by, echoing off the hills and surrounding trees. It was invasive, burrowing under my skin like a tick and digging until it struck bone.

I opened my mouth to yell but stopped. I might have been on the verge of becoming dog chow, but I wasn't planning on going out like some thumb-sucking middle schooler. Clenching my teeth, I concentrated on the narrow stretch of trail in front of me. Up ahead I heard the rush of traffic coming from Stonybrook Drive. Less than a hundred yards away was the exit and my freedom. I doubled down, furiously pumping my legs and pushing beyond my limits. A gust of wind tickled my ears as something large whooshed within inches of my head. Almost there. Another howl of anger bounced through the canyons of the trail as I raced to safety. Doing my best impersonation of Evel Knievel, I launched from the path and rocketed across both lanes, only stopping when I was safe on the other side of the street. Luckily no traffic had been coming, or I really would have been dog chow.

Wheezing in the humid air to douse the fire in my lungs, I looked back and for a few seconds swore I could see a pair of glowing embers hovering in the pitch black. Between breaths I whispered, "Suck it."

The flicker of streetlights drew my attention as they switched on one-by-one.

"Crap!"

Having narrowly escaped both death and stained underwear, I almost forgot the purpose behind my risky move. I rolled down Stonybrook, letting gravity do most of the work. What the hell was that thing? A bear? Not likely. The suburbs of Bowie, Maryland weren't exactly the great outdoors. Maybe a giant dog or just some jackasses with nothing better to do than try and scare the crap out of a kid. Still, the sound it made wasn't something I thought a human voice could replicate.

The greater the distance I put between myself and the trail, the less I thought about my near-death encounter and the more I worried about being grounded. Banking a right onto Spindle Lane, I started the climb up to my house. In the distance Mom was calling out for dinner. I was going to make it.

The smell of oil mixed with paint thinner welcomed me as I glided past our station wagon and into the garage. It wasn't until I opened the door to the house that I felt something wet and sticky on my hand.

Mom called from upstairs. "Chris, is that you?"

"Yes, Mom."

"We're having pork chops tonight! Be sure to wash up!"

I looked at my hand. From pinky to wrist, a scarlet streak was smeared across my skin. Ketchup? Nope. The hot dog I wolfed down outside the 7-Eleven only had mustard on it. Plus, it didn't smell like ketchup. I touched the liquid with my other hand and rubbed it between my fingers. It was greasy. For reasons I couldn't explain, my stomach knotted up into a giant pretzel. Remembering my hand had brushed against the bike's front tire as I hopped off, I rushed back into the garage and flicked on the light. I knelt down and touched the wheel. Pulling away, I saw a slimy red path cut across my fingers. The words, "What the fuuu...," slipped from my mouth and died as I realized the puddle on the bike trail hadn't been filled with water.

It was filled with blood.

Chapter 2

It had been a rough night. Pumped up from my narrow escape, it took forever to fall asleep. When my eyes finally shut, a parade of nightmares quickly followed, marching through my head one after another. Funniest thing, I couldn't remember a darn one of them come morning. That was a bit strange for me.

"Give me room for my legs!"

As if getting no sleep wasn't bad enough, it appeared the chances of sneaking in a little mid-morning nap wasn't in the cards either. On the opposite end of the couch from where I stretched in my semi-comatose state lay my six-year-old sister. With a button nose and chubby little cheeks, Katie could pass for cute when she wasn't being a royal pain in the butt. People said she looked like me when I was her age, but I sure didn't see it.

I stifled a yawn. "All right, stinky. Here, put your legs in front. I'll tuck mine into the cushion behind you."

"I'm not stinky!" she muttered while doing as instructed.

I closed my eyes, fading in and out only half-listening to *Scooby's All-Star Laff-A-Lympics* on the television. I remained in that state until our rattling screen door brought me back to the land of the living.

Rolling off the couch, I flopped onto the shag carpet.

Another round of knocks at the door.

"I'm coming! I'm coming! Keep your shirt on, doofus!"

I wasn't some crazy person cruising for a bruising for insulting one of our neighbors. It was ten-thirty. That meant Paul Perret was knocking on the door. Every Saturday for as far back as I could remember, Paul showed up on the porch between ten and ten-thirty, except for that one time he got explosive diarrhea from a stomach flu and the other when he was grounded for a week. My best bro was as reliable as the finest Swiss watch.

I couldn't help but laugh at the sight of him. My friend had a beach towel over his shoulders, goggles around his neck, and was sporting a bathing suit that ballooned way out below his belly button and extended down to a pair of knobby knees. "Either you're shrinking or that suit is waaay too big for you."

A grimace broke on Paul's thin face, and his blue eyes grew wide. "Yeah, couldn't find my trunks, so I borrowed one of Perry's."

"He let you?"

Paul's smile spread, exposing a set of choppers Bugs Bunny would have been jealous of. "Nope, he was sleeping when I split."

I pushed open the screen door. "Steve's out too. Sometimes he hibernates until noon. So, won't Perry pound you when he finds out you took his suit?"

Paul hunched his narrow shoulders as he entered. "Meh, he'll pound me anyway, so I might as well give him a reason. Besides, I don't want to get to the pool late; otherwise, all the chairs closest to the water will be taken. Now hurry up and suit up."

"I wanna go too!"

In unison, Paul and I sighed and turned to Katie, who was now sitting upright on the couch beaming at us.

"We don't have to take your sister, do we?"

I smiled at her and spoke in a voice only Paul could hear. "That's a big *nooo*. Even if we somehow managed to lug her there, we'd be stuck splashing around in the shallow end all day. Gimme a sec."

I spoke up. "Hey, Katie, Mom is going to the pool in a little while. It would be better if you went with her. See, you can't ride a bike yet, and you're too little to walk all the way there."

Katie's plump face scrunched up. "But I want to go with you! I don't *want* to wait!"

This wasn't working. When reasoning fell flat, experience taught me nothing worked better than a little bribe to help calm my sister. "Listen. If you wait for Mom, I promise to buy you some candy at the snack bar when you get there."

The wrinkles disappeared, replaced with a pair of crescent-shaped dimples. "Can I get a candy necklace? That way I can wear it while I eat it."

Messing up her Dutch-boy haircut, I said, "Whatever you want, stinky."

I crept through the bedroom my brother and I shared so as not to disturb Sleeping Beauty while retrieving my suit. Stubbing my toe on the corner of my bed, I narrowly avoided face-planting into my brother's backside and earning an immediate retaliatory butt whooping. After a quick wardrobe change, I was ready to roll. On the way out the door, I shouted, "Paul and I are going to the pool!"

I wasn't sure if Mom heard because we didn't wait for an answer. We were too pumped. It was the beginning of summer vacation and Belair Bath and Tennis—or BBT as it was known locally—was calling to us to spend the day in a chlorine-infused, water-up-the-nose frenzy of aquatic activities and associated mayhem. With five-feet-deep swimming lanes, a diving well plummeting to twelve, and a snack bar serving the best crinkle-cut fries around, it was the perfect refuge on a hot summer's day in Prince George's County. There was also the slimmest of chances we might spot Melissa Casey and her crew there. Just like Paul and me, Melissa was going to be a sophomore at Bowie High, but with her feathered Farrah Fawcett hair and tight designer jeans, she already acted and looked more like a senior. True, she was light years out of my league, but the last time we saw her at the pool I swore she was checking me out. Paul claims I was suffering from sunstroke.

"Morning, boys! Looks like you two are on a mission."

It wasn't unusual to see Edward Hutchinson in the neighborhood, but it was strange to hear him and even stranger to talk to him. He was always either pruning his rosebushes, watering his flowers, or sitting on his porch in his rocker and smoking his pipe. I'd probably only ever spoken to the old man three or four times in my life, and even then all I said was a simple hello or good morning. It's not that he was mean or particularly creepy. He was just…distant, a background feature of the neighborhood, just like his roses or the streetlights. He reminded me of The Professor from *Gilligan's Island,* but about thirty or so years older with silver hair and skin that looked like you could make a catcher's mitt out of it.

"Yes, sir. On our way to the pool," I answered.

Paul said nothing. He didn't have to. I saw his thinly veiled look of disgust from the corner of my eye.

"Well, don't let me slow you and your tongue-tied friend down." Mr. Hutchison threw me a wink as he passed the two of us. "Remember, son, only that day dawns to which we are awake."

Before I had a chance to think about the old man's strange words, I felt an elbow to my ribcage along with Paul's hushed voice. "You stoned? You know better than to talk to spooky Hutchinson. You get on his bad side and he'll chop you up and shove you in his basement just like he did with his old lady."

Mr. Hutchinson's wife vanished without a trace ten years ago. From what our parents had told us, an investigation that stretched over a year offered no clues as to her fate. Some adults claimed Abigail Hutchinson left her husband of forty-plus years for another man. In those stories, the guy was usually a rich foreigner who whisked her away to his estate somewhere in South America or the Caribbean or someplace like that. Others believed she died of natural causes and that a grief-stricken Mr. Hutchinson took her body to a secret location where he buried it in a private ceremony. As for my friends, the general consensus was Mr. Hutchinson had murdered his wife in some berserk *Texas Chainsaw Massacre* rampage involving a wide assortment of power tools, masks made of human skin, and enough blood to make Stephen King queasy. It made for great storytelling, but I found it the least likely explanation based on the little I knew of the old timer. From what I'd been told, he loved his wife, and her death crushed him.

"I don't know why you're so mean to him. He seems nice to me. I feel kind of bad for the guy."

"*That's* how they get you. You feel all sorry for them, and that's why you don't see it coming until it's too late." Paul slid an index finger across his neck. "Then it's good night, John-Boy, and you're nothing but a three-piece skin suit for the old man."

Having received my morning dose of crazy from Paul, I hopped on the Blue Beast and rode off. Looney Tunes followed close behind on his hand-me-down Huffy. We turned onto Spangler Lane as a summer breeze whipped up, stirring memories of the prior night's events. I fell silent as the hungry shriek of the bike trail beast echoed in my mind. No way in hell a person could have made that sound…

"Ground control to Major Tom."

I looked over at Paul. "Huh?"

"Dude, you've been riding for the past five minutes with that zombie-stare. I'm pretty sure you ate a bug and didn't even notice."

I shook my head to clear it of the bone-chilling cry. "You been over to White Marsh lately?"

"You mean the park? Nah, too far away. If I want to play baseball or soccer, I head to the churchyard."

"How about just on the bike trail part of it?"

"Nope."

We hung a right on Belair Drive and entered the tree tunnel. Fifty-foot beech trees soared to our left and right, reaching out to one another until they meshed into an emerald blanket above us. Picking up the pace, we skipped over the curb onto a dirt path that paralleled the right side of the road.

"Well, I was there last night, and I saw something pretty freaky."

"What kind of freaky? Aliens freaky? Ghost freaky? Third nipple freaky?"

"Dude, what's wrong with you? None of those. There was something in the bushes off the trail. It was hiding from me...I think."

"Why would anyone hide from you?"

"Don't know. I felt like maybe I caught it in the middle of something, something it didn't want to be seen doing."

"Like what, spanking its monkey?"

"No, goober. There were tracks in the dirt like something had been dragged off into the bushes."

"Maybe a body?"

"Maybe...and there's more."

"Keep talking."

"There was a puddle of blood on the ground. I didn't know what it was at first. Thought it might have been water."

Paul's face squished to a frown. "Really? Then what happened?"

"Well, the thing in the bushes must have still been hungry because it came after me."

"Then you did see it. What was it?"

"No. I booked it out of there as soon as I saw the bushes moving and never looked back. By the time I got home, I noticed the blood on my bike's tires. Guess I must have driven through the puddle when I bailed."

Paul's monotone response was annoying. "Uh-huh. Sure."

"What, that's all you have to say? Don't you believe me?"

My friend ignored the question and turned his attention back to the road. "Should be at BBT in a couple minutes. Wonder if Melissa will be there. Hope she's wearing that pink bikini like she did that one time. That was *hot*."

"Paul!"

He glanced back at me with a blank expression. "Look, it's not that I think you're lying to me. It's just this sounds like another one of your stories is all."

And there it was. The knife plunged deep in my gut as Paul twisted it and smiled. I guess I should have expected it by now, but the words still stung, especially because they were spilling out of my best friend's

12

mouth. I pointed to my front tire and went on the offensive. "Okay then. If you don't believe me, look at the tire. I'll bet you a slice of pizza there's blood on it."

Dust and leaves swirled around Paul's ankles as he slammed on the brakes. I stopped beside him.

He flashed a toothy grin as he hopped off his bike. "Okay, sucka! Throw in a Coke and it's a deal."

Taking a knee by the wheel, I motioned for Paul to do the same. My hand glided over its dusty, diamond-patterned surface as I looked for the proof to shut my best friend up. "I'm sure it's all dried now, but there should still be some left. See, look here."

Paul leaned over my shoulder and squinted. "Where?"

"You blind or something? Right *here*. Don't you see the red smudge?"

"Pfft, that could be anything. To be honest, it actually looks a little like a turd. Sure you didn't just ride through a big pile of dookie some dog squeezed out on the trail?"

He was trying to be funny, except there was a time and place for jokes, and this wasn't it. Sometimes I wondered if Paul really took his best bud responsibilities seriously. He was supposed to believe me and have my back when nobody else would. After all, if you can't count on your best friend, who the heck can you count on? I felt my face getting warm. "It's not crap; it's blood. I know what I saw. Guess I should have known better than to think you'd believe me." With nothing left to say, I jumped on the Blue Beast and sped off back down the tree tunnel.

We were exiting it by the time Paul caught up with me. "Hey, c'mon. I was just messing around with you. Be cool, dude."

I didn't feel like being cool. I was trying to be serious, and he was busy trying to be Richard Pryor. Why? I didn't know. It's not like he had an audience.

He finally took the hint. "All right, all right, sorry. It's just you have to admit, you don't exactly have the best track record when it comes to living in a place most of us call reality. Remember the time you thought Mr. Davis was a vampire?"

"That's not *fair*. That was over a year ago, and I had evidence. The guy was pale as a ghost, and we never saw him during the day."

"He was an albino, Chris. He didn't go out in the daytime because he didn't want to get sunburnt."

An excellent point, but I wasn't about to let that stop me. "Fine. But we didn't know that at the time, now *did* we, Paaauul?"

My friend snorted. "You were all set to douse him in holy water you swiped from Saint Pius. I was the one that talked you out of it."

"Yeah, so?"

We zipped past the arched entrance to the Belair Stables where generations of some of the greatest racing horses in American history were born and bred. Now the place was a dusty old museum, and the consensus of my friends was that it was definitely haunted.

Paul flashed his trademark goofball grin. "How do you think that would have gone down explaining to your parents? Gee, Mom, Dad, sorry I nearly drowned our albino neighbor in holy water I stole from church, but I thought he was actually a bloodsucking spawn of Satan."

That actually *was* a little funny. He earned no points from me for his rational argument. Rational was boring. Rational was predictable. Rational was opposite of fun and exciting and, as such, should be considered the enemy. He did get points for his sense of humor though. A smile tugged at the corners of my mouth. "Okay, maybe I owe you a solid on that one."

"Damn right. And don't think I didn't notice the wooden stakes you had stowed in your closet too."

I was positive I had those stashed under the carpeting in the back corner of the closet. If he found them, he may also have seen my stockpile of cherry bombs and the old bra ads from the Sears catalogue. "Yeah, well that would have been our last line of defense if Mr. Davis had turned out to be one of the undead. One of these days you'll thank me for my keen instincts."

"The day that I have to thank you for being nutso is the day we're in a shitload of trouble."

Paul wouldn't have missed a golden opportunity to zing me if he found the other stuff in the closet. As my stomach slowly plopped back to its natural resting place, I decided to make a priority of relocating my incriminating contraband. Mom would have a heart attack if she found my stash.

"Could be," I said. "But on that day you'll be so thankful I saved your life that you'll vow to be my servant for eternity. You'll wash my socks, cook my dinner, and babysit for Melissa Dwyer and me."

"Babysit for Melissa *Dwyer* and you?"

I smirked at him. "That's right. We're gonna get married after high school and have a family. Two boys and maybe a girl. You'll babysit so I can take Melissa out on the weekends for dinner and to the movies."

"Does Melissa know this yet?"

"Of course not, goober! First, we'll date for a couple years and then we'll go steady. For a classy girl like Melissa you have to take your time, spend some money."

Paul snorted a laugh. "You do know you'll actually have to talk to her for any of that to happen, right? Man, I wonder what it's like to live on Planet Chris."

"It's cool. You should come visit sometime."

We spent all day rotating between the pool, ping pong tables, and snack bar. When Mom and Katie showed up, I made good on my sugary bribe and even spent some time splashing around with the ankle biter— much to Paul's annoyance. Despite the absence of Melissa and her pink bikini, we had a good time.

Soon enough the sun was dipping below the tree line, and a pale moon was already rising against a darkening sky. We were pruned, red-eyed, and ready to go home.

Chapter 3

After a quick bite and shower, I was off to Paul's to spend the night. Taking the Blue Beast would have been tricky with the stockpile of board games I was lugging, so I decided to walk the six blocks to his place. On any given summer night, Spindle was buzzing with activity. Whether it was adults walking off second helpings of baked beans or potato salad or screeching packs of kids locked in a heated game of wild hunt—our local souped-up version of tag—chances were you'd run into someone. But tonight was eerily quiet. A full moon floated high above, showering the neighborhood in cool blue light.

In this wonderful netherworld of moon shadows, my imagination began creeping and crawling like kudzu. As I passed the Staubachs' house, my body grew heavy. Eyes were on me, weighing me down with heavy stares. To my left and right, they watched from the inky darkness. A chill swept over me and I shuddered.

"Stop it," I whispered. "Not even five minutes out the door, and you're already imagining sleestak and zombies. Why do you have to be such a freak?"

As if answering the question, snapping twigs drew my attention to a cluster of pines on my right. I froze and stared into the blackness. The logical side of my brain suggested the source of the disturbance was probably a squirrel or maybe a cat.

The other side of my brain was quick to counter. It was the contrary and often crazy side that was constantly getting me into trouble. *Too big to be a squirrel or cat; they don't break sticks.*

Maybe a big dog then?

Maybe…maybe something else.

Like what?

Dozens of pairs of shiny blue marbles fluttered open from the shadows. Unblinking, they watched me with an alien hunger. The eyes had mouths beneath them, mouths with pointy teeth that gnashed up and down as whispers drifted on the night air.

I leaned close to hear them.

Nowhere to run. Nowhere to hide. He sees you.

I was ninety-five percent sure the eyes, teeth, and ominous words were the products of my crazy side, but it didn't make them any less real to me.

My left leg moved forward first, followed by my right. Something pulled me toward the darkness and the mouths. More of them appeared. Teeth and eyes, eyes and teeth. They were whispering again. *He's watching you.* No noses. No ears. Just fangs and glowing blue eyes hovering in the pitch black as if by magic. I stepped off the street and over the curb. They would have me soon.

"Evening, Master Dwyer. Out for a twilight stroll I see."

The *thunk* of a game-packed milk crate hitting the pavement echoed down Spindle as I dropped my precious cargo and threw up my fists. "Whaa!"

The moonlight shined off of Mr. Hutchinson's silver hair. "My apologies. Didn't mean to give you a start. I was just stretching my legs and enjoying the cool evening air. It truly is a beautiful night, don't you think?" He gazed into the sea of eyes and teeth. "Something scurrying around back in there? I would be careful if I were you, son. The Packards said they spotted a skunk in their backyard yesterday. With the moon as lustrous as it is, our normally crepuscular friend could very well be on the prowl."

The only things I heard were moon and skunk. I looked back into the shadows and saw nothing but black. I said the only thing that came to mind. "Huh?"

"Are you quite all right?"

"I'm—I'm fine, sir," I said while leaning over to pick up my crate. Fortunately, the drop had been a clean one and there were no casualties. With my cargo safely secured, I returned to the paved road and started back toward Paul's. "Just thought I heard something messing around under the trees. Must have been some squirrels or maybe that skunk. Thanks for the heads up. Gotta go."

"Take care young man, and stay on the beaten path. And remember, beware the Jabberwock!"

Something was familiar about his warning, but I couldn't remember where I'd heard it before. When I looked back at Mr. Hutchinson, his leathery face was hard. "What?"

"It's said he has jaws that bite and claws that catch."

I stood silent and stared at him, wondering if old man Hutchinson was as nuts as Paul and most of the other kids thought he was.

A smile split across his stony face, and he began laughing. "Just a little levity, Master Dwyer. Compliments of Lewis Carroll."

He was the strangest man I'd ever met. Bonus points for Mr. Hutchinson. "Umm, okay. Goodnight, sir."

With a nod and a wink, he turned and continued on his way up Spindle.

Only minutes back into my journey, the weight of imagined eyes returned. This time I decided not to look into the darkness for fear of falling under their spell again. My parents say I'm blessed with an amazing imagination, but from experience I knew there were times it could go seriously Dark Side and send me on what amounted to a bad trip. A little spook and nudge would push me over the edge, and down into the rabbit hole I'd go.

I started jogging.

Though my street was deserted, there was always traffic on Belair and Stonybrook. If I could just make it to the end of Spindle where it intersected with the busier roads, I would be safe. It was Survival 101. Creatures of the night didn't like leaving witnesses when they attacked. Everybody knew that.

All fell silent behind me, but that meant nothing. There were things that could move without making a sound. There were shadow demons. There were wraiths. Such things, though never heard, could be felt when they approached. The nearer they got to you, the more you tingled. From the base of the spine all the way up to the back of the neck and then the brain, you felt the prickle of impending doom. By the time the goose-bumps broke out, it was too late. I looked down to my forearms and saw an army of tiny hairs standing at attention.

I broke into a sprint. Ahead a car whizzed up Belair while another passed in the opposite direction. Good, it was busy. With refuge just seconds away, an urgency washed over me. I wasn't going to do it. Looking back would be a mistake. It always was. But I couldn't stop myself. I glimpsed over my right shoulder. Something dashed across the street behind me. It was dark and blurred, but it was definitely there. "Fuuaaaaggghh!"

I don't know what the word meant; it just burst out of me. I think I started to curse but—despite my terror-induced state—I still managed to censor myself and utter something completely dorky.

I kept running, being careful not to lose grip of my cargo once more. A few seconds later, I hung a left onto Belair. Once safe, I eased up and jogged the rest of the way to Paul's.

His older brother Perry opened the door. As far as brothers went, Perry wasn't a complete tool. He was okay most of the time, but every now and then he would get a hair up his butt and mess with Paul and me for no reason other than that he could. Of course, Steve did the same thing. It must have been something in the big brother code: be nice for five days out of the week and then a complete dingleberry for the remaining two.

"Why are you all sweaty and breathing heavy?"

"Just getting some exercise," I wheezed out. "Where's Paul?"

A smirk rose on Perry's lightly freckled face, and his blue eyes flared with excitement as he waved me in. "Oh, he's here. Just can't come to the door right now."

Something was up; he was *way* too happy to see me.

At seventeen and fifteen, Perry and Paul were the youngest of the Perret family. With five girls and three boys, it was pretty much guaranteed something was always going on in the house. But tonight it was strangely quiet.

"Where is everybody?"

"Parents are at a dinner party, same one as yours. My sisters are all on dates, except for Mary Ann. She's upstairs sick. Rummy's working."

I plopped the crate down next to the door and asked the obvious question. "And Paul?"

Perry motioned for me to follow him into the back family room. The smile remained fixed on his face as he pointed to Paul's tuba case in the corner of the room.

"So!" Perry shouted. "Learned your lesson yet?"

A muffled "Yes" came from inside the case.

"And what are you *never* going to do again under penalty of a severe butt kicking?"

The same defeated voice spoke. "I'm never going to borrow your bathing suit or any other clothes without asking."

Perry looked at me. The smile grew wider. "Don't forget it! Chris is here now, so I guess you would like to be let out, huh?"

Sarcasm oozed through the cracks in the case. "Yeeees."

Perry thumped the side of it with his foot. "Yes, what?"

Paul responded several seconds later. "Yes…please."

"There, now see? All you have to do is be polite and show a little respect. That's all I ask for, not much."

Perry flipped open the clasps to the case with his foot.

When the final one was unhinged, the lid flew wide. Flush-faced and wild-eyed, Paul looked at his brother and shouted, "I couldn't breathe in there, you jerk! I could have died!"

"You look fine to me. Besides, serves you right. You should know better than to take my stuff. You're lucky I didn't kick your ass in front of Chris."

21

"Yeah, I feel real lucky. Now why don't you split? Go find someone else to bother."

"Fine. But remember Mom and Dad left me in charge. That means don't do anything stupid. Also, I'm coming down to watch *Saturday Night Live* later, so the TV is mine for that. You have until eleven-thirty to watch whatever you want."

Combat was the first in our lineup of Atari games, followed by *Indy 500* and then *Star Ship*. Somewhere between racing and shooting down spaceships, Perry showed up with a large bowl of popcorn. Saying nothing, he dropped it between us as an apparent peace offering and worked his way into the fun. After three and a half hours of nonstop gaming, Perry exclaimed, "Okay, ladies, time for *SNL*! He flipped the television dial to Channel 4 just in time to catch the end of the evening news.

"... *and so there you have it. David Berkowitz, the infamous Son of Sam killer, will be sentenced in less than a week. In local news a gruesome discovery was made earlier today on the White Marsh Nature Trail in Bowie, Maryland. The mutilated bodies of two dogs were found by Boy Scout Troop 1046. The scouts that stumbled upon the animals described them as ripped to shreds and decapitated. The savagery of the attack has authorities perplexed as the wounds are consistent with those caused by a large predator such as a bear. However, no bears have been sighted in Prince George's County in years. Furthermore, such violent behavior is not typically associated with the black bear, which is the only species of bear indigenous to the state. Authorities are urging anyone with information regarding this attack to call the number on the screen.*"

I glanced over at Paul. His slack-jawed stare was a suitable reward for the teasing I'd endured on the way to the pool.

Swimming in self-satisfaction, I nodded and mouthed the words, *Told you.*

"Goatman."

Paul and I turned to Perry. He was staring at the screen with a blank expression. "Definitely the Goatman."

"What's a Goatman?" I asked.

22

Perry's eyebrows rose and his head dipped slightly as it swiveled to me and then Paul. "You guys are joshing me, right? You're telling me you've never heard of the Goatman? Either of you?"

Embarrassed, I backtracked. "Well, sure I've *heard* of him but not a whole lot. Just rumors really. What do you know about him?"

"Uh-huh." Perry didn't sound convinced. "Anyway, this is clearly the work of the Goatman. He's been killing dogs for years now. I remember hearing stories about him when I was younger than you dorks—and it's not just animals he's after. A couple of years ago, they found two bodies out by Allen's Pond, a girl and guy. They were all chopped up into tiny bits by some maniac with an ax. They never solved the case, but everyone says it was the Goatman that got them."

Something about what Perry said wasn't adding up. Although I was all for a good boogeyman story, it needed to be well-constructed for me to invest in it. "Wait a minute. If this is the same guy, then –"

"Goatman," Perry interrupted.

"Right. If this is the Goatman in both cases, why would he be ripping up dogs one day and chopping up kids with an ax on another? It seems weird. If he had the strength to kill two dogs with his bare hands, why would he bother with an ax?"

Perry glared at me like I had a hole bored straight through my head. "Dude, he's a Goatman. *That's weird.* The fact that he kills dogs and people with his hands or an ax isn't that strange."

"So," Paul chimed in, "where did he come from?"

"No one knows for sure," Perry said. "But rumor has it he was a scientist working on some secret genetics testing, and something went wrong."

Yet another sign of poor craftsmanship. I couldn't help myself. "Hmm."

Perry scowled at me. "Hmm, *what?*"

"Well, what kind of genetics testing would you use a goat for? If they were looking to make some kind of human animal weapon, why not use a gorilla or a tiger, or something like that?"

"Or maybe a snake or lizard." Paul added.

"Exactly," I said. "All of those are cool. A goat is just…goofy."

"What, are you two scientists all of a sudden? I'm just telling you what I heard. Besides, it doesn't matter. He's out there, and he's been hunting down people and dogs for a long, long time. Ax or no ax, the Goatman is real, and he's on the hunt."

His words brought with them the memory of my narrow escape on the bike trail and the warnings uttered by the hidden things. *He's watching you.* My silence must have encouraged Perry.

"Come to think of it, you two chumps would make for a pretty good Goatman snack. If I were you guys, I'd stick close to home this summer, probably not mess around much after dark. Otherwise," Perry leaned back in his chair, slowly tilting his head from side to side, "well, you never know."

Luckily for us, the voice of Paul Shaffer drew Perry's attention to the television and away from his taunts. After watching *SNL*, Paul and I crashed out in sleeping bags in the family room, and Perry headed upstairs.

As we drifted off to sleep, I whispered to Paul, "See, I wasn't imagining things on the bike trail."

"I know. Sorry about that."

Silence fell upon the dark room and lingered for a minute until Paul said, "What now?"

Whatever wickedness was stirring up had all started at White Marsh. Yes, it was more of a gut feeling than a brain feeling, but it was still a powerful feeling. "I kind of want to go back there."

"What? You mean to the place you were almost killed? You crazy?"

"I won't go alone, and I won't go so close to nightfall. You'll be with me and maybe a few others. I don't think whatever is there will attack a group of people. Too many witnesses."

"How can you be sure it won't kill us all?"

"I think it's trying not to attract too much attention. That's why it hid from me at first. It didn't make a move until it knew I was alone. Like I said, no witnesses."

More silence.

Paul yawned. "Well if you want me to come, you're going to have to wait."

"Why?"

"Thought I told you. Tomorrow we're heading to Ocean City. Won't be back until Friday."

"Dude! I need you there with me. You're the only person that knows about this."

"Then I guess you have stay cool for a week."

"What the heck am I supposed to do while you're gone?"

"Don't know... maybe you can try and convince Steve to come with us."

"Please?" I begged. "Steve has zero interest in anything I have to say. Now that he's gonna be a senior, he wouldn't be caught dead hanging out with his fifteen-year-old brother. Not that we were hanging out much anyways."

"Yeah, same with me and Perry. Guess they think they're big shots 'cause they can drive and go to parties that have beer and stuff. Anyway, don't do anything stupid while I'm away," Paul said.

"Nah, I'll wait till you get back."

I thought about telling Paul about the walk over to his house, but the details were already getting fuzzy. The sad truth of it was, I wasn't entirely sure what happened myself. Being a little nuts could be frustrating at times—especially when monsters were after you.

Chapter 4

Sunday opened with a gray sky that darkened—along with my mood—as the day progressed. I was bored out of my mind. Although I could hang out with other neighborhood kids, most were older like Steve and Perry or much younger like my sister. I was nibbling on the crust of a PB&J while zoning out in front of the television when I heard my mom's voice coming from the kitchen.

"Chris, I would like for you to do something nice for me today," she said.

A soft groan slipped from my mouth. "Oookay, what is it?"

"A new family has moved into that white rancher on Spiral. They are very nice, and there is a young man there who is about your age. Kevin McNamara is his name. I told his mother you would pay him a visit."

Only eleven-thirty and the day was getting crappier by the second. In response, I released one long, loud sigh.

My mom, Maureen Dwyer, was a sweet and loving mother, but she was nobody's fool and had no tolerance for whining from any of her children. Her New England accent grew thick along with the sternness in her voice. "Christopher Brennan Dwyer, he is new here and has no friends! You *will* go over to his house and you *will* welcome him to the neighborhood. As I recall, his mother said he enjoys some of the same games that you do. What is that one called, Dragons and Wizards?"

Parents were so clueless. "It's *Dungeons and Dragons*, Mom."

"The name isn't important. What is important is you going over there and being a gracious neighbor. Understood?"

"Yes."

"Good."

Dragging my feet along the pavement, I started the two block walk to the new kid's house. Why my mom had to assign me Welcome Wagon duties on today of all days I'll never know. With the way my luck was going, this kid was going to be some kind of glue-sniffing weirdo who'd want to be best friends.

"Hi, Chris."

I smiled at the sound of Tracy Staubach's voice. With her sparkling blue eyes, long brown hair, and perfectly pointed nose, Tracy held the unofficial—and most likely unknown to her—title of Queen of Spindle. At eighteen she was the oldest of our crew. Sure, she had friends her own age, but she always made some time to hang out with the rest of us schmucks, hence her honorary title. And there she was getting out of her convertible VW Rabbit and waving at me.

A high-pitched, "Hey!" escaped my mouth. She caught me off guard, and I didn't have time to think up anything clever to say.

"Where are you heading looking so low?" she asked.

"Oh, um, I'm heading over to say hi to the new kid that moved in on Spiral."

"Gee, Chris, I think that's way cool. Who knows, maybe you'll make a new friend."

My moronic smile widened. She said what I was doing was cool. "Yeah, well, it's important to make friends. I have a lot of friends." Good Lord. I have a lot of friends. More like, I'm a complete spaz.

"Well, that's great. Tell him hey for me. I have to go now—already running late. Smell ya later!"

With that, she disappeared in her house, leaving me with a stomach full of butterflies and a face the color of a baboon's butt. In a goofy voice, I mumbled, "I'm Chris, and I got lots of friends. Adurrrr."

I walked the rest of the way in embarrassed silence. When I arrived at the new kid's house, I hesitated before knocking, dreading what was sure to be a waste of the next several hours of my life.

The door opened. A boy my height with sandy blond hair parted down the middle flashed a metallic smile and said, "Hey."

"Hey, I'm Chris Dwyer. I live over on Spindle."

The glint from the new kid's braces caught my eyes, causing me to blink. "I'm Kevin. You wanna come in?"

"Sure," I shrugged.

I followed him from the front hall through the kitchen to a huge addition built on the back of the house. A monster television sat in front of a pair of leather upholstered couches on the opposite side of the room, and a full-sized pool table occupied its center. To my left was a dartboard and to my right a pair of crossed swords, both mounted on the wood-paneled walls.

"Wow! This is the coolest room I've ever seen. Is that TV twenty-five inches? It's *huge*," I exclaimed with my mouth open.

"It's twenty-five all right. You play pool?"

"Nah."

"I could teach you if you want. It's not that hard."

"Eh, maybe." I pointed to a framed poster of a man in a football uniform. "Who's that?"

"Seriously? You don't know who Terry Bradshaw is? He's the quarterback for the Pittsburg Steelers. Don't you watch football? My dad and I do all the time."

I had the sinking feeling it was going to be a long afternoon. "Sometimes. The Redskins are okay I guess."

"Yeah, they're not bad," Kevin said as he moved to the corner of the room and opened a large walk-in closet. In it were soccer balls, basketballs, footballs, bats, gloves, and shelves of board games. "I played some football at my old school. Don't know if I will here. If you're not into that type of stuff, I got –"

"What's that?" I asked pointing to a book tucked between *Life* and *Operation*.

Kevin pulled it out and handed it to me. "That's my Monster Manual."

"You play *D and D*?"

"Used to before we moved. It's kind of hard playing the game by yourself."

New kid just earned himself twenty bonus points. "No doubt! I'm trying to get my friend Paul into it, but he's just not having it."

"If you like the Manual, you'll *really* dig this."

A shiny smile broke on Kevin's face as he pulled another book from the shelf and handed it to me.

"You got the *Player's Handbook*? Man, I didn't think those were out yet."

"Just came out. I got it yesterday. You can borrow it if you want."

"Really? Sweet! I mean, after you're done with it."

"It's no biggie really. We'll both have to study it if we're gonna do some gaming."

I started flipping through the pages. "This is outta sight. I hear they have more character classes."

"They do. There are paladins and rangers now and other cool stuff."

Now knowing I was in the presence of a fellow gamer, I decided to let my guard down and allow the inner dorkiness to spill out. "Cool. I have a cleric and fighter that I made up a couple months ago. They're okay, but I've been wanting to mix it up a little."

Kevin rummaged through the section of shelf he had pulled the two books from. When he turned back to me, he was holding some paper and a couple pencils in his left hand and a set of dice in the other. "No time like the present."

"What, you mean now?"

"Why not? You just said you've been wanting to create a new character. Besides," Kevin pointed out the window, "it's raining. What do you say? We can try out some of these new classes and see if they're any good. You like pretzels and Mr. Pibb?"

For the rest of the afternoon, we battled troglodytes and drow in the Underdark, gathered gold and experience points, and ate our weight in pretzels, chips, and cheese puffs. Somehow I still found room for a couple of slices of pepperoni pizza when Mrs. McNamara brought us dinner.

Before wobbling my way home, Kevin and I agreed to meet tomorrow to continue our epic campaign. Life is strange. I was sure the day was going to be a flat out bust when I was ordered over to Kevin's, but it turned out to be the most fun I'd had in recent memory. It was well past nine when I left, and the murky night sky was gray and starless.

Buzzed on Mr. Pibb and visions of minotaurs and vorpal swords, I stumbled down Spiral tightly gripping Kevin's copy of the *Player's Handbook*. Kevin was the first person I'd met with an interest in gaming, and his collection of guides and adventure modules was most impressive and would no doubt make for some serious adventuring. Now if I could just get Paul on board.

I froze in my tracks.

Up ahead, in the washed-out glow of the streetlight at the corner of Sexton and Spindle, something sat. I say it was a something rather than a someone because although it looked human in shape, it was easily as wide as a Volkswagen and had a freaky melon-shaped head with spikes protruding from it on both sides. My buzz evaporated. The thing had its back to me and was hunched over with its attention focused on the ground. I fought the urge to go screaming back to Kevin's and, instead, came up with a brilliant plan.

"Hey!" I shouted.

Its melon head shot up, but the thing didn't turn and look at me. Before I could say another word, it stood, stretching up to half the height of the streetlight. I took a step back and was a split second away from setting a new land speed record to Kevin's when the creature darted out of the light and into the Colberts' junipers.

I was alone and shaking uncontrollably as Perry's voice popped in my head uttering two words. *The Goatman.* Ignoring all common sense, I found myself approaching where the thing had been sitting moments earlier. Beneath the light was a pile of bloodied bones and matted fur. The creature had been feeding on something and for whatever reason placed the remains in a neatly stacked mound. The idea seemed a little crazy, but a part of me felt as though the creature left them for me to discover. Under the nasty mess of furry death, I saw something scrawled in red on the pavement. It was a letter, the letter Y to be exact. My stomach bubbled and churned as if it knew something I didn't. Mustering up the courage, I kicked the carnage away and read the words scrawled in blood.

You really should lock your window.

The message could have been for anyone, but in my bones I knew it was meant for me.

A hushed but unmistakable wail echoed down the empty street behind me. It was the same stuttered cry I'd heard on the bike trail.

I ran the rest of the way home.

Chapter 5

By the time I made it upstairs, my breathing had returned to almost normal. I blundered into my bedroom, and papers flew everywhere.

"Hey, come on, spaz!" Steve barked.

"Sorry." I navigated the minefield of notes scattered around the room and made it successfully to my bed without stepping on a single one of them. Plopping down, I stared out the bedroom window. All was still and silent as the grave. I checked the window and blew out a sigh of relief when I found it locked tight.

"What the heck are you doing?" Steve scowled as he gathered his papers and began organizing them into separate stacks.

My mouth opened, but the words turned sideways and wedged in my throat. I wanted to tell him about White Marsh and the thing lurking in the Colberts' bushes, but I couldn't. I knew it would take more than a pile of bones and a warning about a window for my brother to believe me, so I decided to switch subjects. "Just messing around. What about you?"

Steve removed his horn-rimmed glasses and wiped the lenses with a shirt sleeve. Before putting them back on, he shoved his fingers in his hair and ran his hand through it. "Right now I'm cleaning up your mess. What I *was* doing was putting the final touches on the script for *The Jungle of Doctor Dubois.*"

Steve's movies were a big deal in the neighborhood. If Tracy was the Queen of Spindle, Steve was the Spielberg. All of us neighborhood kids wanted to be in his films, and our parents got a giant kick out of watching the finished product. With his Super 8 millimeter camera, my brother made epic adventures, exciting whodunits, and—most recently—a history of the world project for school. Everyone enjoyed the spectacle tied to each cinematic venture, but I got something extra out of every movie. It was an opportunity to hang out with my brother and have some fun, like we did in the old days before he became such a big-headed wanker.

"When do you want to start filming?"

"By the end of the week, when Perry and Paul get back. I'll need them, you, Brian and Mark Johnson, and maybe one more."

"How about Kevin?"

"Who's Kevin?"

"He's the new kid over on Spiral. He's pretty cool and has a sweet collection of *D and D* stuff."

"You think he'd want to be in the movie?"

"Yeah, I think so. I'll talk to him tomorrow. What's this one about anyway?"

"It's science fiction. A mad doctor experiments on people, turning them into half-men, half-animal monsters."

"Oh, kind of like *The Island of Doctor Moreau.*"

Steve frowned. "A little, but mine's way cooler. The movie takes the hero to the jungles of Africa where the doctor's compound is located. I was thinking we could set up the backyard to look like a jungle, maybe use the shed as one of the doctor's laboratories. It's not perfect, but –"

The thought struck me like a lightning bolt. Without thinking I blurted, "What about the bike trail?"

Steve stopped sorting his papers and looked back at me. "The bike trail?"

I inched my way to the foot of the bed, moving closer to where my brother sat on the floor. "Sure, White Marsh. Think about it. It's got a lot of big trees, some streams. Heck, it even has vines. It would make the *perfect* jungle."

"Hmm. You may actually be on to something. The whole crew could bike up there, and we could do most of the shooting in an hour or two. You know, Chris, you're actually a little smarter than you look."

That was the closest thing to a compliment Steve had given me in a long time. "Gee, thanks."

"Don't mention it."

With seven or eight kids stomping around, I was sure we would all be safe. Having a decent idea of how long it usually took Steve to find the perfect shot and organize, I figured Paul, Kevin, and I would have plenty of time to snoop around. Exactly what we would be looking for was another question entirely.

Leaving Steve to fuss over his screenplay, I flopped back in bed, kicked off my shoes, and opened the *Player's Handbook*. After a few minutes of paging through magic user spells, my thoughts drifted back to the bushes. I suppose it could have been someone wearing a costume, maybe one of the neighborhood kids yanking my chain. But still...

"Hey, Steve?"

"What?"

"Ever heard of the Goatman?"

"Of course. Everyone has."

"Do you believe he's real?"

"Doubt it. They've been telling stories about him for years, but there have been no pictures or evidence to show he exists. I think he's more or less a myth."

"Perry says he's real."

"Hah! Let me guess. He told you and Paul he was real when you slept over."

"Maybe. Why? What difference does that make?"

"He was trying to scare you, doofus—you and Paul. I bet it worked too."

"No, it didn't."

"Sure it did. You two suckers probably stayed up all night hugging each other and praying that the big bad Goatman wouldn't drop by and hack you to pieces. Classic!"

Before I could mount a protest, Steve pointed to the book in my hands and said, "Someone like you probably shouldn't be reading that stuff."

"What do you mean, *someone like me*?"

"Gee, I don't know. Maybe I mean someone who thinks the closet is alive and staring at him."

Only a month ago, I swore a pair of bulging eyes was peering out at me from our bedroom closet doors. My scream woke the whole household that night, and it wasn't until my parents showed me what I was actually seeing was just the reflection of headlights off the porcelain knobs of the closet doors that I finally settled down. The most embarrassing part was even after I knew there was nothing to be afraid of, I couldn't fall back to sleep. Buried somewhere deep in the back of my brain, I was convinced the knobs were eyes, and as soon as everyone else fell asleep, those huge, unblinking peepers were bound to turn my way. It was a favorite subject of both Steve's and Perry's and something I wasn't going to live down anytime in the near future.

Steve smirked. "What about someone who believes vampires are roaming the streets of Bowie or—my personal favorite—someone who thinks your stomach will blow up if you eat Pop Rocks and drink soda? You, dear brother, are hopeless."

"Whatever. Mom and Dad say having imagination is a good thing."

"They say that to your face because they don't want to hurt your feelings. Keep it up, and one of these days they'll end up wrapping you in a straitjacket and putting you in a rubber room somewhere."

What Steve said touched a nerve because there was truth in his words whether he knew it or not. Just a few weeks earlier, I overheard my folks discussing the possibility of sending me to see a shrink. It was hard to make out most of the conversation from the top of the stairs, but words like *hyperactive imagination, anxiety,* and *worrier* came up several times. In the end they agreed to wait to see if I grew out of *it*—whatever *it* was. To an insecure fifteen-year-old already prone to thoughts of doom and gloom, the implications were terrifying. For the next several weeks, I'd break out into a cold sweat every day I came home from school, convinced that eventually I would return only to be met by a couple of no-neck strangers in lab coats and then hauled off to the looney bin. I pictured the visits from my family during the holidays. They would stay for an hour or so, watching the clock the whole time as they spoke slowly, using third-grade words so as not to excite me. Then they would split back to the real world to enjoy their lives without Crazy Chris butting in. It all sounds a bit dramatic, but I promise you, it seemed inevitable at the time.

Getting in an argument with my brother never ended well for me, but the crap now spewing from his mouth was simply more than I could stomach. It had gotten much worse over the past couple of years. To him I was either stupid or a nuisance or, in some cases, a stupid nuisance. As if he was so perfect, so brilliant and talented with his precious little movies. Big deal. I could make movies. The thing with my brother was, his calm, cool look was just an act. Beneath the gleaming armor of superiority, Steve was almost as insecure as I was, and by some strange twist of fate, I had a unique talent for finding the chink in that armor. "Crazy or not, at least I know a crappy movie when I see it."

Steve looked up from his script. I knew his blank expression was an act. He was seconds away from going nuclear. "What was that?"

A queasy feeling rose in my stomach, but for some reason I couldn't stop. "You heard me. At least I know a lousy movie when I see it."

My brother had entered a growth spurt when he turned fifteen. When Mongo stood up now, he stretched over six feet tall. I, on the other hand, barely made it to a lame five foot four. "What *lousy* movie are you talking about?"

Now that I had his attention, I had to zing him, let him know he should think twice before dismissing me as his stupid kid brother. I spat out the first movie that came to mind. "Gee, I don't know, maybe *Space Wars*. I mean, talk about a rip off. All you did was take *Star Wars* and switch out the title."

He walked to the edge of my bed. It was just a matter of time. "Everybody liked that movie. Mom and Dad said it was one of the best ones yet." Steve smirked. "And you seemed to have plenty of fun being in it as I recall." He turned and started back to his masterpiece in the making.

Time to poke the bear with a sharp stick. "Yeah, it was fun acting in it, but the whole thing still sucked. They were just being nice to you. The movie stunk it up more than a fart in an elevator."

I sprang off the bed but couldn't escape his hands in such tight quarters. He grabbed me by the neck and slammed me into the closet. The whack to the back of my head wasn't as bad as it sounded, but it still left me seeing stars. Steve was in full-on Hulk mode now. Next, he tossed me to the ground and planted a freakishly large foot on my chest. Leaning down, he smiled. "At least I'm doing something with my life and not daydreaming about fairies and dumbass dwarves!"

I reached up and was able to grab a fistful of hair.

"Wow, look at how the sissy fights! Grabbing hair like a girl!"

Frustrated, I let go. As he straightened up and loomed over me, I did the only thing I could think of. Thrusting my right leg up, I arched my back to get a little more momentum. The result was a well-planted but somewhat lacking groin shot.

Steve grunted and stumbled off me as he cupped his tenders.

I jumped to my feet and swung.

Avoiding my punch by a mile, Steve pushed me back onto my bed.

As he pounced on top of me, I grabbed his shirt in an effort to try and pull myself up. The rip of polyester was unmistakable.

We froze.

"You tore my shirt!" he yelled.

I said the only thing I could think of, "I know!"

As quickly as it started, the brawl was over. Being the biggest and strongest, Steve had the final word when it came to ending our fights. This time it didn't work out so bad for me, so I was more than happy to call it quits.

Steve stormed off to the bathroom to assess the damage to his shirt. Before slamming the door, he shouted, "And don't forget to shut the bedroom window, you little stain! You're lucky I did before the rain came and almost ruined my script!"

Chapter 6

For the next couple of days, I held dominion over the realms of monsters and men as dungeon master extraordinaire while Kevin hunted down the cunning but cowardly drow as he ventured deep into the bowels of the Earth. When we weren't neck-deep in dark elves and gnomes, we were at the pool secretly hoping in vain for a sighting of Melissa Casey and crew. Having a friend as cool as Kevin to hang out with was great, but the sun was never far from my mind or, more specifically, its closeness to the horizon. Another late night encounter with my mysterious pen pal wasn't at the top of my summer bucket list.

Kevin came over Wednesday and crashed at my house. After stuffing ourselves on pizza from Happy Italian, we took a break from gaming and mellowed out in front of the tube watching *Planet of the Apes* on the sofa bed. The next thing I knew, Kevin nudged me awake. I snorted to semi-consciousness while a lone eagle soared across the television screen to a chorus of the national anthem.

"You're not already asleep, are you?"

I yawned out a, "Nooo."

"Good." Kevin rolled off the sofa bed and grabbed his duffel bag. A goofy grin split on his face as he plopped it in front of me and unzipped it. He reached in and then paused for dramatic effect, whispering, "My ass would be grass if my dad knew I smuggled this from the house." He pulled out what looked like a gun.

"Holy crap! Is that a forty-five?"

Kevin squinted and cocked his head to the side. "Yeah, sure. My parents let me have a gun. I got a bazooka under my bed I'll bring over next time." He tossed it to me. "It's a BB gun, Sherlock."

Pointing to a switch on the side of it, he spoke in a matter-of-fact tone. "The BBs go in there—it holds up to twenty. All you do is pull the receiver back to load one. Then just aim and squeeze the trigger."

My interest in all things Bruce Lee led to a rather impressive collection of throwing stars, nunchakus, sai swords, and such, but I didn't own a BB gun. I had to admit it was very cool. The cold steel felt good in my hands and made me feel like Dirty Harry.

"Want to try her out?" Kevin asked.

He knew I did. Only a blind man could have missed my ear-to-ear grin. But where the heck did he think we could shoot? Both the garage and backyard were way too risky. All it would take was a broken window or dinged car door and I'd be grounded until college. "Where?"

"I know the perfect spot. Put your sneakers on."

I felt my stomach drop. Sooner or later I knew I'd have to venture back out into the dark, but I was hoping it would have been later rather than sooner. It was still too early in our friendship for me to tell Kevin about my late night stalker. I didn't want to spook him. For now, he thought I was actually a normal fifteen-year-old, and I wanted to keep it that way as long as possible. At least it was the two of us this time, and we were armed.

The humid night air turned the streetlights into huge will-o'-the-wisps. With great speed and ninja-like stealth, we crossed Spindle and entered the Colberts' side yard wading through the very bushes my pen pal had been hiding in just three days past. I didn't think it was possible, but I'm pretty sure my stomach dropped even lower.

The side yard led us to a wide open field. On the far end stood the Belair Baptist Church. Kevin pointed to it. "That's our objective. There shouldn't be much traffic on Belair this time of night, but if you hear a car coming or see light, drop flat on the ground and wait. We're far enough away from the street that nobody should be able to make us out, but you never know."

He was off, running at full sprint. I took a deep breath and followed close behind. We made it to the rear of the church without encountering any late night traffic and hunched down in the shadow of a fenced-off dumpster to catch our breath.

I couldn't take the mystery anymore. "Dude, where the hell are we going?"

Kevin smiled as his eyes crawled up the side of the church, stopping only when they reached its flat rooftop.

I followed his gaze until it dawned on me. "Uh, no. First, my parents would kill me if I got caught on the roof of the church. Second, how the heck would we get up there anyway?"

Kevin ignored my protests. "Follow me, young Jedi, and be not afraid."

He stood and opened the gate housing the dumpster. Then, with the skill of a level ten thief, he shimmied up the side of the trash receptacle using the neighboring chain link fencing to help support him. Once on top of the dumpster, he waved me up whispering, "You're not afraid of heights, are you?"

With slightly less grace than my spider monkey friend, I managed to work my way up without totally embarrassing myself.

From where the two of us now stood, the roof was little more than chest height. Kevin was first again, jumping up and wrapping his arms around the brick ledge. His legs dangled in midair for a few seconds as he heaved himself over and disappeared from sight. I heard a soft thump followed by Kevin's voice. "It's a little dirty here, so watch your landing."

I didn't get as much vertical action on the launch, but with a little grunting and great deal of swearing, I breached the church's defenses and rolled off the ledge and into a pile of dried leaves and pebbles. "Crap!"

A hand grabbed my arm and pulled me up. "Told you to watch the landing."

I brushed myself clean and looked around. The church rested atop a large hill. From our vantage point, we could see the rooftops of the houses lining both Spindle and Sexton. In the opposite direction lay Belair and, in the distance, the tree tunnel.

I sucked in the wet air and uttered the only word I thought fitting for the occasion. "Cool."

"You can see everything around," Kevin responded. "I've been up here a couple times before. It's a good spot to just mellow out and think if you're into that kind of thing, but it's a *great* place for a little target practice."

"What are we gonna shoot at?"

Kevin started shuffling around, kicking his foot through the piles of leaves that blanketed the church's asphalt roof. "The good news is we're not the only ones that have snuck up here. Bingo!" He reached down and picked up a couple of empty beer cans. "Perfectamundo!"

He set the targets a few inches apart on top of an air conditioning unit on the far side of the roof about ten paces from where I stood. As he came back toward me, he said, "Okay, you get five shots to knock them off. I have the first five. Just watch what I do."

Kevin raised the gun. A hollow *plunk* echoed in the still night air as one of the cans fell. "One down, one to go." He repeated his actions and the second can jumped off the air conditioner.

I was duly impressed. Not only was Kevin the only kid I knew with a BB gun, but he also had the skills to use it. "Nice shooting, quick draw."

"Eh, these cans are no fun. Thought I saw some bottles up here somewhere. Take a look in the corner over there, and let me know if you find any. I'll check over here."

I worked my way to the far edge of the roof, shuffling through the dried leaves and trash from past visitors. That's when the cold prickles first hatched, starting on my forearms and crawling upward until they tickled the nape of my neck. I looked below.

It was standing beneath a streetlight again. This time it was looking up at me. I wanted to shout to Kevin, but I knew if I did, the thing would disappear into the shadows. I was also sure that if I turned and motioned for him to join me, by the time I looked back it would have vanished as well. Instead, I stood motionless, returning its icy gaze.

It was out in the open for all to see, but no one was watching except for me. The shadows cast from the light above managed to mask its features. All I could make out was its immense frame and pointed head. How long had it been there? Did it follow us from my house? Was I now under constant surveillance?

It knelt and scooped up a large clump of dirt with wicked, clawed fingers that acted like a steam shovel. With its other immense hand, it dropped something in the remaining crater. The creature let the earth fall back over the hole as it stood back up. It raised a hand to its face. Though its silhouette was all I could see, I knew in my gut what it was doing. In my mind I saw a single hooked finger pressed against foul lips. What was buried in the ground was meant to be kept secret. Our secret.

Chapter 7

I played it cool the rest of the night and waited until Kevin went home the next morning before going back to see what my stalker had left. It was still way too early in our friendship for me to share this level of crazy with Kevin. Better to break him in slowly.

My hands shook as I shoveled up the loose dirt. Whatever was in the shallow hole was meant for me. It was supposed to be a secret, one shared between the two of us, monster and boy.

Something long and thin was in my hands. It was a leather strap. No, not a strap but a collar. A dog collar. I wiped the dirt away with my fingers and examined the splotches of cracked red covering it. I was still a little sleepy, so it took a few seconds to register. When I realized what I held in my hands, I dropped it. The collar was from one of the dogs on the bike trail, one of the unfortunate canines that had been slaughtered just a week ago. Even though there were no tags or anything to identify the dog or its owner, I knew that's what it was. But why was the creature sharing it with me?

Something else was in the hole. I reached down and grabbed it, letting the extra dirt slip between my fingers. An orange butterfly barrette. This time I immediately knew where the tiny piece of plastic came from. It was one of a matching pair, and its twin was sitting on my sister's dresser.

A cold sweat sprouted on my forehead. "Shit."

The message was twofold, and it was received loud and clear. Part one: yes, I was the one on the bike trail that you interrupted in the middle of a furry buffet. Part two: know that I can get to you or your family anytime I want, so you should keep your mouth shut about what you've seen. But why the warning? Why even send me a message since I had no proof of anything? I had to be missing something. I pocketed the collar and barrette and—for reasons I couldn't explain—filled the small hole back in. I stood up, dusted the dirt off my knees, and slowly started back home.

Closing my eyes, I unleashed my mind and let it wander to the dark places. I needed to figure out what was happening. Why was I being stalked? Who or what was coming for me? Every time I went over it in my head, it all came back to one place. White Marsh. The bike trail was where I first encountered the creature. Just after that it started following me everywhere I went…at least I think it did. Maybe something else was buried on the trail that it didn't want me to find, or perhaps it had a lair hidden somewhere deep in the forest. And, most importantly, when was I going to stop referring to my stalker as a thing, creature, or beast and simply start calling it by its name—the Goatman.

Chapter 8

On the day of the filming, I cornered Paul and Kevin before our group left. By that time I had already told Kevin about my near death experience on the bike trail. I knew Paul would back up my claims in the event he doubted the story, so it wasn't too risky a move. But neither of them knew anything about the ominous messages the Goatman had been leaving me. I guess I figured it would be pushing it dumping so much on them and expecting them to believe it. Besides, if things went as I hoped they would, we'd find some kind of evidence on the trail that would help solve the mystery of the Goatman.

"Remember, when we get to the spot where I saw the blood, I'll give you the signal. We'll have to convince Steve it's a good place to stop and shoot some scenes. That will give us time to snoop around."

"Riiight, and what exactly are we looking for again?" Kevin asked.

"It's like Chris said," Paul exclaimed. "We're looking for the spot the Goatman killed the dogs."

From the moment Kevin and Paul met, it got a little weird. Paul was acting bossy with Kevin, and Kevin was being super sarcastic with Paul.

"I got that. But then what, Paul? What are we looking for other than the spot?"

I watched Paul's face flush and decided it was an excellent time to pipe in. "Wish I knew, but I don't. Guess we're just looking for something that's out of place, something that looks like it doesn't belong there."

"Oh, okay. Well, that's all you had to say."

"That *is* what I said," Paul answered.

I was glad to hear my brother's voice break in before it got ugly between the two of them. "Okay, get on your bikes, and let's head up to the trail. We need to scout out a location for the scene. We're looking for a good jungle setting, so keep your eyes peeled."

Steve whizzed by and then Perry. They were followed closely by the Johnson brothers, Mark and Brian. Mark was the older of the two and also going to be a senior. Brian was a year behind him but just as tall. The brothers were thick as thieves and always seemed to be smiling for one reason or another. Both were things I was a little jealous of given my current fraternal challenges. It wasn't until years later when my eyes were opened to the ignorance and stupidity of racism that I came to understand our friendship with the Johnsons may have been considered by some of narrow mind to be unusual or even inappropriate. The concept of judging someone by the color of their skin seemed as strange to any of us as judging them by the color of their eyes, hair, shirt, or shoes. Black, white—it was all the same on Spindle. Now if you were rapidly approaching sixteen and still wearing Toughskins, that was an entirely separate matter—you would be judged, and judged harshly.

One of Mark's familiar grins blossomed on his face as he rolled by. "Better get pedaling, Chris. Don't wanna be left behind!"

"That's right!" Brian added with a near-identical smile. "Don't want the director getting mad at you for slowing us down. You know how he can get."

I slipped between Kevin and Paul as we cruised down Stonybrook. Despite the sunny weather and cheerful mood of my companions, a familiar chill crept up my spine the closer we got to the bike trail.

"You okay, Chris?"

It was Paul's voice. I realized I was staring at the rapidly approaching trail entrance like a fruitcake. "Sure, just kind of weird being back here is all. I'll be fine."

"Good, 'cause I don't need you freaking out on me."

With Steve still in the lead, our group rolled onto the trail. We kept it painfully slow for some time as the older guys commented on what scenery would be the best fit for the movie. We were about a minute away from the target when our crew slowed to standstill.

I pulled up next to my brother. "What's the deal?"

"Mark and I think this place has potential. We're gonna check it out."

"No!" I belted the word out so loud that Mark jerked his head back. I realized I needed to dial it down pronto if I wanted a chance of winning my brother over. After taking a deep breath, I continued. "I mean, there's a spot just a little farther down the path that is way sweeter than this. We should check it out."

Steve got off his bike. "Keep your shirt on. We'll look at this one first and then yours."

"Man, Chris," Mark added, "just cool it like your brother said."

I watched the rest of them dismount—all except Kevin and Paul. If they chose this site before seeing the other, my carefully laid plans would be down the toilet. I had to think up something fast. "Steve, the other place is much better than this. Why don't you let me show it to Paul and Kevin, and they can vouch for me? You guys have to at least give it a shot."

Steve looked at Perry and the Johnson brothers with a blank face. "What do you think?"

Perry shrugged his shoulders.

Brian said, "Why don't you let the three stooges check it out?"

"Fine, but no goofing around. I want to get this shoot going, and you're already starting to get –"

I began pedaling before Spielberg had a chance to finish. "Thanks, be back soon!"

A couple of minutes later, we rolled up on the underbrush the creature had been lurking. Skidding to a stop, I dropped my bike in the dirt. I heard the rubber from Kevin and Paul's tires as they slid out behind me.

"Is this it? Is this the place?" Kevin asked.

"Yep."

"You think we're okay?" Paul asked. "I mean, it's just the three of us instead of seven."

"I think so. It's the middle of the day, and the other guys are within earshot. I'm sure we're fine." I had absolutely *no* idea whether we were in any actual danger. I was too stoked at the prospect of discovering something about the Goatman to care.

In a hushed tone Paul said, "I don't see any blood."

"Of course you don't," Kevin scoffed. "It's rained a couple of times since Chris said he was here."

"Whatever, numb nuts." Paul mumbled.

"What was that?"

"Ssshh," I said while pointing to the brush. "That's where it was hiding."

The three of us froze and stared at the grouping of stunted trees and bushes as if they were a pack of rabid wolves ready to attack at any moment.

I knew it was kind of a goofy thing to do, but I knelt down and picked up a good-sized branch from the ground. I was sure my friends were going to make fun of me. Instead, Paul grabbed his own stick, and Kevin scooped up a couple of broken chunks of asphalt that had crumbled away from the path.

I raised the branch in both hands and approached as my friends spread out in flanking positions. At least if I was attacked, they would have a chance to strike. Not that sticks and stones would be of much use against an ax-swinging, half-man, half-goat freak show.

The light of the mid-morning sun weakened the forest shadows. About ten feet away from our target, I saw we were in no immediate danger. "Looks like we're clear; nothing's back there. Now let's spread out. I'm not sure how much time we have before Steve comes looking for us."

We sifted the leaves and dirt and crawled through the surrounding bushes and brambles looking for something unusual or out of place. Kevin went so far as to start flipping over several large rocks—what he hoped to find I didn't dare ask. We had all but given up when Paul blurted out, "What the heck is that?"

Kevin and I followed Paul's gaze to a soaring white oak. Carved six feet up into the bark was a symbol:

"Freaky," Kevin said. "Looks like someone must have chiseled that sucker in."

I put an index finger on the design and traced the crescent shape and then the circle below. The cuts were smooth and a good inch deep. Something razor sharp with serious power had to have made those sweeping gouges. "I don't think a knife could cut like that. Look how perfect it is. There are no hack marks or signs of whittling."

Paul was next to touch it. "Maybe some kind of hook did it."

"Or a claw," Kevin added.

I was glad Kevin said it. This time I couldn't be the one blamed for diving off the deep end. For one of the very few times in my life, I chose the path of caution. "What kind of an animal could carve something like this? Look, it's almost a perfect circle and quarter moon."

"If it was a person, they're tall," Paul said. "If they reached out straight in front to make these markings, they'd have to be at least six feet at the shoulder."

"What do you think it means?" Kevin asked.

"Don't know. I've never seen anything like it," I said.

Paul kept his eyes locked on the symbol as he stepped back from the tree. "Sometimes when people are in the woods, they mark things, so they know where they've been. You know, so they don't get lost."

Kevin shook his head. "Lost…on the bike trail? C'mon, dude, it's not like this is the Amazon."

"A warning," I whispered.

"What was that?" Paul asked.

I turned to my friends. "It could be a warning—kind of like a no trespassing sign."

Kevin's eyes narrowed. "What good is a no trespassing sign if no one can read it?"

"Maybe they're initials or something like that," Paul theorized. "Like when you write your name in your school books so people know they're yours."

"Someone wanted us to know the *tree* is theirs?" Kevin teased.

Paul's cheeks turned pink. "No. They wanted us to know the *forest* is theirs. I wonder if we would find more of these if we looked around."

Footsteps came from behind. Somebody was approaching from the bike trail.

"What are you knuckleheads up to? Steve's starting to get pissed!"

Perry.

I looked at Paul and Kevin and shook my head, hoping they would get the point. This needed to be our secret for now. It was too early to share, and with no concrete proof that something supernatural or at the very least fiendish was going on, there was no point in sharing our discovery. All they would do is rag on us.

"What's so great about this place?" Perry huffed. "Doesn't look like anything special to me."

There was nothing more for us here. We found what we were looking for—at least I thought we did. There was no doubt in my mind that the symbol and the Goatman were connected. Maybe the creature was marking its territory like Paul suggested, but whether that proved to be the case or not, we didn't need Perry or Steve poking around yet. "Eh, maybe you're right; guess I remembered it a little differently."

"Yeah, well, you guys better get back. You're holding everything up, and you know how Steve gets."

For the next couple hours, the three of us screeched, hollered, and howled as we relentlessly pursued our prey through the dirt paths and alongside the muddy creek beds of White Marsh. It was funny in a warped sort of way. Just over a week ago, I was the one being hunted here—except then it was real. Now it was just Paul, Kevin, and me sporting a bunch of greasepaint and fake fur glued to our hands and faces as we chased Brian—otherwise known as Professor Benedict Haywood—at the command of the nefarious Doctor Gerard Dubois—aka Perry. Mark was always more comfortable behind the camera and content to serve as Steve's special effects and lighting coordinator. To sum up, the Professor triumphed in the end, defeating the doctor and his furry minions.

Steve had started off filming in a pissy mood, barking orders at me and my friends like we were nothing more than a pack of wild dogs, which we vaguely resembled in hindsight. But by the time we were finished, his mood lightened, and he seemed genuinely pleased with how the shoot went.

Steve pushed his glasses up, smiled, and announced, "Okay, that's a wrap! Let's head back. We have Italian ices and freeze pops at our house. Good job, guys!"

Getting praise from my brother lifted all of our spirits, and the ride back was a loud one filled with jokes and laughter as we took turns mocking each other's acting skills. Turning off Stonybrook and up Spindle, we passed Mr. Hutchinson watering his rosebushes. He waved at us and shouted as we rode by, "Christopher! Do you have a minute?"

Christopher, ugh. I hated it when adults used my full first name; it always made me feel like I was in trouble. I noticed Paul slow down and turn a frowning face to me as if to say, *Ignore the old man and keep pedaling.* I waved him off and circled back around.

Mr. Hutchinson released the hose nozzle and smiled as I approached. "Nice riding, young man. Looks like you guys are having fun today."

I was taught to always respect my elders and Mr. Hutchinson seemed a little cooler than most, but his timing really stank. For the first time in a very long time, I was actually having fun with my brother, and here the old man comes and wants to strike up a conversation smack dab in the middle of it. I swallowed my frustration and put on the best fake smile I could muster. "We were all just making a movie. It was kind of fun, I guess."

Mr. Hutchinson pulled a handkerchief from his back pocket and patted it on his forehead. "That's nice. Sorry to barge in on your merriment, son. I was just wondering if you would like to make a little extra cash this summer."

The annoying conversation suddenly got interesting. "Sure. What do you need me to do?"

"Do you know how to mow a lawn?"

I knew Mr. Hutchinson had seen me mowing our lawn, so the question seemed a little weird. "Sure. Me and my brother take turns doing it."

"Excellent! See, I'm afraid I'm getting a little too old for that type of thing. My knees and back aren't what they used to be. What would you say to coming over every Sunday starting tomorrow and mowing the front and back for let's say…fifteen dollars?"

I had never noticed Mr. Hutchinson having any difficulty with his yard, but I wasn't about to let that get in the way of making some serious moolah, especially since the going rate for a lawn the size of his was ten bucks. "You bet! I mean, I'd have to check with my dad, but I don't think it will be a problem."

"Good man! That's what I like to hear. Please, run it by your father. If he says yes, let's say you drop by tomorrow around ten o'clock. I'll give you a walk-through and then turn you loose."

"Sounds good, sir. I'll ask him tonight."

I'm pretty sure Mr. Hutchinson was still talking when I sped off. I wasn't trying to be rude. I was just pumped at the prospect of a paying job. Also, I was dying for an orange freeze pop.

Chapter 9

By the time I got the mower to Mr. Hutchinson's lawn, I was already sweating. The conversation with my dad started off a bit bumpy. At first he was confused as to why Mr. Hutchinson would ask me to mow his lawn versus Steve or one of the half dozen older boys in the neighborhood offering their services. He also wanted to know exactly what Mr. Hutchinson had to say to me. Apparently, interest in the old man wasn't limited to the younger generation and hadn't faded over time. After repeating our conversation three or four times, I reminded him that this would be my first paying job and the beginning of my journey to financial independence. That seemed to do the trick.

I wiped the sweat from my forehead as Mr. Hutchinson took me on a tour of his property while giving me a lesson on the finer points of lawn care. "Like I said, the front is pretty simple, just back and forth keeping an eye out for that stump I showed you next to the porch. There's no rocket science to the back either, as long as you remember to bag everything to avoid getting clippings in my petunia beds."

After offering several head nods and a handshake to seal the deal, I was mowing. The front yard went off without a hitch, but a third of the way through the back, I realized Mr. Hutchinson left out one major and potentially painful detail concerning its inhabitants. As it so happened, two pear trees bookended the property on its northern and southern sides. Though these trees grew no edible food, they did an impressive job of dropping bushel after bushel of stunted green fruit on the lawn. Pushing Dad's antique mower forward, I approached a bubbling sea of black and yellow. The mass of wasps gorging on the half-rotted fruit was an image born straight from one of the nine circles of Hell. At any moment I was sure to be swallowed by a swarm of yellow jackets and stung until I swelled up like a tick that had struck an artery. I slowed down and pushed the mower as far out in front as possible in the hopes it would scare off at least some of the winged spawn of Satan. Back and forth, north and south, I rolled over dozens of the insect-riddled pears. A few successful passes later, I realized I might actually make it out alive. The noise and smoke belching from the Lawn Boy did an excellent job of keeping the flying terrors at bay. Still, a little heads up from Mr. Hutchinson sure would have been nice. Minus ten points.

After enduring a half hour of white-knuckled fun, I parked the mower out front and knocked on his door.

He opened it almost immediately. His big white teeth seemed to glow against the backdrop of his tanned face. "I heard the mower stop and figured you were done. Why don't you come in for a minute and cool off while I get your money? I'm guessing you could probably use a soda. I have Coke and Orange Shasta."

I wasn't in the mood to jibber jabber with Mr. Hutchinson, but the chilly air coming from inside his house felt amazing, and the offer of a cold drink was too good to pass up.

"A Coke would be nice, thanks."

"You're quite welcome, son. Please, do come in."

The inside of Mr. Hutchinson's house seemed dark compared to the sun-drenched world I was exiting. Passing several paintings, I followed him down the front hall to the dining room as my eyes slowly adjusted. It opened to a room with a large oak table occupying its center. To the right was the kitchen and to the left stood an enormous hutch against the far wall. Below the china and crystal, several portraits rested on the lowest tier of the grand old cupboard. A beautiful black-haired women was the subject in all of them.

Though sparse, his furnishings all looked solid and very old. Somehow it seemed right to me. Here was an old man with equally old furniture. They were made for each other, both worn and scratched up from decades of use but still strong and sturdy. Something was missing though, something I couldn't quite put my finger on. After a few more seconds, it dawned on me. There were no photographs to be seen. No baby pictures, pictures of weddings, holidays—nada. Coming from a house wallpapered with photos of aunts, uncles, grandparents, cousins, and siblings, that seemed strange to me.

"Have a seat at the table."

I watched as he grabbed a can of soda from the fridge. "Do you prefer in the can or in a glass with ice?"

"Can is fine, sir."

Mr. Hutchinson handed me the Coke and took a seat at the opposite end of the table. He looked out of a large sliding glass door that offered a view of the backyard. "I believe I forgot to mention the fruit from those trees can attract bees and yellow jackets. They scatter when the mower comes at them though."

Was he watching me? "Yeah, I found that out."

The old man chuckled. "Sorry about that. Hope they didn't give you too much trouble. Always remember, it's important to keep a level head and your wits about you when something scares you. Though I'm sure you don't need that advice. You seem like the type of boy that doesn't unhinge too easily."

I took a swig of the soda. The bubbles tickled my nose as the cool sweetness rolled down my throat. It hit the spot. "Thanks, sir, but I don't know about that. My brother and his friends say I have an overactive imagination and get freaked out too easy. They're always messing with me about it."

Wrinkles creased the corners of Mr. Hutchinson's eyes as his smile widened. "Yes, well, older kids have a tendency to poke fun at younger ones; it's in their nature to do so. Personally, I never associated a robust imagination with cowardice. Don't sell yourself short, young man. Possessing mental agility is one of the joys of youth. As we get older and our brains harden, we often close our eyes and ears to the fantastic. We get narrow in our views and rigid in our beliefs. Hold on to your fancy, Christopher Dwyer, and remember, a dreamer is one who can only find his way by moonlight, and his punishment is that he sees the dawn before the rest of the world."

The old man had a crazy way of talking. I decided I liked it even though I didn't have a clue what he was saying half the time. Twenty more bonus points for Mr. Hutchinson. "Yes, sir."

"That wasn't me by the way; it was Oscar Wilde. He was a bit of a dandy, but he possessed a cutting wit nonetheless."

"Was he a friend of yours?" I asked.

More laughter. This time it was louder and warmer. "No, son, I'm not quite that old, though I may look it. Just remember, it may be true you have a slightly overactive imagination, but it is just as likely that you are a highly perceptive individual."

Was he reading my mind? "That's what I've been trying to tell people, but they *never* listen."

"They usually don't, but that is no reason to lose heart. Those of us possessing creative thought and verve often find ourselves on the receiving end of mockery—particularly from our siblings. Now remind me, you have an older brother and younger sister, correct?"

"Yep. Steve's my brother. He's only two years older, but he acts like he's twenty. Katie's my kid sister. She's cute and all, but my mom always wants me to look after her, and it can be a bit of a drag, especially when I want to hang out with my friends."

"I'm sure your mother appreciates the help. It's an important responsibility being a big brother."

"I guess."

"How about school. Are you doing well?"

Sometimes I wondered if adults went to a class where they were given a standard set of questions to ask kids. "I'm getting As and Bs, so I guess I'm doing okay."

"Excellent. Favorite subject?"

"Mmm, not sure. I hate math. If I had to pick, I guess I would say history or maybe English."

"Two of mine as well. Now keep in mind, son, one of the easiest ways to let your grades slip is to get involved in delinquency. I hope you're steering clear of all of the drugs and other vices that appear to be corrupting so many of our youth nowadays."

The conversation seemed to be gradually steering into some kind of back door interrogation. If I didn't know better, I'd swear my mom put Mr. Hutchinson up to this. But I was pretty sure he wasn't yet a member of the neighborhood watch commonly known as the Mom Mafia. Whatever the reasons were behind his questions, I had nothing to hide. "No way! No drugs here."

"I'm delighted to hear that. These are tumultuous times. Things are changing so fast, and there are so many opportunities for young men and women to stray from the beaten path."

I watched as his tired eyes turned toward the window and the smile fell from his face.

"It's been almost two decades since this suburban monstrosity took root. In that amount of time, I have witnessed the beauty and serenity of this county turn into acre after acre of houses, malls, churches, fast food restaurants, and gas stations. It's gotten worse since my sweet Abby left."

I kept my mouth shut. Mr. Hutchinson appeared to be deep in thought, and I figured it would be rude to interrupt him. There was something really sad about the way he stared at his freshly cut lawn.

After several seconds of awkward silence, he looked back at me. The smile slowly returned. "Forgive me. When you get to be my age, the mind tends to wander."

"That's okay. My grandma can go on and on talking about the good old days. Sometimes she'll get halfway through a story and forget what she was talking about. I have to remind her."

Mr. Hutchinson gave a little laugh. "Yes, that happens the older you get. I'm not there yet, but my time is sure to come."

"If it's any consolation, I think you're a ways off from that. You haven't repeated yourself yet, and you haven't forgotten my name. Those are both things my grandma does. So, did you live here before Bowie was built?"

"No, but I was here when Bowie was very small, before Mr. Levitt bought everything and ripped up the land to crank out the *marvelous* cookie-cutter homes we live in. I resided a few miles north of here not too far from where the racetrack is now. I had a modest farm where I grew barley and some tobacco. Had a small apple orchard too."

"That sounds nice."

"It was. Was a much simpler time too. People kept to themselves and respected one another's privacy. I remember when I could look out my window and see nothing but oceans of bearded barley and wave after wave of apple blossoms. Now," Mr. Hutchinson waved his hand back and forth, "all you see are rows of carbon-copied houses packed into ill-conceived, alliterative neighborhoods; all you hear are the relentless, mind-numbing drone of streetlights interrupted by the calamitous dirge of automobiles racing this way and that."

The kindness left his face. "In just a handful of years, the living countryside was bulldozed to make way for this ant farm we call suburbia."

As my host's mood slowly turned chaotic evil, my eyes dropped to the money he was holding in his hand. It was half of what I needed to buy my own *Player's Handbook*. I had to stay the course, no matter the cost.

A few painfully long seconds later, his face softened. "Sorry about that, son. I believe I lost myself in time. Aside from some fading memories, all I have left from that bygone age are my paintings, some dusty old furnishings, and a few family heirlooms."

I felt the urge to say something kind to keep him from slipping back to the dark side. "You have a lot of really cool stuff here, Mr. Hutchinson. The furniture looks nice and so do the paintings, like the one behind you with the lady in the white dress. She's very pretty."

The old man glanced over his shoulder at the portrait of a beautiful young woman with dark hair and the whitest skin. A tiny smile split across his face. "Ah yes, that is Mrs. Hutchinson."

I felt like a complete boob. "I'm sorry. I didn't mean to –"

"That's all right, boy. I'm sure you've heard the rumors surrounding Abigail's disappearance."

I began stammering. "I-I don't–"

"Oh, come now! What's the prevailing theory?" His smile stretched wide. "That I murdered her during some marital spat and buried her in a secret place or perhaps that she absconded with her Latin gigolo? Or is it something else entirely? I have to admit, I haven't heard anything original in some time, so I'm curious."

All I wanted to do was slide under the table and crawl out of the house. Nothing I could say or do would make things better. Did he actually expect me to tell him my friends were convinced he was an ax-wielding psychopath who killed his wife and chopped her up into itty-bitty pieces? "I don't know about all of that stuff. My folks said it's not nice to–"

Low, wheezing laughter cut me off. It was like he was remembering an old joke he'd heard a thousand times before. "I'm sorry, son. That wasn't fair of me, but you see I don't get much company anymore, and I'm afraid my social skills have suffered all the more for it. Please understand I'm not trying to be cruel, and I'm fairly certain I'm not going crazy—inasmuch as any man can be sure. Sometimes, though, when memories festering of failure, regret, or anguish leak into my thoughts, I turn to laughter as a balm. Do you forgive me?"

Any hard feelings I might have had disappeared with his words. "Sure. It's okay. I think I get it."

"I thought you would. As for all my wonderful paintings, you may have guessed I'm not a fan of photographs, never have been. I believe something is lost in the process of taking a snapshot of one's life and immortalizing it forever on film. To me it detracts from the full beauty and quality of the subject. With a little oil and some canvas, a true artist can capture not just the literal but the spiritual aspects of the individual. All of that is lost in the antiseptic practice of photography."

He stood and stretched both arms to the ceiling. "Now as promised."

He extended the hand clasping the fifteen dollars.

I got up, took the money, and swiftly pocketed it. "Thanks!"

"Of course. You earned every cent. Also, I appreciate you entertaining my rants. I imagine I gave you a little more than you bargained for. You, Chris, have the patience of Job and wisdom of Solomon. Same time next week?"

"Yes, sir! And really, it was no big deal. It was actually kind of nice talking to you."

"The feeling's mutual, son. Now go have some fun before you turn into an old, doddering fool like me."

Chapter 10

My summer reading list served as the perfect cover for a trip to the Prince George's County Library. If not for *Fahrenheit 451* and *Lord of the Flies*, I would've had to convince my mom I'd developed a sudden interest in being cooped up with a bunch of dusty old books instead of burning away the summer days poolside or gaming at Kevin or Paul's while working my way through a mountain of cheese puffs and Twinkies. It's not that I didn't like reading. I just believed there was a time for it, and summer was definitely not that time. I thought about asking Paul and Kevin to join me but reconsidered when I remembered how they'd been going at it like a couple of grouchy old biddies. Hopefully they'd mellow out once they got to know each other better.

After getting some help from the librarian, I found my books. With that junk out of the way, I began exploring the shelves and card catalogue in pursuit of my true mission. The symbol we saw carved into the oak meant something—it had to. Whether it was a warning or some kind of territorial marking remained to be seen, and I hoped to find a clue to its origin and how it was linked to the Goatman somewhere within these walls.

The musty smell of aging paper followed me as I wandered for a half hour through rows of science fiction, history, geography, horror, and mythology. I focused my efforts on books tied to symbolism, religion, and the occult, but I wasn't having much luck. I was fried, frustrated, and very close to calling it quits when I heard a voice from behind.

"Dude, you've been creeping around these aisles for a while now, but it looks to me like you're still lost. Am I right?"

The guy was older than Steve by a couple years. He had long, gnarly hair and wore a pair of round sunglasses, which I thought was odd since we were indoors. As he approached, an invisible cloud of funk followed. The hippie smelled like he'd been camping for a week, got in a fight with a skunk, and then decided to stand by the campfire in the hopes that the smoke would help cover up the skunk smell. If that was his plan, it didn't work. I knew enough not to ask for help from anyone who worked there in case the symbol I was looking for was tied to something dark, maybe even satanic. The last thing I needed was some nosey librarian telling my parents their son was a devil worshipping freak, but something told me this guy wasn't the judgmental type. I decided to take a chance. "I'm looking for a book on symbolism."

He snickered. "There's a lot of books on symbols here, little man. You're gonna have to be more specific."

I guessed the direct approach would be the best one with Cheech and Chong. I put my finger in the air and made a loop. "What I'm looking for has a circle," I continued with an arc up and to my right and then another just above it back to the left, "with a crescent moon sitting on top of it."

The stoner's eyebrows perked beyond the rims of his sunglasses. "Groovy. Think I know what you're after. Follow me."

We skipped by a couple rows and then turned down an aisle as my guide extended his hand and ran his fingertips across the book spines. He slowed down. "Aaand we're here."

He pulled a thin black book out from a shelf and tossed it to me. "You'll find what you're looking for in there."

I flipped it to the front. In gold lettering were the words *Pagans and the Occult*. "Pagans? What are pagans?"

"Open it up and find out. Expand your mind beyond what you've been brainwashed to believe is the truth." Cheech and Chong turned around and waved a hand as he walked away. "Good luck finding what you're looking for, dude, and remember, don't ever let anyone tell you what to think. Peace in the Middle East!"

"Okay...thanks." I had no idea what he was talking about. I focused back on the book. It was written by some fancy pants professor who claimed to be an occult expert. Skipping all that junk, I dove right into the good stuff. Each chapter appeared to be about a particular symbol. There were triangles and stars, hearts, and a bunch of swirly circles. Three quarters of the way through, I found it. The chapter was titled *The Horned God*. Beneath the words was my circle with the crescent moon resting above it. My heart broke into a gallop and my hands went clammy. Even though I wasn't doing anything wrong, I glanced up to make sure no one was watching. Satisfied that none of the surrounding people cared a lick about me, I read on.

The horned god is a relatively new personification of an ancient entity. In Wicca he is the masculine form of the divine and is both equal and opposite to the goddess. The origins of the being go much, much deeper, however. From the Celts to the ancient Greeks and Romans, versions of a powerful horned divinity are a frequent occurrence. Whether he is called Cernunnosor or Pan is irrelevant. What he represents is key. He is a personification of the male side of nature, both powerful and chaotic. In Judaism and Christianity more sinister origins are ascribed to him under the monikers of various demons and devils such as Baphomet, Behemoth, and Lucifer.

I swallowed hard, trying to push my heart back down out of my throat. *Lucifer. Wonderful.*

"Did you find what you were looking for?"

I almost dropped the book as I jerked to attention. When Mom wanted to, she could be as stealthy as any ninja. Holding the book in my left hand, I casually let it drop to my side and tried to sound as cool as possible. "Eh, not a whole lot here that I'm interested in."

"Oh really?"

Mom glanced at the book and then looked back to me. She had the tiniest smirk on her face. "What do you have there?"

"It's nothing, just a –"

"Then why don't you let me see what *nothing* is?"

Busted. With my head hung low, I handed her the book.

She read the cover. The tone of her voice was more curious than stern. "Why are you looking at this? Does it have something to do with that dungeons game?"

Bingo. That was it, my way out. "Well, yeah—I mean—yes. I was doing some research for a campaign I'm putting together."

Mom sighed. "If only you put half as much thought and effort into your studies as you do that game. You need to spend more time on your assigned reading, understood?"

"Yes."

"Good." She handed it back to me. "I also don't like the look of that book. It stays here in the library."

Over the years I learned to be extremely careful when expressing a difference of opinion with my mom. She could outthink Einstein and outwit Columbo. It was only on rare occasions and in the most desperate of circumstances when I dared challenge her, and even then it almost always ended bad for me. This was not one of those times. The book went back on the shelf but not before I memorized the title and author.

Chapter 11

The next few days flew by. I split my time between acting in Steve's movie, splashing around at BBT, and plotting with Kevin on ways to brainwash Paul into liking *D and D*. Although I shared what I discovered at the library with both of them, with no more dead dogs showing up on the evening news and no messages scrawled in blood or buried barrettes, the subject quickly faded from our thoughts. In retrospect, the sudden silence should have aroused my suspicion, but in truth, we were having too much fun for me to notice.

We finished the last shots of *The Jungle of Doctor Dubois* in our backyard. When we were done filming, we celebrated with a feast of RC Cola and lemon and cherry fruit pies. The whole crew was there: Perry, Paul, Kevin, Steve, Mark, Brian, and even Katie, who made a brief appearance in the film as the evil doctor's assistant. Tracy also dropped by to watch us wrap up. With my dad at work and my mom running errands, we had the run of the place.

It was in this state of super-caffeinated, sugared-fueled mania that someone decided it would be a good idea to commence with the next engagement in our never-ending apple war with the Drake Boys. There were three of them, all dirtbags ranging in ages from twenty to twenty-four. The border in our skirmishes was our back fence. A mix of chokeberry and Virginia-creeper grew thick and wide at its base and gradually thinned as it stretched upwards. The wall of weeds blocked all direct visual contact with the enemy. The implied weapons of choice for both sides were crab apples that grew in abundance on both our properties, but sometimes ice cubes and the occasional rock found their way into the fray. For the life of me, I can't remember who started the war, but to call it such might be a bit of an exaggeration. Most of the enemies' assaults were of the hit and run variety. One might end up with an apple to the head while mowing the lawn or playing in the backyard with friends. Steve and I fell victim to these cowardly attacks on multiple occasions, but Tracy had been the most recent casualty. For that reason, I'm pretty sure it was our queen who launched the first apple.

None of us could tell if she got lucky with her throw, but a quick volley of returning apples let us know at least one of the Drake Boys was there. Game on. This time would be different though. We had eight fruit slingers on our side—eight and a half if you counted my sister—and, more importantly, Tracy was *pissed*. We grabbed handfuls of apples and let loose, peppering the sky with green. For the first few seconds, it was fast and furious as we exchanged a barrage of quarter-sized fruit, but soon we overwhelmed the enemy and the return fire ceased.

"Take that, suckas!" Paul screamed as he flung six apples in rapid succession.

"Yeah, you dicks!" Tracy added as she unloaded her own arsenal.

The Johnson brothers broke out laughing while emptying their hands of the tiny fruit.

Then it happened.

From over the fence came a shout. "Son of a bitch! Which one of you little shits are throwing rocks?"

We looked at one another with blank expressions—except for Tracy, whose lips were pinched tight.

"If one more apple, rock, or anything else flies over this fence, I'm coming over, and I'm gonna kick all of your asses!"

Only one of them was back there, but it sounded like Russell. At twenty he was the youngest of the bunch but also the meanest.

This time I witnessed the act. With an evil little grin popping up between her plump little cheeks, Katie made one final attempt to lob an apple over the fence after many unsuccessful tries. Time seemed to slow down as we watched the tiny fruit skirt above the barricade with hardly an inch to spare. Squeals of delight followed as my sister howled and started hopping in place.

The fence started quivering. The festive wave we were all riding crashed hard and a general panic followed. Stampeding out of the backyard, we poured onto the street. It wasn't until we were halfway to the Johnsons' house and safety—their mom and older brothers were home—that I looked back and noticed Katie was way behind. I shouted to my brother and took off after her. By the time I caught up with my sister, it was too late.

Russell Drake stepped between us and shoved me down on the pavement.

I landed hard, scraping a hand in the process.

"How you like that, you little pansy?"

I started to get up but froze when he moved in and cocked his right hand. I could smell the beer on his stale breath. "Try and stand, and I swear to God I'm gonna knock the taste right outta your mouth! Now," he pointed to a thin stream of blood that trickled down his greasy, pockmarked face, "which of your friends threw the rock? If you tell me, I'll only break their arm. If you don't cough it up, I break yours, your little sister's, and everyone else's I can get my hands on!"

Before I could answer the creep, I heard Steve's voice from behind me. "Leave him alone!"

Tracy spoke next. "Yeah, Russell! Feel like a big man picking on someone half your size?"

"Look who it is! Four eyes and his little girlfriend. How'd a fag like you land a fox like that?"

The sneer on Russell's face twisted up into a Grinch-like smile. He looked at Tracy. "Why don't you dump that loser and upgrade to a real man? You look like you could handle it. Oh baby! The things I could show you!"

Tracy's nose scrunched in disgust. Her mouth opened wide, preparing to unleash what would no doubt have been the mother of all comebacks, but she never got the chance.

"Problem here?"

Mr. Hutchinson must have learned his ninja skills from my mother. He was staring at Russell with hard gray eyes.

"This is none of your business, geezer. Stay out of it unless you want a smackdown."

Ignoring Russell, he looked down to my kid sister and smiled. "Katie dear, go ahead and get behind your brothers."

Katie hesitated for a few seconds before scooting around Russell to me.

"Hey, old man! I said—"

Mr. Hutchinson's eyes shot back to Russell Drake. A tiny sneer curled on his face. "Trying so hard to play the tough guy but can't even manage to scare a bunch of children, huh Russell?" He turned around and winked at me. "Why don't you four skedaddle. It's time Mr. Drake and I had a heart-to-heart about where his life is taking him."

It was the strangest thing. Even though Mr. Hutchinson had to be in his eighties, a part of me almost felt worried for Russell. There was a fire in Mr. Hutchinson's eyes and strength in his voice that convinced me the old timer could clean the floor with the creep if he wanted to. He looked ten feet tall at the time. I nodded and got to my feet. Together the three of us rejoined the group half a block away. 100 bonus points to Mr. Hutchinson.

By the time we got there, everyone started talking at once. My brother raised a hand to hush them. "All right! All right! One at a time."

Perry started. "What did Mr. Hutchinson say to Russell? Is he going to call the cops on him?"

Brian chimed in before Steve could respond. "Does he have a gun in his hand? Thought I saw a gun."

"No, no gun. All he said was..."

With his own brand of dramatic flair, my brother described the exchange between man and goon. As he did this, I looked back and watched the continuing altercation. The two faced off a couple feet apart. Unfortunately, they were too far away for me to hear anything, and Mr.

Hutchinson had his back turned to us. A few seconds into their conversation, the oddest thing happened. With no apparent baiting from Russell, the old man lunged forward a foot. At the same time, Russell stumbled backward, almost tripping over himself. His eyes bulged and the color drained from his face. Even though Mr. Hutchinson had stopped moving, Russell kept retreating, muttering something the whole time. Finally, he turned tail and bolted through our yard back to his house. With the curious confrontation over, I forced my attention back on our group just as Steve finished his story.

"…and that was it. He told the four of us to come over here and that he was going to have a heart-to-heart with Russell."

Brian pointed to Mr. Hutchinson. "Guess he's done. Looks like Russell didn't dig whatever Mr. Hutchinson had to say. I've never seen white trash blow away so fast."

I noted the only one not captivated with Steve's story was Paul. He was looking at me with a puzzled expression. He mouthed the words, *What the heck?*

"Everybody okay over here?"

Mr. Hutchinson was once more wearing his familiar smile.

"We're fine, sir," my brother said. "Thanks for bailing us out. He said he was going to break our arms."

"Yes, I heard. I don't think that's anything you are going to have to worry about from here on out. But still," he glanced over the lot of us as his smile stretched wider, "let's refrain from tossing rotten fruits or rocks into the Drake's backyard. We don't need to have any more misunderstandings, do we?"

We responded in unison. "No."

"Excellent. I knew you were a smart bunch. Now is anyone hurt?"

No one answered until Kevin pointed to my hand. "Chris, you're bleeding."

In all the chaos and excitement, I forgot about my scrape.

"He is indeed," said Mr. Hutchinson. "Steve, Chris, I take it your mother is not home?"

"That's right," Steve said.

"Okay then. Chris, let's get that hand cleaned up and bandaged. As for the rest of you, please try to keep the mischief to a minimum for the remainder of the day."

Back at his house, Mr. Hutchinson retrieved a wide bandage and bottle of Mercurochrome from his medicine cabinet. "This is going to sting a little, but we want to make sure the wound is clean."

I nodded and braced myself as he dabbed the rust-colored liquid on the wound with a cotton ball. Wet and cool was quickly followed by a mild burning sensation.

"What did you do to earn this battle scar, son?"

"I went back to get Katie. She got left behind by accident."

"Ahh, so you returned to rescue your sister."

"I don't know about that. We just forgot about her; that's all."

"Hmm. Brave and modest. I suppose that shouldn't surprise me. There, all bandaged up."

"Thanks."

"You are quite welcome, young man. A word of advice though. Be more careful on your bike."

"My bike?"

"That is how you injured your hand, right? Unless, of course, you have another story you would like to tell your parents. One that involves throwing things in a neighbor's yard and almost getting into a fight with a thug?"

"Ohhh, yeah. A bike wreck, that's definitely what happened."

"You may want to share your story with you brother and sister to make sure there is no confusion."

"Yes, sir."

Since getting to Mr. Hutchinson's house, I'd been dying to find out what he said to Russell to make him bail so fast. Now that we were alone, I summoned up the courage. "Can I ask you something?"

"Certainly."

"What did you say to Russell? See, I know he's bad news and has even been arrested before. I just don't understand how someone that mean and angry can suddenly become so…"

"Scared?"

"I guess."

A soft laugh. "Let me tell you something about bullies, Chris. For all of their bark, their bite is usually rather weak. I have lived a long time and encountered people far more dangerous and intimidating than that foul-mouthed miscreant. Most of the time all they need is a good thump on the nose with a rolled up newspaper, and they whimper away."

"Huh?"

"They just need somebody to call their bluff and expose them for the true cowards they are."

"And that's what you did, called his bluff?"

"Precisely. However, don't get me wrong. You should avoid Russell Drake like the plague. Though he is craven, he is also violent and petty. That was the reason he attacked you kids in the first place. No, the lot of you would be better off tiptoeing around the Drake's. At least until his comeuppance."

"Comeuppance?"

"That's right. Everyone that has ever wandered down the road of vice, cruelty, and larceny eventually gets their comeuppance. Remember, my boy, in the end all brutes, hoodlums, and murderers owe the devil his due."

Chapter 12

After a couple days of editing the film down to size and splicing it back together in all the right places, Spielberg was ready to premiere his masterpiece. The neighborhood kids and their parents were all invited over for the first ever showing of Steven Dwyer's *The Jungle of Doctor Dubois*. It was a catered affair complete with hot dogs, burgers, and all the baked beans you could eat—courtesy of my folks. Neighbors brought bowls of potato and macaroni salad, crockpots of chili, molds of gelatin, and a ton of chips, cheese puffs, and pretzels. We kids enjoyed being in the movies, and most were thrilled to see themselves on the silver screen, but the films served a greater purpose, bringing pretty much all of Spindle—and portions of Spiral and Stonybrook—together for what amounted to one heck of a block party.

The evening's festivities would commence with the movie followed by the chow down. The living room was packed wall-to-wall with kids and parents. While the adults relaxed on the motley mix of sofas, recliners, and folding chairs brought out for the event, my friends and I were reduced to fighting over the tiny scraps of shag carpet closest to the screen.

As the lights were turned down, Steve gave Perry a slight nod. Having received his silent instructions, Perry placed the needle on the forty-five and let Credence Clearwater Revival's *Run Through the Jungle* play. This was the seventh movie Steve had shown with Perry's technical support, and the two had it down to a science. I had to hand it to my brother. With Fogerty setting the mood in the background and Steve's spot-on narration, I almost forgot I was watching a silent film. I'm pretty sure all of us did.

Not even thirty seconds into the movie, I got an elbow from Kevin. "You hear they found another body with no head?"

"Where?"

"Not too far from the railroad tracks out by Fletchertown Road. The guy on the news said the man may have been hit by a train. He didn't sound convincing."

"Ssshh!"

I turned to Steve. Even in the dimly lit room, I saw the whites of his eyes as he glared at me. We were interrupting the premiere, and there would be hell to pay if we didn't zip it.

Clueless, Kevin continued. "The news guy said about two years ago they found a couple of bodies in the same area also missing their heads, and the police never solved the case. But you want to hear the freakiest thing about the deaths?"

"No, I *don't*," I said in a hushed tone.

A sound rolled up Kevin's throat but died on his lips. He stared at me with his mouth wide open, clearly confused by my lack of curiosity.

"Not right now," I said. "Steve's going to beat the crap out of me if we dork up his movie. Tell me after."

For the next fifteen minutes, we listened as our parents tossed question after question at the director. Steve handled them like a pro, answering each one while never missing a beat on the narration. When everything was said and done, *The Jungle of Doctor Dubois* turned out to be a smash hit. Everyone laughed where they were supposed to, gasped when the heroes were in danger, and showered the cast and crew with applause as the movie ended. In that moment of celebration, I felt a pang of guilt for the below-the-belt shot I hit my brother with the week before—the verbal one, not the kick in his doodads. I didn't mean what I said about him ripping off other movies, but it was a way to get his attention. It was kind of funny, I guess. I'd rather have him furious with me than ignoring me.

At the end of the movie, everyone headed to the backyard to pig out. With half a cheeseburger still in his mouth, Kevin finished relaying the news story to Paul and me. "…and the creepiest thing was, they never found the heads."

"*Any* of the heads?" Paul asked.

Kevin swallowed hard as his eyes locked on Paul's. "None."

The sound of my dad's voice interrupted. "Grab some marshmallows, guys! That is of course, unless you'd prefer to skip the s'mores!"

After impaling our puffy treats on sticks we found in the backyard, we gathered around the campfire pit my dad had blazed up as soon as the movie ended. The fire was now low but steady and perfect for toasting. As the sun dipped below the horizon and the firelight glowed on all of our faces, my brother said in a low voice, "You guys ever heard the story of Crybaby Bridge?"

I knew the name and remembered hearing bits and pieces of the story from years ago but couldn't remember exactly how it went. From the hushed "Nos" and "uh-uhs" of my fellow actors, I wasn't alone.

"So," Steve said, "it begins a long time ago—before the Civil War. The slave of a rich family became pregnant and had a baby. As it turned out, the baby's father was the owner of the plantation. He was already married and didn't want another kid, so he banished the woman, sending her into the forest with her newborn baby and just a little bit of food."

In respectful silence we passed the Hershey Bars and graham crackers until they made their journey around the circle of fire. Some were desperate to bite into their crunchy, chocolatey treats and pulled their mallows out too soon. Those of us in the know, those true s'more experts, understood you had to wait until the marshmallow was a crispy golden brown before removing it from the fire and tucking it in its chocolate and graham bed. This tried and true practice assured optimal gooeyness and flavor.

"After a couple of days in the bitterly cold woods, the woman got desperate. She thought that if she got rid of the baby, she might be allowed to return to the plantation. That's when she came across this bridge. Checking first to make sure no one was looking," Steve thrust both of his hands forward over the fire, "she threw the baby into the water, and let it drown in the raging waters. On dark and lonely nights, they say you can still hear the baby crying if you go to the bridge."

"Man, that's messed up," Brian mumbled.

"What happened to the lady?" Kevin asked.

"When the plantation owner found out what she had done, he wouldn't let her come back. The woman was so upset she went crazy. She ran back to the same river she tossed her baby into and jumped in herself, never to be seen or heard from again."

"That's *really* messed up," Brian said.-

I thought about the story, unaware of the sound escaping my big, fat mouth. "Hmm."

"Hmm, what?" Steve demanded.

Busted, I tried to backtrack. "Nothing. It's nothing."

"No, you said, 'Hmm.' That was definitely something. Out with it, dungeon master. Is the story too boring for you?"

I knew he wasn't going to let up until I responded, so I decided to tell him the truth. "No, it's not boring. It's just…it doesn't sound that scary. It's more sad to me."

"You say that now, but let's see if you'd feel the same way if you heard a baby crying late at night in the middle of some dark forest next to a bridge known to be haunted."

I didn't want to get into with my brother, not in front of all my friends. "I guess."

"So, it's a scary ghost story you want to hear?"

We all looked to Perry.

A dab of melted chocolate and marshmallow clung to the side of his mouth as he cleared his throat and began. "If that's the case, I got a good one for you. It's about our friend the Goatman. You know, the guy that's been busy this summer killing dogs and chopping people's heads off."

"Ohhh brother," Paul moaned. "Is this the same story you tried to scare Chris and me with a couple weeks ago?"

Perry scowled at his kid brother. "No and shut up! This is an old one you haven't heard before. It's about the Goatman's first known victim, and it happened about ten or so years back. Yeah, that'd be about right."

A hush fell on the group. By now we all knew about the recent body discovered near Fletchertown Road and the specter of the Goatman was in the back of all of our minds.

Perry started. "Back then there was this guy and girl on a date. They're driving along this lonely dirt road, and all of a sudden their car breaks down. Turns out they had run out of gas, so the guy says to his girlfriend that he'll head down the road to get some. Just before he splits, he tells her to lock all the doors and not to open them for *any* reason. A couple hours pass, and it's getting real late, so finally the girl climbs into the backseat and goes to sleep. She wakes up a few hours later, and it's still dark. That's when she starts hearing this sound coming from above. It's a swish-swish sound like something is brushing against the roof of the car. She's about to open the door to check it out but remembers her boyfriend's warning, so she plays it cool instead. The sound continues and she ends up falling back asleep listening to it, swish-swish, swish-swish. Time passes and there's a knock on the window. She wakes up and sees a policeman there, so she rolls down the window. She asks him if there is something wrong and where is her boyfriend. But the cop doesn't answer her questions. Instead, he tells her to get out of the car and not to turn around—no matter what. The girl thinks it's a weird thing to say, but the guy is a cop, so she does what he says. Except... after she gets out, she gets too curious and looks back."

Perry paused for dramatic effect.

A voice gushing nervous energy asked, "What was behind her?"

I turned to Paul. His wide eyes reflected the flames from the fire. Guess he hadn't heard this story before.

The right corner of Perry's mouth twisted up. "Hanging upside down from a tree directly over the roof of the car was her boyfriend. At least the clothes the body had on were her boyfriend's. See, there was no head; it had been chopped clean off." Perry picked up a paper plate. He made a fist and started brushing his knuckles against the back of it. "The sound the girl heard was the hand of her dead boyfriend scratching back and forth across the roof of the car as his body swayed in the tree. On the trunk of the car was a message written in the boy's blood. It said, 'Beware the Goatman.'"

Paul continued his line of questioning. "Is that a true story? It's not... right?"

Perry shrugged. "Can't say for sure, but I heard it from a guy who was dating a girl that knew the girl from the story. They say she went nuts after that and had to be checked into an asylum."

With the parents having moved back inside to enjoy a wide variety of adult beverages and a puff or two of their Camels, Salems, and Newports, silence descended on our group. The crackle and pop of the fire seemed to grow louder in the stillness. The golden glow of the dying sun had vanished, and a darkness you could almost touch crept into our camp. I looked around at my friends and noticed the same haunted expressions on all of their faces as they stared into the flickering flames.

Mark finally broke the silence. "I heard a story about the Goatman too. Except it was my mother that told it to me." His eyes stayed fixed on the fire. "Mom's story happened a long time ago though, like the olden days when there was nothing but farms around here. The story went that there was this man—a kind of traveling handyman—that would go from farm to farm looking for work. He would offer to do chores, paint fences, plow fields, feed pigs—all kinds of things. In trade for what he did, all he asked for was a bed, some food, and whatever money the family could spare. See, this was in Depression times when everyone was down on their luck and stood in long lines just for bread and toilet paper. Most of the time the man would be on his way once the work was done and he was paid. But sometimes after he left, something would end up killing every man, woman, and child in the home within the next couple of days. Mom said they found a sole survivor at a farm that was attacked. It was a little girl who had jumped in a well to escape whatever was after them. When they got her out, she had a real bad fever and was ranting and raving about a half-man, half-goat beast that tore her mom and dad to pieces. Soon after, they found out her home had been visited by the stranger, so they asked her if anything weird happened before he left. The girl said no, but went on to say that her dad kept bragging about how he tricked the man into doing a bunch of work for him and only ended up giving him a little bit of money and some moldy old food. The girl said when the stranger split he was smiling and almost seemed happy that her dad had gypped him."

"Were the stranger and the Goatman the same person?" I coughed out as a blast of warm, smoke-filled air blew in my face.

Brian spoke for his brother. "The stranger never showed back up after that last attack. Mom said there were different ideas on what was going on, but she believed the man and monster were the same. She said the man was some kind of demon or devil, and anyone that tried to cheat him out of his due would end up paying what was owed in blood. Mom said it's important to treat people fair—even strangers."

The more I thought about Mark and Perry's stories, the more confused I got. "This doesn't make any sense."

"What doesn't?" Brian asked.

"How could your Goatman and Perry's Goatman be the same? First off, he'd have to be very old, like my grandpa's age. Second, the stories are totally different. In one he's a shapeshifting demon punishing people that try to cheat him. In the other he's some psycho chopping up teenagers."

Brian's face scrunched. "You calling my mom a liar?"

"No, no, it's just —"

"It's just what it always is with you," Steve said. "You let your imagination run wild and start spazzing about stupid things. These are just ghost stories; don't get all literal on us."

The sudden warmth in my face had nothing to do with the fire. "I know they're just stories, *Steve*. But still, you figure there would be some sort of pattern or consistency between them. They should at least agree on whether he is a man or a monster. I mean, give me something to *work with* here."

Kevin whispered in my ear. "Cool it. You're taking this too personal."

He was right, and I knew it. I was letting my obsession with the Goatman get the better of me, but I just couldn't help myself. I had to get back to the library and somehow get hold of that book.

"Well," Steve said, "that's the great thing about ghost stories. You believe what you want to. Kind of like closet monsters, right Chris?"

And there it was, Steve's perfectly timed revenge for my earlier cheap shot on his movie-making abilities. I should have seen it coming.

He continued. "You can either believe there is some giant, spooky monster staring at you from our closet or grow up and realize it's just doorknobs you're looking at." Steve stood and began wiggling his fingers in front of his face as he wailed, "Whooo, Chriiiis! It's the haunted door handles coming to get youuuuu!"

Laughter rippled through the group.

Doing my best to fight back tears, I stood up. Getting slammed by my brother in front of my friends was bad enough. I sure as hell wasn't going to give him the satisfaction of seeing me cry. "You're an asshole!"

You could have heard a mouse fart.

"Daaamn, Chris," Mark muttered over the hiss of the fire.

Steve's jaw dropped for a split second before clamping shut like a vise. His eyes flared wide. He looked *extremely* pissed.

Never before was I so bold, but the resentment that had been building up in me for the past several months finally exploded. "You think you're such a big shot, and that you're so smart, but you're not! Yeah, you got a nice movie camera. Whoopty-freaking-do! I could make movies as good as yours if I had a camera like that, probably better. And guess what? I wouldn't be a fat-headed, tight-assed, fart face to everyone either!"

Paul stood and placed a hand on my shoulder. "Take it easy, dude."

My mouth opened and a string of curse words flowed out, all directed at my big brother. I knew what most of them meant, but I threw in a few new ones I was a little sketchy on. Judging by Steve's pinched face and white-knuckled fists, I used them right. If Perry and Mark weren't holding him back, I would have been obliterated. When I finished my rant,

84

I stormed off and headed inside to my room. Why did Steve have to be like that, always messing with me in front of the other kids? Why didn't he want to hang out anymore? What did I do to make him not want to do stuff with me like we used to?

Why didn't he like me anymore?

As I lay in bed, I slowed my breathing and listened to the muffled racket of music, laughter, and conversation coming from the boozed-up adults below. Eventually my eyes grew heavy, and I faded out.

Chapter 13

I would have sworn it wasn't possible, but the next Sunday seemed twice as hot as the last. In spite of the flood of salty sweat dripping down my face and blurring my vision, I navigated the minefield of yellow jackets with the style and grace of a Harlem Globetrotter and finished mowing both the front and back lawn in under two hours.

As I rounded the corner of the backyard and pushed the Lawn-Boy toward Mr. Hutchinson's driveway, I froze in my tracks while passing a large elm. Was the heat playing tricks on me? Was it messing with my vision? Turning around, I circled the twisted old tree, looking at its scarred skin. Halfway around it I forgot to breathe. Carved into its thick bark was the mark of the horned god. It was identical to the one at White Marsh with smooth slashes gouged deep into the wood. Despite not having breathed in, I found enough air to blow out an, "Ohhh crap." Was this coincidence or something more? Could it be that many more of these markings were scattered around Bowie? Were any in my yard? I fought the urge to tear through the neighborhood looking for more of them, but I had fifteen hard-earned bucks coming to me, so the search would have to wait—for now.

Mr. Hutchinson greeted me at the door with an open bottle of Coke. "Here you go, my boy. Looks like you need it. Come on in and cool off a spell."

"Thanks."

The effects of the soda and air conditioning were immediate. I let out a long sigh while plopping down into the same chair I sat in last time.

"It's a killer out there—the weather that is," he said.

"Yes, sir. It sure is."

"Now you understand why I hired you. Mowing lawns is a younger man's game as far as I am concerned."

"I guess."

This time the payoff came quick. Mr. Hutchinson pushed the money across the table to me as he took a seat. "So, you have anything you're saving up for?"

"There are a few things I'd like. Some *D and D* stuff for starters."

"D and D?"

"*Dungeons and Dragons*. It's a role playing game that's really cool. You can be a fighter, magic user, cleric, and some other classes. You fight monsters, explore dungeons, and get treasure and magic items."

"I see. You enjoy works of fantasy?"

"I guess you could say so."

"Have you read any of Tolkien's books?"

I accidentally snorted a laugh before blurting out, "Of course! He's the best. I'm halfway through *The Two Towers* now."

"Excellent, you're a reader, eh?"

The familiar quiz-like nature of our conversation returned. "Sure. I used to like C.S. Lewis, but now that's kind of kid stuff. I like Tolkien, King, Bradbury, and lots of others. *Something Wicked This Way Comes* is one of my faves."

"Yes, all gifted authors to be sure. Don't be so quick to dismiss Mr. Lewis though. He has written many intriguing tales aside from the fantasy works you are undoubtedly familiar with. Both *The Screwtape Letters* and *The Great Divorce* are fascinating pieces of literature. The narratives have a different flavor than what you are accustomed to, but something tells me you're ready for them."

After taking a long swig, I burped and said, "I'm always looking for good stories, so I guess I could give him another shot. Oh, and excuse me."

Mr. Hutchinson laughed. "You are quite excused. Now as I seem to recall, Mr. King can write some pretty gruesome fiction. Do you enjoy a good heart-pumping, hair-raising story?"

"Sure. As long as it's not too twisted. I can deal with ghosts, zombies, and ax-wielding nut jobs, but no clowns please. Bozo the Clown always freaked me out."

"Truly? You suffer from clourophobia, do you?"

"If that's a fear of big-haired, red-nosed, super creepy clowns, then you bet. Also not a big fan of anything to do with possessed kids. A couple years back my parents let me stay up to watch *The Exorcist*. I had to sleep with them that night. It was highly embarrassing."

"Ah, I know what you mean. That was a very graphic movie. It's amazing what they are allowed to put on the big screen nowadays."

"You got that right."

"How about what's been going on around here lately? Has that got you or any of your friends worked up?"

"You're talking about the body they found?"

"Precisely."

"I don't know. I guess we're all a little freaked out, but these things usually end up getting solved, right?"

Mr. Hutchinson's eyes slipped to the backyard. "They often do, though not always. Pardon me for being a little morbid, but a man of my age finds so few things to entertain him. Tell me if you would, what is the prevailing theory among your cohorts? What do all of you think is the cause of this most recent unfortunate event?"

It seemed like a weird question to ask a fifteen-year-old, but I was quickly learning Mr. Hutchinson was different than the other adults in the neighborhood. He made no efforts to censor himself or treat me like a kid when we spoke. It was almost like he considered me another adult. Maybe it was because he didn't have a lot of practice talking to kids, or maybe he didn't think it was necessary to talk down to someone just because of their age. Whatever the reason, I decided to trust him.

"This is going to sound a little goofy, but a lot of kids are saying the Goatman killed the guy."

Mr. Hutchinson grimaced before releasing a dry chuckle. "The Goatman. I've heard that name bubble up in conversation off and on through the decades—from when I was your age as a matter of fact. Years would go by with no mention of the horned fiend, and then a body would be found. If no attributable cause could be identified within a narrow window of time, everyone started blaming the Goatman. You'd think someone would have come up with a better name than that by now."

"You mean you know about the Goatman?"

"Most assuredly. Anyone who has lived in this area for more than a few years has heard of him. That said, none seem able to agree on exactly what the Goatman is."

"Do you think he's for real?"

Mr. Hutchinson's eyes crept across the lawn before sweeping back into the house and zeroing in on me. For a few seconds, his face was a total blank. It was like his brain had checked out from his body and was off visiting some distant planet. Then he cracked a warm smile. "Bah! The Goatman's an urban legend, son. A myth. You might as well add him into that dungeon game you play. Now don't get me wrong. I'm not belittling you or your friends' theories. Part of the joy of youth is having an active imagination, but when you've been around as long as I have, you tend to take a more pragmatic view of the unexplained. I would venture to guess that sooner or later another more mundane explanation will be provided for the condition of the body."

"Some of my brother's friends told us stories about the Goatman, but they didn't make a lick of sense to me."

"How so?"

"For starters, Perry says the Goatman was a government scientist who got all messed up in some top secret experiment that went and turned him into a half-man, half-goat creature."

"And?"

"Brian says the Goatman has been around since the olden days and is some kind of shapeshifting monster."

Mr. Hutchinson reached into his pants pocket and retrieved a small leather pouch. He stood, went to the kitchen counter, and picked up an old wood pipe. He spoke as he emptied a pinch of tobacco into it. "I have listened to those same stories told time and time again over the years. I've heard a few others as well. Some of them are a little more composed and thought out."

The aroma from the pipe was surprisingly pleasant. I expected the same ashy odor that came from the cigarettes puffed by my parents and most of the other adults on the street, but this smoke had a rich, baked smell that reminded me of oatmeal cookies.

"There was one story that grabbed me in particular. It's very old, going back to a time before the war between the North and the South. Back then this whole area was part of the Ogle Estate. The tale begins with the arrival of a new slave on the planation. She was exceptionally beautiful and a recent acquisition made by one of the Ogles—Richard I believe—during a trip he had made to the deep south. As the story goes, this young woman gave birth to a child rumored to have been fathered by Richard. Well, the gossip proliferated and was soon bolstered by the decidedly light complexion of the baby. In a jealous, murderous rage, Richard's wife grabbed a rifle and set out to kill both mother and child. Fortunately, she turned out to be a bad shot, and with a little help from the other slaves, the woman managed to escape with her child. That would probably have been the end of the story save for one thing. This woman had been educated in the dark arts, Palo Mayombe to be specific, and was considered a witch of some renown. Now this was not the benign root magic or Hoodoo common throughout the region, mind you. No, the woman had been taught the secrets of this most powerful, malevolent form of sorcery while growing up on a plantation in Cuba. Hungry, cold, and alone save for her wailing child, the witch sought revenge upon her former master. Using her gifts, she summoned a demon from the abyss with the intention to strike a bargain and bring the Ogle family to ruin. However, a steep price had to be paid for such a request. By the rubrics of Solomon, blood pays for blood. The demon demanded the woman sacrifice her child as payment. In the heat of passion and desperate for revenge, the witch agreed, dropping her child into a nearby river as an offering. But as the baby let out one last, pitiful sob before disappearing beneath the icy waters, the witch was overwhelmed with grief and regret. She jumped in the river and fought its powerful currents in a futile attempt to save the doomed infant. And so it was that both the witch and child perished."

"What happened to the demon?"

"You have a vivid imagination, don't you? What do you think happens to a demon once the one who summoned it is dead and no contract negotiated?"

I considered the question for a few moments as the smoky haze in the room thickened. "I guess with no one to control it or send it back, the demon would be free to do whatever it wanted to."

Mr. Hutchinson tilted his head forward. "I knew you were a smart one."

"But wait. How does this story connect to the Goatman? Are you saying he's actually the demon?"

The old man leaned back and took another puff before he spoke. "That is one of the many stories I have been privy to over the years."

"I hadn't heard that one before."

"Like I said, it's very old."

Ever since I could remember, I felt like an oddball because of my willingness to believe in the fantastic. A part of me saw something similar in Mr. Hutchinson. He was both old and wise but also open-minded with a knowledge of the supernatural that most adults didn't have. I held out a glimmer of hope that he might be an adult I could confide in if push came to shove. Maybe he could be the Obi-wan to my Luke. He even looked a little like him but without the beard. "Do you think any of the stories might be true? I mean, just a little?"

"Let us consider the alternatives. Is it likely that some demon, changeling, or genetically altered aberration has been traipsing around the woods, fields, and neighborhoods of Bowie for the past hundred-plus years slaughtering teenage lovers and mutilating dogs? Or is it more probable that a rich tradition of storytelling has led to the evolution of a Goatman urban legend that has adapted and evolved over the years to reflect the culture and mores of the times?"

Was I looking for something in Mr. Hutchinson that just wasn't there? For a few seconds, I had dared to dream the old man could be a sort of teacher guiding me through the world of the supernatural as I tried to solve the riddle of the Goatman. A feeling of embarrassment grew from a suspicion that he might be having fun at my expense. "Yeah," I said meekly, "I guess so."

He laughed. It wasn't a mean laugh, but it still stung a little. The sour expression on my face was impossible to hide.

"Oh, Chris, I do envy you. You are young, strong, and have your whole life in front of you. You are also brave and keenly attuned to your environment. That is a rare trait in this day and age when so many walk around with blinders on."

The compliments made me feel a little better.

"Although I'm a skeptic when it comes to the plausibility of a Goatman, I do hold a deep appreciation for those who aren't afraid to wonder and question the status quo. In other words, never stop questioning and never stop exploring...unless it's late at night."

I frowned. "Huh?"

"I'm not a proponent of the Goatman mythos, but there is wisdom in caution. There are people in this world who can be just as cruel and vicious as any Goatman. With these recent events happening so close to home, I urge you and your friends to abstain from late night adventuring. I imagine your parents have already advised you as such."

"I have to be home by dark unless I'm over at a friend's house."

"Good. Heed your parents; they know what they're talking about."

His warning made me think about Russell Drake again. I knew he was one of those cruel people the old man was referring to. What had caused him to turn tail and run like a whipped dog?

My sudden silence drew my host's attention. "What is it, son?"

"I guess I just wanted to thank you again for helping us out with Russell. If you hadn't shown up when you did, I'm pretty sure he would have beat the snot out of us."

Mr. Hutchinson's head tilted to one side as he puffed out oatmeal-scented smoke. "I believe you may be correct on that assumption. Russell Drake is a brute with a retarded intellect."

A laugh escaped me. "You can say that again!"

He smiled and whispered, "I don't think you have to worry about Mr. Drake anymore."

The comment seemed strange to me. For someone as smart as he was, I believed Mr. Hutchinson was underestimating the cruelty of my neighbor. Sooner or later I was sure to bump into Russell Drake, and payback was a bitch.

Chapter 14

Out of fifteen shots fired, Kevin had thirteen in the bullseye. True, it was his BB gun, and knowing him, he had no doubt racked up a thousand hours of practice, but the far out way he pulled the spring-loaded receiver back, took aim, and fired—all in less than five seconds—left Paul and me in awe.

"Man, Kevin, you should enter a shooting contest!" Paul exclaimed.

The narrow patch of land running behind the two sheds in the Perrets' backyard made for a pretty decent shooting range. The tree-of-heaven and chokeberry bordering the fences of the neighboring yards gave us cover from prying eyes. Also, with his dad at work and mom running ragged trying to keep his seven brothers and sister in line, the chances of being busted by Paul's parents was slim to none.

Kevin hunched his shoulders. "Eh, once I shot a crayon from over twenty feet away. It was with one hand too. See I –"

Wailing sirens interrupted Kevin's suspicious story. As they got louder, we realized they were coming down Stonybrook toward Paul's house. Kevin stashed the gun in his waistband, and we bolted to the front of the house just in time to see a swarm of police cars converge on Russell Drake's home three houses down. A team of four officers jumped out and approached the front door with their guns drawn.

"Whoa!" Paul shouted. "What do you think is going on there?"

We watched in silence. After a great deal of shouting, two officers entered only to emerge seconds later escorting a young, handcuffed man between them.

"Son of a bitch," Kevin whispered. "They're arresting Russell."

"Sweet! In your face, Russell!" Paul crowed.

Kevin and I turned to our friend.

He looked at us and grinned. "I'm just saying what we're all thinking. That guy's the biggest jelly brain, fart sniffer, douchebag on the planet."

We turned and looked on, mesmerized with the scene unfolding in front of us.

"Think it's drugs?" Kevin asked.

"Could be," I said.

A minute later another officer brought out something the size of a basketball in a trash bag. I noticed he held it as far away from his body as possible as he walked back to his cruiser.

Paul took a few steps closer and cupped a hand above his eyes to shield them from the sun. "What do you think that is, his stash?"

No one answered.

Several seconds passed before the fourth officer emerged. He was wearing gloves and holding a huge machete. The blade of the weapon was stained red. He proceeded to the back of another one of the squad cars.

Paul turned to us with a crazy, wild-eyed expression. "Holy crap! Did you see that?"

We watched as two of the officers drove Russell away. The gears were turning in my head as I tried to make sense of it all. Was Russell really the monster that had been terrorizing Bowie? Sure he was a druggie and petty criminal, but a murderer? I thought about the look in his eyes when he pushed me down and threatened to break my arm. He was definitely capable of violence, but was he a stone cold killer? I wasn't convinced.

"What do you guys think?" Kevin asked. "We have a bloody sword and a garbage bag with something big and round in it. I'm guessing it's a head."

Paul's noggin bobbed up and down. "Yep, yep, yep. Gotta be. That was the head of the guy they found on Fletchertown Road, and Russell Drake is the Goatman. Right, Chris?"

I wanted to agree with them, but it all seemed too simple. "Maybe."

Paul was all riled up. "Maybe? Maybe? C'mon, Chris! Of all people, I never expected you to be a doubter."

"It's not that; it's just all a little too...clean. Besides, Russell never seemed like the psycho killer type. Y'know?"

"You're kidding me, right?" Paul rolled his eyes. "Just a week ago the creep was going to wipe the floor with you. He's been in and out of jail for all kinds of things. I even heard he was into devil worship."

Kevin nodded. "Paul's got a point, Chris. Ever since I moved in, all I've heard is freaky stuff about Russell and his brothers."

I was outnumbered. It was interesting how just a couple weeks ago Paul and Kevin were at each other's throats, bickering about everything like a couple of old ladies, but now they were thick as thieves. I should have been happy they were getting along so well, but at the moment I was just frustrated. I raised my hands. "Fine. Maybe Russell is the Goatman. I'm just saying I'm not entirely convinced. That's all."

"So," Paul continued, "if you don't think Russell is the Goatman, then who is?"

Since first seeing them haul the Drake kid away, a question had been crawling around in the back of my brain. Was Mr. Hutchinson's prediction about Russell just coincidence? There was something going on with the old man, but what it was I couldn't say for sure. And what was the deal with the carving on his tree? I hadn't yet had a chance to scour the neighborhood looking for more of them, but I had a hunch if I did, I would come up with squat. In his own wordy way, he'd made clear that he thought the legend of the Goatman was a bunch of bull, but his eyes said something else. He was holding out on me. Next thing I knew, my mouth was moving and words were coming out. "I saw one of those symbols in Mr. Hutchinson's backyard. It was identical to the one on the bike trail."

"Weird," Kevin said. "Maybe Russell carved it on his tree because he was planning on taking out the old man next."

I shook my head. "I don't think so. Don't you remember the look on Russell's face when Mr. Hutchinson saved our butts? He was scared of him. And there's more..."

"Like what?" Paul asked.

"Yesterday he told me we wouldn't have to worry about Russell anymore."

"What's that supposed to mean?" Kevin asked.

"I'm not sure, but how would the Mr. Hutchinson know he wasn't going to bother us any longer?"

"Okay, that does sound a little strange," Paul said. "But what do you think? The old man somehow set Russell up? Framed him? Sounds like a stretch to me."

"Yeah, but there's this as well. He also said we should stay in at night—not go out."

Kevin sighed. "So? All our parents have been saying that to us. That doesn't mean anything."

Paul nodded in agreement.

"Ugh! You guys are missing the point. It's not any one thing; it's everything together." I started counting off with my fingers. "First, I found the horned god carving on his tree. Second, he said we wouldn't have to worry about Russell anymore. And last, he said not to go out at night." I lifted the three fingers up to them. "Those clues make Mr. Hutchinson suspicious."

Kevin shrugged. "Even if we give you that, what do you want us to do about it?"

"I've been thinking. What if we set up a surveillance of Mr. Hutchinson? You know, spy on him at night to see if he sneaks out and does anything strange."

Paul snickered. "What, you mean like start chopping people's heads off?"

"I don't know, maybe."

"Look," Kevin broke in, "even if we wanted to, we couldn't. Back in by the time the streetlights are on, remember? My parents used to cut me a little slack with that, but since the body was found out on Fletchertown, they brought the hammer down. I'll be grounded for life if I stay out too late."

"Me too." Paul said.

I knew I would have to sweeten the deal, make it worth their time if I was going to get them to back me up. "C'mon, just think about it. If we borrow my brother's camera and are able to get Mr. Hutchinson on film doing something suspicious, maybe the police won't close the case on the Goatman murders."

Kevin squinted. "Suspicious? What kind of suspicious?"

"Well, might be we catch him putting an ax in the trunk of his car or coming back home with blood on his hands, or something like that. Point is, we won't know unless we give it a try. What do we have to lose?"

"A month of summer if I end up being grounded," Paul said.

"What he said," Kevin added.

"Listen, no one is getting grounded. I've been thinking. You guys can come over to my house Friday night. It's my folks' turn to host their dinner club, and they'll be too busy entertaining to worry about us."

"You mean too busy getting toasted," Kevin teased.

"Exactly. I'll put the tent up, and we can crash out in the backyard. We'll wait until around midnight, sneak out, and head over to Mr. Hutchinson's."

"That could be kind of cool," Paul admitted.

Kevin cast Paul a sideways glance and then looked back at me. "It isn't the worst idea you've come up with, and your plan may actually work. But I think we're wasting our time watching that old man."

Kevin was on the fence. I needed something to seal the deal. "We could play a little *D and D*. I'll even let you be the dungeon master. What do you say?"

Paul's head pumped up and down.

Kevin scratched his chin. "Give me your ring of vampiric regeneration, and it's a deal."

"Done! Also, bring all black or camouflage clothes."

"Why?"

"Because this is gonna be a covert op. Paul, pack your binoculars too; they might come in handy."

"You're forgetting one thing," Kevin broke in, "how are you going to get your brother's camera without him noticing?"

"Leave that to me. I have a plan all worked out."

"Really? It better be a good one. If you get caught, your ass is grass."

Kevin was right, and I actually had no plan. Zilch. Getting caught by Steve wasn't high on my list of concerns at the time. There were bigger stakes on the table. If our operation proved successful and we found evidence that Mr. Hutchinson was the Goatman, we'd be the heroes. If we got busted and it turned out the old man was the same creature, we'd no doubt end up his next victims.

Chapter 15

Things were still frosty the next few days between Steve and me. We must have said all of five words to each other since my fireside meltdown. Deep down I knew I should have apologized, but in all honesty, I was too scared to. I was worried that bringing up memories of my trash-talking rant would be about as smart as taking a baseball bat to a hornet nest. Instead, I took the wimpy way out and kept my trap shut, hoping that with each passing day any the hard feelings would fade.

On top of all that drama, I was having serious second thoughts about "borrowing" Steve's camera. Somehow I would have to snatch it, shoot the footage, take the film out, and then replace it with another film cartridge with him none the wiser. Then there was the whole developing issue, but that was something to worry about later. The immediate mission was to obtain the incriminating evidence. If we actually caught Mr. Hutchinson red-handed, I was sure Steve would forgive my little indiscretion. At least that's what I hoped.

Luck turned out to be on my side Friday. Steve had gone over to the Perrets' house to hang out with Perry for most of the night. With sweat-soaked, quivering hands, I slipped his Canon 310XL out of its case and placed it in my duffel bag.

By the time my parents' guests started showing up, Kevin and Paul had already arrived. The adults watched in obvious delight as we hauled our provisions of cola, corn chips, and Suzy Qs to the old canvas tent I had set up in the backyard. Mr. Blanchard clearly believed he was the funniest person in the room when he shouted, "Really roughing it, huh boys?"

All was going according to plan.

As the sun dipped low in the sky, the voices inside the house grew louder and the smoke thicker. At a quarter of ten, my dad poked his head in the tent and said, "Okay, boys, have a good night, and don't do anything I wouldn't do."

We swore we wouldn't.

Despite his somewhat bland impersonations of the non-player characters, Kevin did a decent enough job as dungeon master. For a novice level player, Paul proved a quick study, and his character steadily advanced under my guidance. We lost ourselves in role play as the night drew on and the rowdiness inside the house gradually faded.

"The cavern is dark, and you can only see about ten feet into the room. What do you do?" Kevin asked.

Paul looked over at me. "I listen for any sort of sounds."

"You hear a gurgling noise coming from the far end of the cavern. It sounds like it could be a small river or maybe stream."

Paul kept his eyes fixed on me. "I'll lead the way 'cause I'm the fighter. But first, I'll toss a torch into the middle of the cavern to light it up for us."

I gave him a slight nod.

Paul cracked a crooked smile.

Kevin cleared his throat for dramatic effect. "The torch lands dead center in the room, lighting up the cave. You see things scurrying along the floor to your left and right. They look kind of like giant greenish centipedes and seem scared of the light. They circle around the cavern walls and approach you from both sides."

Paul kept watching me. "What do I do now?"

I had a good idea we were facing a couple of carrion crawlers based on Kevin's description. If that was the case, it wouldn't be too hard for us to take them out, but I wanted Paul to make the call. "What do you think?"

"Roll for initiative?"

"Works for me."

Kevin broke character. He looked at his wristwatch and said, "Uh, guys, hate to interrupt the fun, but it's eleven forty-five."

The plan was to set up our surveillance post in the mess of juniper trees in the Blanchards' yard directly opposite Mr. Hutchinson's house. But in order to do that, we would need to suit up, grab our gear, and high-tail it there by midnight. With a fifteen-minute window, it was gonna be tight. The time I picked wasn't random. Though the dog mutilations happened early in the evening, every report of human death rumored to have been the handiwork of the Goatman occurred sometime between one and three in the morning. That being the case, midnight seemed like a primo time to stake out the old man's property. We stripped down and slipped on our stealth gear. Kevin looked sharp in all black. Paul was also respectable, covered from head to foot in camouflage clothes he most likely took from Perry and would end up serving hard time in his tuba case for later. I, on the other hand, was feeling a tad self-conscious in black church pants and a charcoal sweatshirt that belonged to Steve.

The night had cooled down and a haze settled over everything like a wet, clammy blanket. We hopped the fence into the adjoining back-yard to avoid any possible encounters with tanked neighbors leaving the dinner party and crawled our way across until we made it back around to the front of the house. From there we stayed in the shadows, weaving through the trees, bushes, and driveways. Sweaty and out of breath, we arrived at our target location and hunkered down behind a wall of evergreen.

"Kevin," I whispered, "what time you got?"

He shined his flashlight on his wrist. "A couple minutes past twelve."

Holding my brother's camera, I said, "That's okay. I don't think a few minutes will matter. Paul, got the binoculars?"

"That's a big ten-four, good buddy. Also brought this."

Paul pulled a tiny silver canister out from his waist.

"Why are you carrying a bottle of hairspray? Worried about getting frizzy hair?" Kevin asked.

"It's not hairspray, tinsel-teeth. It's mace. I swiped it from my sister's room."

Kevin snickered. "What do you need that for?"

"Protection, what else?"

"You really think that's gonna stop the Goatman?"

Paul shrugged. "Don't know, but it might slow him down if I get him in the eyes."

"Ssshh," I whispered. "Someone's coming."

A couple of adults were walking our way. Well, one of them was walking—the other was doing a crab-like shuffle, zigzagging left to right as he stumbled forward. We sat in silence and listened as they approached.

"I told you, you shouldn't have had that third Wallbanger!"

It was Mrs. Blanchard, and she did not sound happy. Mr. Blanchard, on the other hand, looked like he was feeling downright groovy.

"Do you know what your problem is, Helen?" Mr. Blanchard slurred. "You need to lighten up. Since we got to the Dwyers', you've been on me like a crow, just cawing and cawing." In a shrill voice the drunk man yelled, "Caw! Caw!"

"For the love of Mike! You're sleeping on the couch tonight…and maybe tomorrow night too!"

"Oh, you mean—hic—you mean I don't get to sleep with my wife? What a shame. 'Cause *that* was gonna lead somewhere."

Clueless to our presence, the lovebirds continued arguing all the way up to their front doorstep, at which point Mr. Blanchard began speaking in tongues. As they entered the house, his religious experience ended, not with an amen but with gut-churning heaving.

The last words we heard were Mrs. Blanchard's. "Well, that's just lovely."

As soon as the door shut, the bushes erupted in muted laughter.

"And gooood night John-Boy," Kevin muttered.

"Guess my parents really can throw a party," I whispered.

Before we had a chance to enjoy a round of jokes at the Blanchards' expense, Mr. Hutchinson's door opened. We fell silent.

In the darkness of our hidden nest, I fumbled with the controls of the Canon 310 XL while lifting it to my eye.

The old man walked to the driver side of his Mercury and reached for the car door but paused. He stopped, stood up straight as a rod, and turned around, looking outward into the night, tilting his head up and scanning his surroundings as if he were sniffing out trouble.

I held my breath.

After a few seconds of searching for God knew what, he strolled back to the front porch, reached a hand into his pants pocket, and pulled out his pipe. With the other hand he flicked something against the porch post. In the amber glow of the match flame, I swore I could see his eyes. They were looking directly at us. The flame went out, and darkness swallowed him. All that remained was a steady stream of gray smoke curling out from under the porch roof.

"That was freaky," Paul whispered.

"Ssshh. He's still out there," I said.

We watched in silence for what felt like forever but was probably closer to five minutes. Finally, Mr. Hutchinson turned around and went back in his house.

As the door closed, Kevin asked, "What the hell was all that about?"

"That was *really* freaky," Paul said a little louder.

I put the camera down, just then realizing that I never started filming. "He saw us."

I noted the shared *here we go again* look exchanged by my friends.

Paul spoke first. "What do you mean, he saw us? We're butt-deep in the bushes, and there's no moon out. With the stuff we're wearing, no way he could have seen us unless he has bionic eyes. Heck, *I* can barely see you."

"Paul's right, Chris. No way the old man could see us."

I shook my head. "I'm telling you, somehow he knew we were here. Why else would he stop in his tracks, decide to light up, and then go back inside? It's because he figured out he was being watched."

"All right, all right," Kevin said, "it was strange the way he froze up, but that doesn't mean he did it because he knew we were here. Maybe he went out to his car to get something and then remembered he left it somewhere inside. Old people do that all the time."

"What about when he started looking around with his nose in the air?" I asked. "It was like he was sniffing, you know, like a dog."

"Are you saying he smelled us?" Paul asked.

Kevin chuckled. "Maybe he smelled Paul; he's got Frito breath. I can smell it from here."

Paul leaned over and blew into Kevin's face.

"Sick! Get away from me, you Frito freak!"

I knew what I saw. Whether from sight, smell, or hearing, Mr. Hutchinson somehow sensed we were there, which was why he decided to postpone his midnight cruise. Even though my plan didn't work as intended, I had gathered enough evidence in my mind to continue with the investigation. But not tonight. "Okay, let's get back. The longer we stay out, the better the chance we get caught."

We made our way back to the tent with slightly less zip than we had set out with. Even though our stakeout didn't last that long, I was wiped out and looking forward to crawling into my sleeping bag and staying there for the next ten to twelve hours. Unfortunately, that would have to wait. As we entered the tent, Kevin's flashlight fell upon an uninvited guest.

Steve's cheeks actually looked like they were painted red. His words came out fast and clipped. "Having fun, guys?"

Shitty, shit, shit.

With an unblinking glare, he looked at me and thrust out a hand.

I was so screwed. I avoided his burning eyes and cautiously offered him the camera. I had to be careful. The wrong choice of words would guarantee a pounding—and worse, in front of my friends. Our relationship was strained at best and this last act, this theft of Steve's most precious possession, might prove to be the straw that broke the camel's back. "I'm...I'm sorry, Steve. It's just –"

"It's just nothing!" he snapped. "You better pray to God you didn't damage it!"

Steve gave the camera a once-over as we waited in humbled silence. He had us by the cojones. If one word of this got out to any of our parents, we'd spend the rest of the summer in lockdown. Once satisfied that no noticeable damage existed, he looked back at the three of us. His scowl softened as he soaked in our wardrobe choices. "What the hell were you dorks doing anyway? Filming some kind of ninja movie?"

From the moment I saw Steve's beet-colored face, my mind started scrambling for a believable excuse. Fortunately, I found the answer in the question my brother asked. "Um, kind of."

"And?"

"It didn't turn out too well. As a matter of fact, we didn't even film a single scene— everything was way too dark."

My brother snorted laughter. "No duh! You guys are wearing all black, and it's after midnight. Geez, haven't you learned anything after watching me make movies? Proper lighting is *key*."

"I guess."

"And you said you didn't use any of my film?"

"That's right."

"None?"

"Uh-uh."

"Good. Because if you did, you'd have to pay for a new roll."

"I know."

I fought the urge to come clean with my brother. Despite trash-talking his creative abilities, I actually admired him. He was the smartest non-adult I knew, and his big brain could prove helpful in solving the mystery that was Mr. Hutchinson. Unfortunately, I had a growing suspicion he truly despised me and simply tolerated my existence like a person tolerates an annoying, clinging dog. On rare occasions I may serve as cheap amusement, but by and large I was a nuisance and part-time responsibility he would rather do without.

Steve sighed. "Listen, if you want to learn how to use the camera the right way, I can show you. But if I ever catch you trying to take it again without my permission, I'm going to pummel you severely. Do you understand?"

This was unexpected. By the unspoken brother code, he was well within his rights to pound me, pants me, wedgie me, or at the very least leave me to the fate of parental justice. Maybe I had once more jumped off the deep end and unfairly assumed the worst of Steve. I nodded repeatedly. "Yes, of course! Got it! Sorry for messing with your stuff."

Steve's eyes turned to Kevin and Paul. Paul held his mace while Kevin had the binoculars. "Ninja movie, huh? Is that *all* you guys were doing?"

Though I was experienced at fibbing to my brother, Kevin and Paul weren't. I held my breath and watched, convinced one of them would crack under the pressure.

Kevin's eyes circled around the tent but refused to meet Steve's. "Yep, just trying to film a movie."

Paul said nothing. He just bit his lip and pumped his head up and down.

Steve flashed one of his *I'm-smarter-than-you* smiles at us. "Okay. If that's your story, that's your story."

As he brushed past us and made to exit the tent, he turned around. The smirk was still on his face. "By the way, Chris, you'll be taking my chores for the next two weeks. That includes cleaning the bathrooms and mowing the lawn. Any objections?"

Now *that* was the Steve I remembered. For some strange reason a tiny smile broke on my face as I said, "Nope."

For the second time that strange night, we had narrowly avoided disaster. As I crawled into my sleeping bag and drifted off, I wondered whether our luck would hold out.

Chapter 16

My friends and I kept a low profile for the next couple of days. It wasn't a hard trick for me to pull off because I now had double the amount of crap to do. As if the added work wasn't enough, Steve's chores needed to be done when both Mom and Dad were out so they wouldn't get suspicious. To add insult to injury, I had to stand by and listen to the parade of compliments showered on my brother for the "wonderful" job he did cleaning everything from the toilets to the car.

While out back mowing along the borders of our lawn, I imagined what was sure to follow. "Great job on the grass, Steve! Never seen it looking so good!" The icing on the cake would be, "Maybe you could teach your younger brother a thing or two about mowing." I almost felt the barf rising in the back of my throat. Lost in my nauseating thoughts, I rolled over a bare spot beneath the tire swing hanging from our willow. Before the tree was blotted out by the dirt-filled air, I saw it. Opening my hands, I released the mower's stop lever and approached. I placed a hand on the tree's bumpy surface. There, just above the swing, a hand-sized patch of bark had been stripped away from the willow. In its center was the mark of the horned god.

Oh, crap.

The wood was still damp, meaning the carving couldn't have been there more than a couple of days. It definitely wasn't when I setup the tent for the sleepover—I would have noticed. Then it occurred to me. It was no coincidence the carving showed up in my yard within days of our stakeout. So far, we'd found the mark along the White Marsh Bike Trail, the old man's house, and now mine. Was Mr. Hutchinson making them or was someone else? Or—just maybe—some*thing* else. An idea sparked in my mind. I fired the motor back up and quickly finished mowing. I knew I'd catch some heat for the sloppy mow from my brother, but at least I wouldn't have to listen to my parents praising him for yet another amazing job.

As soon as I was done, I headed out front and started down Spindle in the general direction of Paul's house. Along the way I spot-checked the maples, oaks, pines, and elms scattered throughout the yards on both sides of the lane. A few had initials carved into them, some had hearts or the year chiseled as well, but none displayed the mark of the horned god. I burned a good twenty minutes weaving my way through my neighbors' yards playing tree inspector. When I finally got to Paul's house, he was finishing a heated game of *Risk* with his brother. For the next half hour, I had to sit and watch as Perry hoarded armies on Siam in preparation for a massive invasion of Paul's last strongholds in Australia and Indonesia. It was a brutal war that lasted much longer than it should have due largely to Paul's luck with the dice.

I was on my feet the second Perry's six, five, and five beat Paul's five and two. "Okay, let's go."

"What's your hurry? How about I take you both on?" Perry suggested. "The only thing I ask is to start with all of green."

Before Paul could accept the challenge, I blurted, "Maybe later; we're busy now."

Perry raised both arms and meshed his hands together behind his head. He leaned back, resting his fat head in his open palms. "Tell you what, I'll leave the setup here. Anytime you feel like getting the crap beat out of you, you know where to find me."

"Yeah, sure," I said while dragging Paul out the back door.

Once we were outside, Paul stopped. "What's got your panties in a bunch? I think we should go back in there and kick Perry's butt. There's no way he could beat both of us."

I headed to the cluster of pines on the far side of the yard adjacent to where Paul's dad stacked wood for their fireplace. "You're probably right, but we have something more important to do."

"Like what?"

I ducked beneath the branches while running my hand along the rough, sappy surfaces of the trees. Nothing.

"What are you looking for, Chris? Did something happen?"

"Kind of." I looked around his backyard and spotted no more trees. Knowing that Paul's front yard had just one lonesome crabapple tree, I turned to the wide section of lawn wrapping around the side of their house and pointed over the fence to a cluster of poplars and pines. "We have to go there."

I jogged toward my target as Paul shouted, "Dude! What the heck are we looking for?"

Not stopping, I waved for him to follow as I skirted over the chain link fence and disappeared into the dense gathering of trees. The smell of pine hit me as hundreds of tiny needles tickled my face. It was a little after noon and the summer sun was high in the sky, but the spider web of branches above blotted out much of the light, turning the world around me a murky gray. Paul followed close behind me, softly grumbling. I'm pretty sure he was muttering something about me being on drugs. My hand felt it before my eyes saw it. The carving was deep and oozing sap.

I could tell Paul spotted it from the way his voice jumped a couple of octaves. "Is that what I think it is?"

"Yep."

Paul moved in close to get a better look. "What does it mean? I mean, why would someone carve that here?"

I remembered what Paul said when we first discovered the marking in White Marsh. *Something wants us to know this forest is theirs.* The more I thought about it, the more I was convinced Paul's theory was not just possible but probable. For some reason the Goatman was marking our yards, letting us know that we were not safe or protected—even in our own homes. *You really should lock your window.* The image of the bloody message sprang into my mind causing me to shudder. I turned to Paul. "I found the same thing on a tree in my backyard."

His eyes grew wide. "Maybe they're on a bunch of trees! Maybe this whole neighborhood–"

"Nope. I checked out all of the front yards of the houses between yours and mine. None of them had any carvings on them."

"Yeah, but you couldn't have done a good search without checking in the backyards. There might be more."

There was one way to get to the bottom of it quickly, to find out if we were being targeted. I looked at Paul's pale face. "Kevin's house. Now."

Paul didn't bother to let his mom know where we were going—something we both knew he would regret later. But this was important, and we both felt time was of the essence. Breaking into a steady trot, we wound our way from Stonybrook to Kevin's house in a little under ten minutes. By the time we reached his driveway, we were panting like dogs.

Kevin answered the door with a frown. "What's up?"

Between gulps of air Paul sputtered, "Can't talk. Need to get in your backyard."

He moved to enter, but Kevin planted a hand on the doorframe blocking him. "No can do. My English tutor is here."

Kevin had never mentioned any tutoring to me. From the look of surprise on Paul's face, I could tell it was news to him too.

Before we could say anything, Kevin continued. "I squeaked out a C in English on my last report card, and my mom went all bananas on me. She hired this old school teacher to help jack up my grades next year, but the lady is a real ballbuster. If I don't get back to my lesson, she'll probably rat me out."

"So, when's the battle ax gone?" I asked. "Paul's right, we need to get in your backyard pronto."

"Why? What's so important about my yard all of a sudden?"

Paul opened his mouth, but Kevin raised a hand in front of his face before he could get a word out. "Wait. Just stop. Listen, guys, I don't have time for this now. Mom said that if I did good with the tutor, we could go to Shakey's for pizza. Whatever wild goose chase you knuckleheads are on is gonna have to wait until tomorrow."

A scratchy, ancient voice carried down the front hall. "Master McNamara, now is not the time for tomfoolery."

I looked at Paul, and he looked at me. Simultaneous smiles popped up on our faces.

I put on a terrible British accent. "Master McNamara, if you're a good chap, we'll have tea and crumpets after the lesson. Now please, bring your big bum back in here. Hip-hip now."

Paul cracked up as the frown lines on Kevin's face deepened.

Kevin cocked his head to the side and shouted over his shoulder, "I'll be right there, ma'am." He looked back at the two of us. "Cool it until tomorrow morning. Come by around ten."

Before we could bust his chops further, Kevin shut the door in our faces.

The two of us stood there giggling like a couple of boobs for some time before reality sunk back in. With no access to Kevin's backyard, we would have to wait until tomorrow to see if the mark of the horned god had made its way onto his property.

The smile dropped from my face. "Nuts."

"What?" Paul asked between chuckles.

"Don't you remember why we came here?"

His amused look vanished. "Oh yeah."

"Now we're going to have to hold on until tomorrow to find out if Kevin's in the same boat as us."

"And then?"

I scowled. "What do you mean?"

"Let's say one of his trees has the same marking on it. Then what? What does it mean, and what the heck can we do about it? The police can't help and neither can our parents."

With no hard evidence to share with Paul, I hesitated to share my theory with him. An eerie silence descended as we started down Kevin's driveway and back the way we came. It lasted for half a block before I said, "No one can help us. We're on our own for now."

Paul didn't respond. We kept walking until we reached the intersection of Spindle and Belair. Though the sun was bright and warm on my face, a chill clung to my bones. I turned to my friend. "Listen, we'll find an answer to all this—the three of us will. It's important we stick together. One for all and all for one. Maybe we can convince the older kids something is going on."

"Yeah, but what? We don't know what's going on ourselves, other than there's some crazed tree carver stalking us. For all we know it could be one of them jerking our chains. It could be Steve decided he was going to teach us a lesson for the way you tore into him at the cookout."

The accusation hit a nerve, so I lashed back. "Well, what about Perry? He was the first one that told us about the Goatman, and he seems to get a real kick out of scaring the crap out of us. Could be he's been the one whittling on the trees."

"You might be right," Paul said. "I guess it could be either of them."

I was pretty sure neither of them were involved, but Paul had got me riled up when he started talking about Steve. True, he could be a real butthead sometimes, but he was still my brother. "I'm not sure. Y'know, I kind of doubt either of those guys would do something like this." I squeezed the display button on my watch and looked at the glowing red numbers. "Anyway, I have to go."

"Why?"

"I have another lawn to mow."

Chapter 17

I was on autopilot as I rounded the mulched beds of azaleas. This time I paid no attention to the hordes of yellow jackets gorging themselves on rotting pears—more important things occupied my mind. The sign of the horned god was spreading like crabgrass. It had made its way from the bike trail all the way to Spindle and Stonybrook, and I was willing to bet a million bucks we'd find it at Kevin's too. The *real* question was what was Mr. Hutchinson's tie-in to everything. To this point he was the only one other than Paul and me to have the horned god symbol on his property. He had also known something was going to happen to Russell Drake right before it did. As if that wasn't enough, his bizarre behavior last Friday was irrefutable evidence he was up to no good. So why didn't Kevin and Paul see any of this? It was all so painfully obvious.

The logical voice inside my head interrupted. *Do you really have to ask that?*

It continued. *What evidence do you truly have against Mr. Hutchinson anyway? A bunch of scribbling on trees? Anyone could have done that. Or was it the creepy look he'd thrown at you when you were spying on him? And don't forget, Russell Drake had been in and out of jail since he turned fifteen. Was Mr. Hutchinson's comment really so unusual?*

I paused but kept the mower running. "No," I whispered, "this time is different. This time I have facts. I have evidence to back it up."

The voice countered. *Just like with Mr. Jenkins, the vampire? You thought you had facts then too. But as it turned out, you were wrong. Seems like you've been wrong a lot. Maybe your Mom and Dad were right. Maybe it's time for you to see a shrink.*

"Shut up." I started mowing again, trying to block out the infuriating voice of reason. Sometimes I hated the voice. It was so critical, so condescending. Who cares that it'd been right to date. That didn't mean it would always be right. Besides, this time was different. Wasn't it?

For the next hour and a half, the voice taunted me as I plodded back and forth in tight formation, neatly trimming the lawn. By the time I was done, it had worn me down, chipping away at my confidence and eroding my self-esteem. Was it all just in my head, or was Mr. Hutchinson hatching some evil scheme? Or was there something else going on I was blind to?

The old man opened the door after just one knock. He had a big smile and was holding a bottle of Coke. "It's another hot one today. Have a soda and cool off a minute."

I took the drink and went inside to my assigned seat. We had been through this routine several times now, but something felt different this go-around. A nervous energy buzzed in the air, putting me on edge. Of course, it might have just been that hateful voice poisoning my conscience and infecting me with guilt for spying on and judging a man who had been nothing but kind to me.

Mr. Hutchinson pulled out his pipe and pinched some tobacco into it. "How's tricks? I haven't seen you around the neighborhood for the past couple of days."

"Yeah, I've been a little busy doing chores around the house."

Striking a match, he lit its contents. Smoke wafted out of his mouth as he said, "I see. Get into a little trouble maybe? Been sentenced to some manual labor?"

"Not exactly."

"Oh." Mr. Hutchinson settled in a chair across from me and continued. "Well, I'm glad to hear you weren't up to any mischief. You don't strike me as that type of boy. I suppose you heard what happened to our friend Mr. Drake."

"Sure. We actually saw him get arrested. It was crazy."

Mr. Hutchinson chuckled. "I'm sure it was."

Thick, gray smoke curled out of the old man's pipe and hung heavy in the air. The familiar oatmeal aroma from his usual tobacco was gone, replaced by a stronger smell that reminded me a little of the incense they burned at Mass.

"Interesting isn't it?" he said. "You and I were just talking about the Goatman, and next thing you know, the police are arresting him—at least the man they are alleging committed the most recent murders attributed to the beast. And on top of it all, the fiend was living in the house right behind yours. Fascinating, don't you think?"

It took me a minute to track what he was saying. A combination of smoky air and mild dehydration was making things fuzzy around the edges. "Yeah, weird."

Mr. Hutchinson's eyes narrowed. "Why, Chris, are you all right? You look a little peaked."

"I'm…I'm okay. Just need to drink a little." I had to concentrate to lift the soda and direct it to my mouth. I took a tiny sip and let the bottle plonk onto the table.

"So, do you suppose that will be the end of that, and things will return to the relative peace and quiet we're accustomed to?"

I heard his words, but it was taking longer than usual to process their meaning. Several seconds later I said, "I guess."

"Ah, well let's hope so. It's been rather helter-skelter around here these past few days, if I do say so myself. Which brings me to the next issue at hand. Chris, I have to ask what you and your cohorts were doing these two nights past nesting like a parliament of owls in the Blanchards' bushes. Were you spying on me? If so, what were you expecting to find?"

In the confines of the hazy room, it took a moment for my brain to register the allegation. We were busted; that much I was sure of. But for reasons I couldn't understand, I really didn't care.

"Well?"

"Yes, we were."

"Why?"

"We thought you might be, thought you might be…"

"Come now, out with it."

"The Goatman."

And there it was. I should have braced for the scolding to follow, but I found myself unusually mellow. I wasn't scared. I wasn't embarrassed. I simply felt…nothing. There was laughter. Not the warm, friendly kind I was used to hearing from Mr. Hutchinson. This laughter was cold and bitter.

When the old man spoke next, his voice was hard. "You really are a gem, boy. You know, the more I think about it, the happier I am I didn't tear that little head of yours clean off."

The words were threatening. Something important was happening, but it was hard for me to focus. "What?"

"White Marsh, child. It was me you interrupted in the forest, indulging in a little repast. Though it is true I prefer the flesh of Adam and Eve, beggars can't be choosers, right? Especially now that the need to feed has grown dire. Which, of course, is why you are here."

Despite the drug-induced daze, my revelation arrived fast and hard. I was right. I had been right all along. Sitting in front of me, smoking a stinky, old pipe, was the Goatman. And it looked like I was going to be his next meal. A sudden anger brewed inside me. The rage didn't come from having been tricked by the old man; he had played his part well. My rage was directed inwards for having doubted my instincts in the first place. I tried to get up but stumbled and almost fell over. "N-no, I–"

Mr. Hutchinson reached over and put a hand on my shoulder to steady me and then force me back into my chair. "You misunderstand, child. You are not my prey. In fact, you are the guest of honor. Think back, Chris. Do you remember that tired old urban legend I regaled to you during our last visit? The one concerning the witch and the demon?"

I allowed a moment for my heart to slow before answering. "I think so."

"As it is, that tale is true in its entirety. Furthermore, as you may have surmised, I am the demon from that story."

Mr. Hutchinson placed his right hand over his heart. "Allow me to introduce myself. I am Corabas, though I have gone by many names over the centuries."

"Like the Goatman?"

Corabas spit the words out as if they were poison. "The Goatman! For millennia my ilk has been called many things, sa'ar, ordogs, leshy, as well as the names of various gods and demons, yet now we have the Goatman. It is a vulgar moniker, but I suppose it is a sign of the times we live in."

He leaned back in his chair and took another puff as he sized me up.

I felt like a piece of livestock up for auction. He said I wasn't on the menu, but it sure as hell didn't feel that way.

"You, Chris, are truly something special. You possess youth, good health, intelligence, but most important, you are a highly perceptive child. You alone deduced that I was the one responsible for the killings, that I was the infamous Goatman. Tell me, have you seen the trees?"

I couldn't focus. My toes and fingertips were numb from the poison in the air. "The trees?"

"Yes, child, the trees. Have you solved their riddle? I know you must have seen them by now. I made them rather hard to miss."

I closed my eyes and tried to concentrate. In the darkness of my mind, the pagan image burned. I whispered, "The horned god."

Corabas wheezed out a chuckle. "That's right. That's what it is called now. But in truth, it is my mark, and there is power in it. The mark serves as an anchor, binding me to the land and the land to me. Understand, Chris, this is my domain." The demon turned his gaze to the backyard, but I could tell from the distant look in his eyes the place he envisioned was far beyond his freshly-mowed lawn.

"I was summoned here in the years before the Great Rebellion when this countryside was lush and untamed, and I thrived for generations in relative peace. This was my Eden before the serpent, before the soot-spewing, ear-rattling contrivances of industry rolled through and laid waste to so much. It was where I lived with Abby—the Eve to my Adam—for many golden years."

Corabas remained lost in another time. A weak smile rose on his face. "When I first asked for Abby's hand, my intentions were entirely practical in nature. Though there is no denying she was an attractive woman, my interests resided solely in her usefulness as a prop to bolster my masquerade. Beauty and intelligence aside, Abigail's most desirable qualities were her docile tendencies and appeasing nature, both of which proved useful in constructing the façade of a happily married couple. Of course, Abigail's motives and affection were sincere from the start. Then the oddest thing happened. I found myself growing increasingly accustomed to her presence. The way she hummed off-key every time The Carter Family came on the radio, how she rolled my socks into tight little bundles, her insistence on a morning kiss before I set out to work—these things were all at once insufferable yet on some perverse level endearing to me. Over the months and years to follow, tolerance and polite indifference slowly yielded to true affection. Her simple manners and charms worked their magic on me until I found myself utterly beguiled. Thus the marriage born of lies and deception turned in to something different than expected…"

His eyes slowly turned back to me. They were not sad like I would have guessed. Instead, they burned with unnatural energy. "It must seem odd to you. The notion that a demon can fall in love."

I opened my mouth to speak, but my tongue was lagging behind. I wanted to ask him what he was going to do with me, but I'm pretty sure all I got out was something like, "Whaju gon do." With each gulp of polluted air, I slipped further under the demon's spell. I was eight miles high and felt like I was in some crazy dream.

A long sigh slipped from the demon. "The greatest single regret of my life was ripping my darling Abby's throat out. You see, the older this body gets, the greater the hunger and more often I have to feed. It takes much to sustain such a frail form. On the ill-fated night in question, Abby somehow got it in her head to follow me. Looking back, I imagine my frequent snacking must have aroused her suspicion. If I had to guess, I would say she suspected infidelity." Corabas shook his head. "To think she could have imagined I was capable of such a thing."

Why was he telling me all of this? Unless, of course, he knew no one else would ever find out...

"So there I was in all my majesty, this tired old shell of flesh cast aside. The fever was upon me, and I was seconds away from dining on some plump little hen walking her equally obese dog. Then there came a scream. Oh, that scream! If my wits had been about me, I would have recognized the shrill pitch. But alas, it all happened so fast."

Corabas raised an arm and whipped it through the air. "Out of instinct I lunged and slashed. It wasn't until her lifeless body dropped to the ground that I realized my folly."

He fell silent while I sat frozen, paralyzed with fear and unable to speak. What was he going to do with me? Kill me and stash my body in some hidden crypt beside the mummified remains of his wife? Serve me up for a late lunch and then bury my bones in his backyard?

The seconds seemed to stretch into hours. Finally, the demon turned to me and blinked as if waking up from a dream. "But all of this is of no real import to you. On to the matter at hand."

He stood and disappeared into a room off to his right that had been closed every other time I was in the house.

I fought the smoke-induced spell I was under and rose in my seat to peer through the crack in the doorway to the room beyond. In the dim light seeping through, I saw an old roll-top desk, a chair, and stacks upon stacks of books piled up to the ceiling. A moment later Corabas returned to the table. He was whistling and holding a leather-bound book in one hand and a large canvas sack in the other. He sat back down and placed both objects in front of him. For the better part of a minute, I watched in silence as he flipped through page after page of the book, all the while whistling that annoying tune. Finally, he stopped.

"Ah, there it is!"

He opened the sack and retrieved a strange mix of items. The first thing he pulled out was a short, fat candle and then a polished green and red stone followed by a jar of what looked like peppercorn. Next came some twine, dried twigs, another jar containing tiny bones or maybe teeth, and an evil looking vial of dark liquid. After assessing the ingredients in front of him, Corabas stepped into the kitchen only to reappear a few seconds later with a stone bowl in one hand and a small club made from the same substance in the other.

I watched as he dumped some twigs, bones, and peppercorn into the bowl. With great care, he ground the contents with the club while chanting something under his breath. The smell of crushed pepper hit my nose, but it wasn't as strong as I thought it would be. Apparently, the smoke from the demon's pipe was messing with my sense of smell too.

Corabas looked to me. "It's time for you to know the true reason you are here, child. I have chosen you to be my vessel. Through you I will walk upon the earth for yet another generation. You see, in order for a spirit or demon to remain on this plane of existence, we must find a terrestrial creature to inhabit. Most choose a human, but on occasion lesser animals such as dogs or birds are selected. After all, any port in a storm."

I should have been in full panic mode, but I was too spaced out to care. I concentrated this time to make sure the words came out right. "W-Why me?"

"For the reasons I have already explained to you. You have both the physical and cerebral qualities I desire in a host vessel."

"But what if I don't want to be your vessel?"

Corabas smiled. It was the same smile I had seen dozens of times before, but the warmth was now gone. The friendly face Corabas wore was nothing more than a mask. "It is not as bad as you might think, Chris. Though I will be in control, your consciousness and senses will remain intact. You will still be able to enjoy meals, music, and all varieties of physical activities; you just won't be steering the ship. To put it in terms you can relate to, it's similar to watching television or a movie but a much more stimulating experience."

He was trying to make it sound like it wasn't that bad, but I wasn't sure why. Was it some lame attempt to keep me calm before he swooped in to take up residence? "But I'll never be able to talk to anyone or do anything again on my own?"

"No, you will not. However, there are other benefits to serving as my vessel. You will have increased strength and stamina and live a long, healthy life. You need never fear sickness or disease again. And also there is *the hunt*."

The added emphasis he placed on the last two words disturbed me. "The hunt?"

The demon's eyes flared. "Yes! It is a most marvelous sensation. The adrenaline trickles into your veins when first you catch the scent of your prey. Slowly the spigot opens as you stalk it. When the time is right, you fall upon it, rending muscle and tendon, crushing skull and spine. Then comes the *feasting*. I have to tell you, there is nothing more embracing than dining on the flesh of the fallen. From the first time you sample it, you will be ruined for all other manner of sustenance. My current vessel enjoys it immensely."

"You were the one that left me the message in blood and buried the dog collars and barrette for me to find."

"Ah, yes. It's all part of the dance, you see. There are certain things that need to be shown and particular secrets shared in order for the magic to work as intended. Our connection is delicate at this point, but it will grow much, much stronger."

"I-I don't want anything to do with this." I tried to shake my head, but all I could manage was a sluggish tilt from side to side. "You-you can't make me do this."

Corabas smirked. "That...is actually correct. I cannot enter into an unwilling vessel. Fortunately, there are always enticements. For example, I promised Mr. Hutchinson here I would rid his diseased body of the consumption that was ravaging it. For you another approach will be necessary. Tell me, Chris, what is your sister's name?"

"What?"

"You heard me. What is her name? The cherub that clings to your leg almost as tight as she clings to that filthy little dolly she constantly carries."

"Katie."

"Katie! Such a cute thing. And you have a brother too, older than you as I recall."

"Yes."

"What a beautiful family. So full of love, I imagine. Then there are your friends, the gangly, blue-eyed boy and the one with the sandy hair and braces. The three of you seem thick as thieves. Friendships like that don't come along every day."

I kept my mouth shut. There was no need to say anything; it was clear where he was going.

"I don't normally resort to blackmail, Chris, but you are quite right. A vessel must, of their own volition, relinquish control to me. For this transaction to work, you must cooperate. I'm sure by now it is becoming abundantly clear you have no choice in the matter if you value the lives of your family and friends. I would hate to have to make an example of one of them to entice you, but if that's what is necessary, so be it."

I was stuck in a nightmare. Corabas had my number, and he knew it. I started thinking about it, about being stuck in a prison in my own body, watching as the demon pretended to be me. I was probably better off dead.

As if sensing my hesitation, he spoke. "You should know that the possession is not immediate. There is a special day and time on which it must occur, when the barrier between the spirit and material world thins."

"When's that?"

"Sunset on Samhain, or Halloween as it is better known. This year the black moon comes with it, and so my power is all the greater."

It was July second. That left me with just under four months before I would have to surrender myself to the demon.

"Think of it this way, Chris. In all of the games you have played with your friends, the books of fantasy you have read, and movies and television shows you have gorged upon, how often have you imagined yourself the hero, the one who saves the day and protects the lives of the innocent? Now is your chance. Through your sacrifice your family and friends will be spared from gruesome fates. You have my word. They shall remain untouched and will pass from this world by either natural causes or their own misadventure."

The room fell silent as the demon waited for my answer. I had to hand it to him. Corabas had done his homework. He clearly chose me a long time ago, steadily learning all he could about my habits, likes, and dislikes to guarantee his success…and it was going to work. Even in my brain-fried state, I knew I had no choice. If I refused him, he would kill someone close to me as an example and then make the offer again. If I turned him down a second time, he would kill another until everyone I loved was dead.

"So, I have until Halloween?"

Corabas smiled. "Yes, I will come for you then. But first, the pact must be made." He reached back in the sack and retrieved a first aid kit. He opened it and took out a hypodermic needle, antiseptic, and a plastic bag of cotton balls. "Be calm, child, and this will be over quickly. A small amount of blood is needed for the invocation."

He reached over and gently turned my left arm palm up. "Make a fist."

It didn't take him long to get what he needed. Soon after, I was left holding a damp piece of cotton over the pinhole in my arm. I watched as he lit the candle and began whispering in a strange language. He took the syringe and emptied its contents into the bowl. Next, he drained the oily-looking liquid from the vial. The chanting continued as he struck a match and placed it over the nasty mixture. The flame fell, and green fire flared up followed by a stench that reminded me of rotten eggs. My body shuddered as something icy pricked my heart.

Corabas stood. "It is done. Your head will begin to clear as soon as we get some fresh air in you." He grabbed both of my arms and gently pulled me up. Reaching an arm around my back, he guided me to the front door.

The effect of the warm summer air was immediate. The cobwebs cleared from my head as my senses gradually returned. I started taking deep breaths.

"Remember our treaty, Chris Dwyer. You have entered into a blood agreement that cannot be broken. Any attempt to do so would have catastrophic consequences for both you and your loved ones. Do you understand?"

I nodded.

"Good. Now go home and rest. The ritual can prove taxing on a body, even on one as young and resilient as yours. And remember...I'll be watching."

Chapter 18

By the time I woke the following morning, sunlight was already pouring into my room. It was my mother's voice that woke me; she was talking to someone at the front door. "That's right, boys. Chris is still asleep. He came home exhausted yesterday and went straight to bed."

"It's okay, Mom!" I shouted through a yawn. "Who is it?"

"Paul and Kevin, dear!"

I sat up in bed and rubbed the crusted up dirt from the corners of my eyes. My sleep had been deep but troubled. Something happened, but I couldn't remember what. There was smoke and a terrible smell—there was green fire. For some reason, I put a hand over my heart. Though I felt well enough, I had a sinking suspicion something awful had happened. My mom's voice came from downstairs.

"Are you feeling all right? Mr. Hutchinson came by to check on you this morning, but I didn't want to disturb you. He said you looked a little pale yesterday when you left his house and thought you might have gotten too much sun."

Images flooded my brain. It was all real. The Goatman was real. No, it was Corabas—that's what he liked to be called. "I'm okay. Just needed some rest."

"That's fine, but I want you to take it easy today. It's going to be another hot one. Maybe you boys should head to the pool."

My feet felt like lead weights as I stomped downstairs. With each step, more of the previous day's events resurfaced. Corabas played me like a violin, using my friends and family against me. I was completely, utterly screwed. How long had he been planning it? A month? A year? Ten? The demon had lived on my street for as long as I could remember.

Had he been plotting to steal my body since I was in diapers? It was all too much to think about. When I got to the screen door, Kevin and Paul were waiting for me on the other side.

From their wide-eyed, spooked expressions, I knew something was up. They said nothing and motioned for me to come outside.

I opened the door and stepped out. "What's up with all the hush-hush?"

Paul spoke. "Did you have any dreams last night? Or more like nightmares?"

"I don't know. I might have, but I can't really remember that much. Why?"

"Think hard," Kevin said. "Do you remember any faces or anything somebody might have said in your dreams?"

Both of my friends had them, but the dark circles under Paul's eyes stood out more. For a split second, I considered telling them about Corabas but quickly thought better of it. "No. Like I said, it's hard to remember."

Kevin looked to Paul and muttered, "He didn't see it."

I was groggy, confused, and running on zero patience. "Seeing as you guys dragged me onto the front porch in my pajamas, I'd appreciate it if one of you dorks would tell me what the heck is going on."

"We saw it last night," Paul whispered.

My friends fell silent, as if the words Paul mumbled held some great significance.

After a few seconds of dead air, I spoke. "Saw what?"

"The Goatman," Kevin said. "We both saw him in our dreams."

"Come again?"

"It was late last night, probably after midnight," Paul said. "I heard a scratching sound. At first I thought it was a branch rubbing against the window screen, but when my eyes adjusted, I saw a face staring back at me..."

Where Paul stopped, Kevin picked up. "It was the same for me. I heard a noise at the window and peered out. The face was kind of hard to see—except for the horns."

Paul nodded. "Horns!" He pointed to the sides of his head and began swirling his fingers around like a lunatic. Giant, curvy ones like some mutant ram was knocking on my window."

Kevin shook his head. "Not a ram. It was more like a minotaur. Its face was long and mean, and it had blood in its eyes. They were swollen and shiny and looked like a couple of cherry jaw breakers."

"The eyes," Paul mumbled.

Kevin put a hand on Paul's shoulder. "It was the freakiest thing I've ever seen, and it spoke to me."

Fearing I already knew what their late night visitor had to say, I hesitated to ask. But after a few seconds of silence, I realized they were waiting for me. "So out with it. What did it say?"

Paul spoke like he was talking to himself. "I don't think it said anything to me."

Kevin's nose crinkled. "It said something like, 'If he is true to his word, you will be safe.'"

The message couldn't have been any clearer if Corabas had advertised it on the side of the Goodyear Blimp. If I shut my mouth and waited to be possessed like a good little boy, my friends would be safe.

"You were right, Chris," Paul blurted. "Right about everything. The Goatman is real, and he *knows who we are*."

"Do you have any idea what that might mean?" Kevin asked me. "Who needs to be true to his word, and what the heck does it have to do with us?"

It was the first time anyone ever actually bought in to one of my theories on the supernatural. Under normal circumstances it would have been the perfect opportunity for a well-earned *told you so*. But these weren't normal circumstances, and I couldn't afford to be selfish. I was bursting inside, but all I could say was, "You got me. Are you sure you heard right? I mean, it was the middle of the night, and Paul said the thing didn't say anything to him."

"I may have been scared and a few seconds away from dropping a Baby Ruth in my underwear, but I know what I heard. C'mon, Chris, you're usually really good at this stuff. I bet the key to this whole thing is finding out who the Goatman is talking about. Maybe we should start with some hardcore research. You know, like the kind of stuff they do on *Kojak*."

"Kevin also found one of those carvings in his backyard," Paul said. "That means there has to be a connection with the Goatman, right, Chris?"

This was all heading south fast, and I was the one to blame. I started my friends on the hunt for the Goatman, and now that they had caught his scent, they were all fired up. But this wasn't a game of *D and D*; this was real, and these guys had absolutely no clue of the scale of evil they were messing with. I needed to reel them in quick, so I could have some time to think. What I had to do made me want to barf, but I saw no other way. My stomach churned as the poisonous words spilled out. "Be cool, guys. Let's just think about this. Kevin, you said the Goatman spoke to you in your dream, but he didn't in Paul's."

Kevin corrected me. "Not a dream, Chris. It was real, and yes, he did talk to me. What's your point?"

I raised a hand. "Right, sorry. That's what I meant. Anyway, the guy spoke during your... encounter but not in Paul's. So, they were different."

"Okay, first, not a guy but the Goatman," Kevin huffed. "Second, what the hell are you getting at?"

"Yeah, Chris," Paul added. "Where are you going with this?"

"All I'm saying is, let's think of this logically and not go diving into anything blind. Something happened to you guys yesterday that got you all worked up, but if this is really the Goatman, why didn't he show up knocking on my window? I was the one that started the whole thing after all." My stomach moaned in protest. Was it as loud as I thought it was?

"I don't know," Kevin answered.

"Maybe there wasn't enough time," Paul said. "Maybe he'll visit you tonight, or soon. You should get a camera, and keep it by your bed, so you can get a picture of him."

"That could be the case, and I guess the camera's not a bad idea, but let's take it easy for the next couple days."

The accusatory tone of Kevin's voice was unmistakable. "Why, Chris? Don't you believe us?"

This sucked. I felt dirtier than a used car salesman with each word oozing out of my mouth. Another growl came from my belly. "Sure I do. I mean, I believe you *think* you saw something, but we should keep open minds is all I'm saying. See, I can't help but wonder if me dragging you guys all around the neighborhood looking at trees, spying on Mr. Hutchinson, and all the other crazy stuff I've been shoving down your throats has something to do with this. I hate to say it, but maybe I've pushed you guys to the point of seeing things that aren't actually there."

Kevin turned to Paul. "I knew it. He doesn't believe us."

"No, that's not what I said."

"Then you do believe us?" Paul asked.

I felt like I had to fart. All the lying was making me super gassy. "It's not that simple. Let's just cool it, and give it a day or two before we take this investigation to the next level."

The disappointment on my friend's faces hit me like a sucker punch to the gut.

"Look, I have to go. I have a butt load of chores to do because of Steve."

It was a lie, but I needed to scram before I came unwound and confessed everything to them. Also, I really did have to fart.

"C'mon, Paul," Kevin said. "Let's split."

"I'll see you guys tomorrow at the parade. We can talk more about all of this then."

Paul slapped me on the shoulder before joining Kevin. "If I was you, I'd keep that camera close tonight. I have a feeling you're going to be singing a different tune come tomorrow."

After I was sure they were out of earshot, my butt sounded off like a motorbike. I spent the rest of the day moping around the house, drowning my worries in a sea of Twinkies and Dr. Peppers. I had bought some time but not much, and I was going to have to make a decision: come clean with my friends in the hopes we could somehow stop Corabas or bail and cut all ties with them so they would be safe forever.

Chapter 19

For as far back as I can remember, we spent our Fourth of July mornings at the Perrets'. Being on the corner of Stonybrook and Belair, their house was primo real estate for front row seats of the parade. Steve, Katie, and I headed out before our folks. As soon as we stepped foot on their lawn, Katie ran toward a pack of squealing six-year-old girls, Steve split to go find Perry, and I headed to the curb to meet up with Kevin and Paul, who were watching the fife and drum corps march along.

I headed in their direction then froze. I'd been up half the night trying to come up with the pros and cons of spilling the beans to my friends, but all I ended up with was a major headache and a lot more gas. The logical side of me argued the truth should remain under wraps at all costs, but I was never much for logic. To keep the secret until I came under the demon's power seemed to me a fate worse than death. At least with death people know you're gone; they'll miss you. I would be a prisoner trapped in my own body with no one the wiser. Adios freedom. Bye-bye life.

Paul glanced back and caught sight of me. He tugged on Kevin's shirt before running over. "So? Did you see him? Did you get a picture?"

"No. No late night visitor."

"You sure? You look kinda crappy, like you didn't get any sleep."

"Thanks."

"Paul's right," Kevin said. "You look like a turd. An old, dried up turd."

Kevin had been pretty steamed yesterday, so I was just glad he was talking to me. "Look, there's something I need to tell you guys, something important."

Just getting those few simple words out already had me feeling better. I was going to share everything. "I know I've been a bit of a jackass lately."

"You got that right," Kevin said.

Ignoring them, I continued. "I've been debating whether or not to tell you this, to tell you the truth about what's going on."

"What do you mean?" Paul asked. "You been holding out on us?"

"Kind of. But there's a reason for that. See –"

"Hold that thought!" Paul shouted. "We got clowns at eight o'clock, and they're throwing candy!"

Kevin and I watched as Paul squirmed his way between the wall of younger kids lining the sidewalk. A dozen grease-painted, red-nosed clowns were tossing out fistfuls of sweets to the onlookers. Like the complete spaz he was, Paul started jumping up and snatching sugary bombs of Dum Dums, Bit O'Honey—which no kid ever liked—and Now and Later. I guess I couldn't blame him. After all, when you have seven brothers and sisters fighting over every last Twinkie and Oreo in the house, getting your grubby hands on a little extra candy was a priority.

"There's something not quite right about that boy," I mumbled.

"That's a roger," Kevin said.

Paul came back with a handful of the clown candy. "You guys want in on this?"

I took a couple of grape Now and Later.

Paul raised a candy-laden hand and pushed it in front of Kevin's face.

Kevin pointed to this braces. "Really?"

"You could have a Dum Dum," Paul said.

"No thanks, dumb dumb."

I felt like I was forgetting something. I looked around the Perrets' front yard. Katie and her group of chattering friends were nowhere to be found. "Hey, guys, either of you seen my sis?"

Paul's head swiveled as he gnawed on a rock-hard Now and Later.

Kevin's hand shielded his eyes from the sun. He pointed across the street. "There she is."

Breathing a sigh of relief, I followed his finger. Katie was holding Baby Jackie up for Corabas to see. The mangy doll had survived more tea parties, makeovers, and nights left out in the pouring rain than any other toy Katie owned, and it now resembled one of the zombies from *Night of the Living Dead*. My stomach knotted as I watched the demon pretend to show interest in the thing. He lifted Baby Jackie next to his face and made it wave to me. Though he was smiling, his unblinking stare was anything but friendly. Corabas grabbed Katie's hand and cautiously made his way across the street, worming his way between a Boy Scout troop and a trio of Shriners driving miniature cars.

"Mr. Dwyer, you appear to have misplaced your sibling. Do try to be more careful. It's quite chaotic here and would be easy for a child to become lost or—even worse—get hurt."

His message was received loud and clear. "Yes, sir."

I knelt down and looked at Katie. "You okay?"

"Yes, but you've been bad. You and Steve should have kept a better eye on me."

"I guess you're right. I'm sorry."

"If you promise to play Hungry Hippos later, I won't tell Mom and Dad."

It was a small price to pay for my screwup. "You got it."

"I promise not to tell too."

I stood back up and looked at the demon. He was taunting me, letting me know that he could get to my sister or anyone of my family or friends if I tried to weasel out of our deal.

"So," Corabas said, putting on his best fake smile, "what have the Three Musketeers been up to?"

"Nothing," I said. My voice sounded small and weak. Paul and Kevin remained silent.

"Oh, I doubt that very much. You three clearly look to be hatching a scheme or collaborating on some form of treason. That's quite all right though. I suppose it's in your nature as with all boys your age."

Corabas gave Katie's hair a tussle before he started backing away. "Just remember, it is a big brother's job to look after his sister…no matter what." His eyes zeroed in on me. "Understood?"

At a loss for words, I simply nodded.

"Good man! Now take care boys, and try to stay out of trouble—any *real* trouble that is."

My friends both answered with a hushed, "Yes, sir."

After Corabas was out of earshot, Paul muttered, "I don't know, Chris. The more I think about it, you may have been right about the old man. Another stakeout is probably a good idea. How about it, Kevin?"

Life is funny. Just when you know you're in control and you've made up your mind about something important, it comes along and says, "I don't think so," and kicks you square in the cojones. I was seconds away from confessing all to my friends before Corabas issued his not-so-veiled threat. Now I knew for certain what had to be done. Before Kevin could be tempted down a road that might end in gruesome deaths for both him and Paul, I blurted, "It was me! I made the whole thing up!"

There it was, the big, ugly lie. I had to continue before I lost my nerve. "The whole thing was a hoax. I thought it would be a fun adventure for us over the summer. Kind of like our own real-life *D and D* campaign. It just got a little out of hand."

"What are you saying?" Paul asked.

"Geez, Paul, do I really have to spell it all out for you? It was all fake. From my escape on the bike trail to the carvings on the trees. I did it all to shake things up from the same old boring junk we always do."

Paul's twisted, confused expression was one of the saddest things I'd ever seen. "I like the boring junk we always do."

I felt like I was going to toss my cookies.

"You're just joshing, right? Kevin blared. "You've got to be joshing us!"

Now was the time to shut my mouth. The damage had been done; I just had to ride out the humiliation without springing a leak.

The gleam from Kevin's braces nearly blinded me as he shouted, "So, you're telling me," he paused and motioned to Paul, "you're telling *us* that for the past month you've been jerking us around on this whole Goatman thing?"

I stood my ground and did the only thing I could do. I nodded.

"What about the carvings?" Kevin asked.

"I made them," I lied. "I used one of the tools from my dad's garage and carved the first one on the tree on the bike trail. Then I marked up my own tree and next yours and Paul's."

Paul started with a high-pitched stammer. "W-W-What about the Goatman? Kevin and I saw it. You couldn't have faked *that*."

"C'mon, Paul, think about it. That happened right after you all got riled up about the symbols carved into the trees in your yards. You guys were so freaked out about the markings you must have had dreams about the Goatman."

Kevin spit at my feet. "Un-freaking-believable!"

"This is a joke. Tell me this is some lame, stupid joke!" Paul shouted.

I said nothing. Even if I wanted to, the knot in my throat would probably have made me sound like some whiny baby. If I could just hold out for a few more minutes, it would all be over.

Kevin leaned in as he stepped past, making sure to catch a chunk of my shoulder in the process. "Well good night, John-Boy! That is messed up, man. I think you need help—maybe a shrink. I mean, I knew you had a crazy imagination and liked to make up stories and stuff; I used to think it was kinda cool. But this is *way* too much. I don't think I can hang out with someone that gets off on playing mind games on his friends. I'm out of here."

What I was doing was the right thing, but it didn't make it suck any less. Having my friends hate me for something I didn't do wasn't what I wanted, but it was the only way I could think of to keep them safe and get them to drop the whole Goatman thing. "I'm sorry. I was just trying to have a little fun, that's all."

Kevin looked to Paul. "You coming?"

Paul had fallen silent. He shook his head as he followed Kevin.

And that was the day I lost my two best friends.

Chapter 20

The next couple of weeks sucked something fierce. Now lacking in the whole friend department, I started spending more time at the library. Sometimes I would tell my parents I was heading there, but mostly I would lie and say I was going out to hang out with my non-existent friends. Because it was a close-knit neighborhood, my mom would soon discover the truth, but I didn't sweat that too much. After all, by Halloween none of it would matter.

Day after day, aisle after aisle, I combed the library looking for a clue that might help me get a better grip on what I was dealing with. I started with the book on paganism that first steered me in the direction of the horned god. It offered little more on the subject and pretty much proved to be a waste of time. From there I worked my way through almost every book they had on Christianity, Judaism, Hinduism, Islam, and all sorts on mythology. There were occasional references to demons that could possess people, but nothing looked to be of any practical value when it came to my unique situation, and there was no mention of a creature named Corabas in any of them.

My Sundays with the demon included increasingly invasive interviews. He had questions on everything from favorite foods to girlfriends—of which I was sorely lacking. He was friendly as long as I fed him the answers he wanted, but if he thought my responses were too slow or vague, his mood quickly turned frosty. Occasionally, he would take a break from his interrogations and start reminiscing on the good old days before Levitt destroyed his beautiful countryside. Other times he would get all school-girl chatty and rant about his up and coming occupancy of my body. He was in one of these moods during our last conversation and mentioned something that turned my investigation in a new direction.

Turns out he had been waiting for some time—years in fact—for a special lunar cycle. According to him, on Halloween a second new moon would rise in the sky. He called it a black moon and said with a fire in his eyes that the power of Palo Mayombe would be at its peak then. Corabas was convinced if the possession occurred on that day, his strength would be increased tenfold.

Palo Mayombe. It was the type of witchcraft used to summon him, and I was willing to bet it was the same magic he used on me. Though the library had several books that mentioned the religion, there was only one devoted to its study. Fortunately for me, it wasn't checked out.

Doctor Trevor Langley's *Study of the Evolution of Palo Mayombe from Africa to the Americas* wasn't the type of book one would see on the summer reading list for a tenth grader, so I was careful to find a private reading area with partitions on three sides. I was also sure to keep another book close by in the event some nosey neighbor spotted me and decided to ask what I was reading. So, with *Something Wicked This Way Comes* playing alternate, I dove into the wonderful world of Palo Mayombe. The stuff was as dry as the Sahara. Most of the book was just a description of the practices of the religion and how they changed over time. Given a choice between reading the good doctor's work and my old high school algebra book, I probably would have picked the textbook. But seeing as how my butt was on the line, I gritted my teeth and carried on. After dragging myself through the book one painful page after another and nodding off on at least a couple of occasions, I finally stumbled on something. Buried on pages 258 and 259 was a compass pointing me where I had to go. The text explained that each priest or priestess had their own spell book and *nganga*—or cauldron. These relics were the source of the witch's knowledge and power. Where the spell book showed the words to be spoken and the ingredients to use, the *nganga* served as the source of the witch's power and also as a type of altar on which sacrifices were made to please the dark gods and goddesses.

I already knew where Corabas kept his spell book. He likely kept the cauldron in the same room. If I could somehow get my hands on the book, maybe I could find a way to undo the voodoo he put on me.

"Hi, Chris."

I jumped a couple of inches before fumbling to swap out books. Looking up, I saw Tracy Staubach smiling at me. "Oh, hey."

She giggled. "Didn't mean to startle you. That book of yours must really be interesting."

"What, this?" I waved the decoy in front of me. "Just catching up on a little Bradbury."

Tracy smirked. Clearly my sleight of hand was lacking. "Riiight. Well, sorry to disturb you. I know how gripping that kind of stuff can be."

Knowing I'd been flat-out busted, I quickly changed the subject. "What are you doing here?"

"Meh, I got a C last year in English lit. My folks said that if I want to keep the keys to the Rabbit, I have to do better at Maryland. Sooo, I'm getting a bit of a head start. Tell you what, there are few things lamer than being stuck in the library when your friends are spending their summer in Ocean City—no offense."

"None taken. My summer reading is a real pain in the butt."

"Really? I always thought you and your friends liked to read. Y'know, Paul and that new kid that moved in over on Spiral. What's his name, Kevin? It's kind of cool the way you guys always hang out together."

Ugh, she thought I was some dorky bookworm. "Well, Kevin and Paul are okay, but they can be a bit clingy sometimes."

The coy smile remained on Tracy's face. "You don't say."

"Yeah, they're always wanting to playing games and goof off. It wouldn't hurt them to grow up a little. Take me for instance. I'll be starting Drivers Ed soon. That way when I start driving, I can get a part-time job and earn some decent coin. By the end of the year who knows? Maybe I'll be able to get my own ride, something cool and classy like a Camaro."

Her grin grew wider. "Wow, that's great! The new Camaros are way cool. I'm sure if you put your mind to it, you could do it."

She dug me. Even a blind person could see it. "It is not the mind, but my heart that drives me onward, onward with the promise of seeing your smile and hearing your voice."

The words slipped from my mouth as if spoken by someone else. Usually when talking to Tracy, I'd get so tongue-tied I could barely string five words together. Where I now found the vocabulary and intestinal fortitude to say such a thing was beyond me.

Tracy's mouth fell open before an ear-to-ear grin spread across her perfect, pretty face. "Gee, Chris, that's just the sweetest thing I've heard in a long time. It's nice to talk to talk to someone who knows how to speak to a woman."

"It's like I always say, women are made to be loved, not understood."

With those words whatever ghostly poet had taken over temporary residence in my body promptly departed, and an awkward silence followed as I began bobbing my head up and down and smiling like a complete boob.

"Really! Well that's a quite a saying, Chris. I think maybe there are a few things you could teach some of the older boys in the neighborhood. I'm not sure what it is, but there's definitely something going on with you. You seem a little...older than the last time I saw you." Her sky blue eyes narrowed for a moment before she spoke again. "Why don't you give me a call when you get that Camaro. You can take me for a ride."

As she turned to leave, Tracy threw a wink my way.

I must have run the scenario through my head a million times before coming to the realization I had actually been flirting with an eighteen-year-old girl. Scratch that. An eighteen-year-old *woman*. And from the look of things, I'd done a damn fine job of it. I still had no clue where the words came from, but I wasn't going to complain about the results. For the next few minutes, I made a half-assed attempt to read until coming to the conclusion it was useless. All I could do was think about those blue eyes and that wink.

Chapter 21

One of the side effects of our arrangement Corabas failed to mention concerned my dreams. The control I once wielded over them was now weakened to the point where I was little more than a passenger, riding along through whatever crazy fantasies my subconscious whipped up. At the same time, their vividness intensified until I couldn't distinguish the dream world from the waking one. The sounds, colors, and even the smells all seemed *so* real. For a while the subject matter stayed within my usual repertoire of narrowly escaping hideous monsters, saving a very grateful Melissa Casey—or sometimes Tracy Staubach—from the filthy clutches of one of the Drake boys, or showing up for social studies, English, or history sporting nothing but my Fruit of the Looms. Then one night everything went sideways.

I was kneeling. Looking down, I noticed I was wearing my cassock. Bells were ringing. I turned slowly to my left and saw another boy in identical vestments scowling at me. "You missed your mark," he whispered. "Pay attention for the next one." It was John Sanders, one of the altar boys at St. Pius the X that I sometimes served with. I glanced up and saw Father Calhoun in the middle of the consecration. Beyond him pew after pew of parishioners were watching the priest with great interest. Some I knew, but most were strangers. There was one though, standing at the back near the entrance to the church, that I recognized immediately. Corabas.

I heard the priest say, "This is my body," and panicked. Believing that I would once again miss my cue, I rang the bells. It took me a few seconds to realize I was too early.

"Hey, retard," John scolded in a hushed tone, "you're hosing up the Mass. Just do what I do."

Something inside me snapped. A wicked smile split across my face. "Zip it, Johnny, or I'll shove these bells so far up your ass you'll jingle every time you take a shit."

John's face turned pale. His mouth flapped open and closed, but no words came out.

Where did that come from? The priest must not have heard because he continued with the Mass. Looking back at the congregation, I noticed Corabas had taken out his pipe and was now smoking. He took a step forward and then strolled down the center aisle like he owned the place. Halfway to the altar, he stopped. I glanced to my left and right to see if any of the parishioners noticed the smoking man. That's when I saw the faithful weren't doing too well. The color had left many in the crowd, making them pale and thin. Others appeared to splotch and swell. Bloody tears trickled down the swollen cheeks of men, women, boys, and girls. Those few who still looked normal stood shoulder to shoulder with these zombies and ghouls, totally unaware of the condition of their neighbors. The charred smell of incense filling the church began to thin and a sickly sweet stench surfaced.

Corabas took a long tug on his pipe and then blew a puff of bluish smoke. He turned it over, dumping the still smoking contents on the carpeted floor. Crushing out the smoldering remains of tobacco, he said, "Don't want to start a fire, do we?"

The priest was talking, but his words faded to a steady stream of background noise.

"Why are you here?"

The demon ignored the question. He looked around at the horde of undead parishioners and shook his head. "Goodness, child, you do have a macabre imagination. I suppose this is a byproduct of your generation. Too many nights spent with your face planted in front of a television screen watching rubbish movies with flesh-eating zombies and the like. I believe you and I can do better than this."

144

It was my dream, but I no longer had control. His presence was like a virus infecting everything around me, including the citizens of Bowie who had come to hear the good word. We were all in his world now.

The light shining through the stained glass windows dimmed. The demon's shoulders suddenly lurched forward as his hands popped open and arms spread wide. A low laugh croaked from Corabas's throat while silver fur sprouted from muscles that swelled and tore at his shirt. Coils sprouted from both sides of his skull, spiraling round and round to form a wicked pair of horns on a head that stretched long and thin like a horse's. A pair of glowing red eyes flickered with hellfire.

I swore I must have been gazing at the devil himself.

It was dark. I was in the forest and on the hunt. A terrible thirst and hunger gnawed at me as I silently moved between brush and branch. No twig snapped, and no leaf crunched. It was warm and humid, and the moon was full with a smoky haze surrounding it. The dank, marshy smell of earth and rotting wood hung heavy in the air. There were other odors too. The forest was full of life invisible to the naked eye. I smelled the feathers of a horned owl and the blood of the field mouse it held in its beak as it perched twenty feet above. A few yards off to my right under a blanket of ferns, a black snake slithered.

Such creatures held no interest for me. Something else hovered on the night air that made my pulse race and mouth water. It was a tinny, salty smell mixed with a powerful blast of mint that reminded me of my dad's aftershave.

I followed it through the forest until I came to the edge of a large clearing. In front of me was a freshly mowed field. To my left and right, white soccer goals bookended the turf. A man in a red sweat suit walked along the side of the field picking up bits of trash and tossing them in a bin that stood between a pair of wooden benches. He was thirty yards off but slowly heading my way, all the while humming a strangely familiar tune. I listened in the darkness as he drew closer and the aroma of Aqua Velva grew greater. To my surprise the man paused and let out a crazy howl. Warren Zevon's *Werewolves of London*! That was the song! Though the face I wore wasn't mine, I felt it peel back into a deranged smile. With each step the stranger took, my heart quickened. An overpowering hunger grew from within, giving me immense strength. When my prey approached to less than fifteen feet, I moved in for the kill.

He turned in time to shout, but it was too late. With one swift and ferocious swipe of my claws, half his throat was gone. He made a gurgling sound as he dropped to one knee and tried to stop the river of blood gushing from his neck. Licking my drenched claws, I shuddered as the slick, warm fluid coated my tongue. I grabbed a fistful of the man's hair with one hand and tore with the other, taking his head clean off. His decapitated body slumped to the ground. I moved quickly, dragging the evidence of my crime deep into the woods where I feasted in the shadows.

Ever since that terrible night, I've tried to convince myself countless times that it was all Corabas and not me. Though I was just a tagalong on the hunt, a hitchhiker inside the demon's head, I've never been able to trick myself into believing the pleasure all came from Corabas. From that moment on I was changed.

I woke with a start and began crying, knowing that no matter what happened, no matter if by some miracle I was saved from the demon, I was only delaying the inevitable. I would have to pay for my sins. Sooner or later, I was going to Hell.

I stayed awake the rest of the night fearing that if I fell asleep, I might slip into the mind of the demon again. When the sun broke over the tree line and poured into my bedroom window, I was finally able to close my eyes. A few hours later I woke to the sounds of Mom in the kitchen and Katie playing with one of her neighborhood friends in the family room. I went downstairs and snuck outside still wearing the sweats and T-shirt I went to bed in, hoping the fresh air and warm sun would thaw the chill within me.

A familiar voice called to me. Along with it, the sights, sounds, and tastes of last night's horror show flashed back in my mind. I looked down the street and saw Corabas in his front yard watering a bed of flowers. He motioned for me to come to him. I would rather have been anywhere else in the world than near that monster, but for some strange reason I found myself walking toward him.

"Good morning, Chris!" he said in a cheery tone.

Why he felt the need to keep up the act, I didn't understand. We were the only two people on the street as far as I could tell.

The smile was fixed on the demon's wrinkled face, but a darkness lurked in his eyes when he spoke. "Enjoy our late night repast?"

I found it hard to speak but somehow managed to mumble, "It was…horrible."

Corabas chuckled. "I suppose that's something you have to say. Being brought up in a decent Catholic family, it's only proper to claim that rending a man's head off and devouring his flesh are things one ought not enjoy. But you and I know the truth, don't we?"

Corabas dropped to one knee and leaned in close enough for me to catch a whiff of the tobacco smoke that clung to his clothes. He whispered, "We both know there is no greater pleasure on earth than that of a fresh kill. The feeling of tendon and tissue surrendering as you tear into the neck. The salty taste of warm blood pouring down your throat as it's still pumping from your prey's heart. Given time you will learn to relish such things. It didn't take Mr. Hutchison long."

I felt like I was going to barf.

"Understand, child, the older this body gets, the more frequently I have to feed to sustain it. When you and I join, that won't be necessary. If it makes you feel any better, we won't have to dine in this manner until you have matured to manhood. That said, I have a feeling you're going to be missing it. Once you've enjoyed a fresh kill, there really is no going back."

Corabas stood back up. "Of course, you don't have to convince me of your disdain regarding my dietary choices. That's an argument to be had with your conscience."

The demon started watering his plants again. I took it as my signal to leave. Before I got a dozen steps down the road, he called out after me. "Oh, and lest I forget, the closer we approach the black moon, the more you will notice other changes. Your perception, mood, tastes—even your passions—will gradually become more as mine. It's a side effect of our arrangement, you see. I suspect you may have already noticed some of this."

I remembered my conversation with Tracy. Could that have been Corabas talking? If so, how much more would I change before the end? I walked back to my house and returned to my room. As I plopped face-down in bed, I noticed Steve was up and thumbing through an old copy of *Mad*. I was surprised when he put the magazine down and spoke to me.

"Rough night?"

I rolled over and looked at him. "I guess."

"Must have been having some funky-ass dreams. You were snarling and making slurping sounds. Very creepy."

He hadn't been sleeping when I woke from the feeding. That means he must have heard everything—including the crying. "I had a nightmare."

He smiled. "Guess it was a doozy."

"It was."

Steve pushed himself upright and scooched over until he sat on the corner of his bed. "Haven't seen your dorky friends around lately."

My eyes fell to our carpet. I always found it easier to lie when I wasn't looking the person in the face. "I've been kind of busy lately with chores and summer reading. There hasn't really been much time to hang out."

"Uh-huh. Perry told me you and Paul got in some kind of fight. It must have been a good one because he said Paul was super upset. He couldn't get anything more out of him though."

I sighed. "Guess it was just a matter of time before you found out."

"How bad is it? I mean, you guys have been best friends ever since you could walk. It's kind of weird not seeing his goofy face around. Is this fight the same reason you're not hanging out with Kevin too?"

"Maybe."

"Want to talk about it?"

This was the longest conversation Steve and I had since he busted me with his camera. The funny thing was, I had been waiting forever for a chance to hang out and talk, and now that I had it, I couldn't tell him a damn thing. First of all, he would think I was nutso, and second, it would put him and our whole family in danger.

He must have sensed I was conflicted because he kept talking. "Look, I know I've been a bit of a turd for a while now. I want you to know it's not because of anything you've done or said. See, it's just high school has been a bitch for me. Around here people think I'm a big shot and all, but school's different. It's been hard for me trying to fit in, to find my place. I don't make friends as easily as you do. It's just," he paused and shook his head, "I don't know. It's nothing personal is all."

For as far back as I could remember, Steve was always the man with the plan, the guy that every kid in the neighborhood turned to for direction. To have him open up and share that he was just as clueless and unsure as the rest of us schmucks was mind-blowing. I felt I had to say something.

"What would you do if you had to tell a lie to protect someone—like a friend maybe—but you knew that by telling the lie you would probably lose that person as a friend?"

"That's a tough one. Sounds like a no-win situation. If you lie, you lose your friend, but if you tell the truth, they may get hurt."

"Exactly."

"I guess that would depend on the specifics. You know, the stakes. If the friend could get seriously hurt or might even die, the best thing to do would be to lie to them, but if the consequences were less serious, maybe telling them the truth would be the better choice."

Even though I pretty much knew what he would say, it still felt good talking to someone. The real problem buzzing around in my brain like a beehive was that the deal between Corabas and me was based on the understanding that the demon would honor his promise. I had no guarantees, no way to be sure Kevin and Paul would be safe. All I had was the word of a flesh-eating spawn of Satan. I nodded. "That's kind of what I thought too."

He frowned. "Are you telling me that Paul and Kevin are in danger and you're protecting them from it?"

I don't remember what the hell was running through my head when I answered Steve. It might have been that the terrible secret weighing me down for the past several weeks had simply become too much to bear. It could also have been that sheer loneliness was driving me to share with someone—anyone—my unique problem. But looking back, I probably just didn't trust the demon. Whatever the reason, it slipped out. "I think Mr. Hutchinson is the Goatman."

I had no idea crickets could chirp so loud.

Steve's face tightened up until he looked like Dirty Harry's four-eyed twin. "Are you yanking my chain now? I'm trying to make an effort here, and now you start talking about –"

"It's true. He told me so. He confessed one afternoon when I finished mowing his lawn. He was very specific on his victims, and he said if I told anyone he would kill Kevin and Paul."

And there it was out in the open. I knew I would most likely regret it, but getting the secret off my chest felt great.

"But they already caught the Goatman killer, remember? That creepy Drake douche. They found a murder weapon and body in his backyard."

I decided to stick with the story of Mr. Hutchinson being your typical garden-variety killer and not a bloodthirsty demon born of Hell. That would have been a tad too much for Steve to believe...at least for now. "It was all a setup. Mr. Hutchinson planted the evidence and called the police on him. He never liked Russell and figured this was an easy way to kill two birds with one stone."

"Okay, let's say this whole thing is true. Why the heck would he tell you? What's the point of that?"

"I'm not sure there was a point. I really think he just wanted to brag to someone. He said he could tell me because he knew no one would believe me if I squealed. He also said that if I ever *did* say something, he would kill Kevin and Paul."

"And that's why you stopped hanging out with them?"

"Yep. They already suspected he was the Goatman, so I had to tell them that everything I'd said about him was a lie. I told them I was bored and just messing around. They didn't take it too well."

The scowl on my brother's face softened. "I bet. But back to the bigger issue. Do you have any proof to back up what you're saying? And remember, this isn't some goofy game. We're not talking about vampires or monsters in the closet. You're calling one of our neighbors—a person we've known for our entire lives—a psycho murderer."

A plan bubbled up in the back of my mind. If I was able to convince Steve of Mr. Hutchinson's guilt, maybe there was a chance I could slip into his house and get my hands on the spell book. "I know, and the answer is no. But the proof is in his house. There's a room on the first floor that I think he keeps some evidence in, like mementos from his victims and maybe some of their bones. He's gone in there a couple times when I was over, and I was able to catch a glimpse from over his shoulder."

"And what did you see? Bones?"

I had to be careful. If I told him I'd seen bones, Steve would push for us to call the police. One of two things would then happen, neither of which was cool. If the police found enough evidence to arrest Corabas, they would take the spell book and everything else in the room and tag it as evidence. With the book in lockup, nothing I did could stop the possession from happening. I suspected that even from jail the demon would be able to leave Hutchinson's body and possess my own. On the other hand, if there wasn't enough evidence to hold Corabas, he would come looking for me as soon as the coast was clear and exact his revenge, most likely by shedding innocent blood. My only chance stood in convincing Steve to help me get in the house without Corabas knowing.

"Not exactly," I said, answering his question.

"What do you mean, not exactly?"

151

"It was kind of dark and smoky. I'm like ninety percent sure there is evidence in that room that will tie Mr. Hutchinson to the murders, but I can't guarantee it. But…if we could get the old man out of the house, I could sneak in and –"

"Chris."

"What?"

"Haven't we been down this road before? Remember Mr. Jenkins? Don't think I didn't see the wooden stakes you hid in the back of the closet."

You make one mistake about your albino neighbor and no one will ever forget it. "I know, I know. But this is different. He told me with his own mouth."

"Are you sure the old man wasn't messing with you? After all, you have a reputation for going off the deep end when it comes to witches, ghosts, and vampires. Maybe he was just having some fun. He is a weirdo after all."

The accusation stung, mainly because it hit close to home. "I knew it."

"Knew what?"

"That it wasn't worth talking to you. That you would never believe me." I rolled back over in bed to face a blank wall. "I don't know why I even bothered."

Playing the guilt card was a gamble, but I was desperate. I needed someone to believe me. I needed *anyone* to believe me. The last few weeks had been the longest of my entire life.

"All right, all right. Just cool it. I'm not saying the old man didn't say something to you about the Goatman, but you have to understand how weak your case is. If only you had some concrete evidence. That would be something else entirely."

Now was my chance. I flopped back over to face him. "That's what I'm saying! Maybe if I could sneak in his house and get some –"

"No way! I'm not helping you break into anyone's house based on what we have so far. What if you got caught? You could be arrested for trespassing."

"Or worse," I mumbled.

"Look, I can tell this whole thing has got you more worked up than usual. You're not hanging out with your friends, and you're definitely having some freaky-ass nightmares. Just give me a little time to figure out a better plan."

Time was one thing I didn't have. I had to think of something quick that Steve might agree to. If I couldn't get him to help me sneak into the house, maybe there was another way.

"What about a confession?"

Steve snickered. "What, are you going to walk Mr. Hutchinson over here and get him to tell me he's the Goatman?"

"No, doofus. I'm talking about Dad's microcassette recorder, the one he uses for work. If we borrowed it, I could record Mr. Hutchison talking about how he is the Goatman. Wouldn't that be enough evidence?"

"I don't know. Maybe. But how are you going to pull that off?"

"Don't you worry about it. Just be prepared to eat your words, and help me out when I come back with a recording of the old man fessing up."

Chapter 22

The best time to try and get a confession out of the Corabas would be after I mowed his lawn. His interrogations were now routine, and I figured it wouldn't be too difficult to sucker him into some sort of admission while he was questioning me. The demon had grown comfortable during our sessions and was obviously convinced he had broken me. As far as he was concerned, I was little more than a talking piece of real estate he was about to move into. I hoped to use his cockiness against him.

Sunday was still two days away though, and in the meantime, some major butt-kissing was in order. I wasn't sure what I would say to my friends, but I knew it sure as heck couldn't end this way. My fake confession was done with the best of intentions, but it wasn't exactly the brightest idea I ever had. Over the past several weeks, I'd come to know Corabas better, and based on this, I began to doubt his promises. As silly as it may sound, there was a time I was open to the idea of an honorable demon. I believed it was possible that a monster, no matter how bloodthirsty and vicious, could still have its own code of conduct and principles. At first, my theory seemed correct based on the promises made by Corabas, but over time I noticed something wrong. Despite his noble, fancy words, some of his actions had no good explanation and could only be described as cruel. The most extreme example was when the demon lassoed me in to joining him on one of his feedings. Why Corabas decided to introduce a fifteen-year-old to murder was beyond me. There was no need for it; the demon could have fed on his own. There was also no lesson to be learned. Corabas brought me along solely for his own twisted enjoyment. For that reason above all others, my view of our arrangement had changed. It was time to talk to my friends—if they would listen.

Mrs. Perret answered the door, smiling at me as she opened it. "Mr. Dwyer! It's been quite a while since we've seen you around here."

"Yes, ma'am."

"Well, I for one am glad you decided to finally pay us a visit." Her head tilted above her left shoulder as she shouted, "Paul, you have company!" She gave me a quick nod and wink before disappearing down the hallway.

Paul showed up a few seconds later.

"Hey," I said.

"Hey," he said back.

Before it got too weird, I blurted, "I know I've been a major jackass, and I'm sorry. I really wasn't trying to jerk you and Kevin around."

A weak smile broke on Paul's face. "Kind of figured that."

"I also want to tell you something. It's some pretty serious stuff, and I'm not sure it's fair to pull you into it. That's why I haven't come around to see you guys."

Just a couple of weeks back, Paul would have already pushed the screen door open and invited me in. It stayed shut for now. "Is it gonna be the truth or more BS?"

I deserved that. "No more lies. I've been thinking it over and here is the fairest way to do this. I have just one question for you. If you had a choice to make, tell your friend the truth and possibly put him in danger or tell him a lie to try and keep him safe knowing it would cost you the friendship, what would you do?"

"You're talking about us, aren't you?"

I stayed silent.

Paul smiled. "What's the point of having friends if you can't tell them the truth? Friends are supposed to count on each other—especially if they're in trouble or danger."

Paul always had a way of getting right to the heart of things. "Okay then, here's the deal. Mr. Hutchinson *is* the Goatman. He *did* carve the markings on your tree, and he *was* at your house scratching on your window."

156

Paul pointed at me through the screen door and shouted, "I knew it! I knew it! You had Kevin convinced it was all a dream, but I knew it was real."

I put a hand up. "All right, be cool. Anyway, the reason I lied to you is Corabas said he would hurt anybody I told. I figured if I stayed away from you guys, you'd be safe, but honestly I think he's full of crap and can't be trusted. I mean there's nothing to stop him from doing anything he wants after he's possessed me."

"Okay, so what the hell's a Corabas, and who is possessing you?"

"Can I come in?"

Paul looked at the screen door like it was the first time he was noticing it. "Huh? Oh, sure."

On the way to the family room, we passed by Perry. "Thought I smelled something. Good to see you, dorkus."

That was as close to a welcome back as I was going to get from Perry.

Even though no one was in the family room except for the two of us, Paul turned up the television volume before whispering, "Okay, out with it. What the heck is going on?"

Over the next twenty minutes, I told him everything, from the spell Corabas placed on me all the way up to my conversation with Steve and my plan for getting a confession out of the demon. Paul didn't make a sound or even blink until I was finished.

"Holy crap! You're telling me that unless we do something before Halloween, you're going to turn into the Goatman?"

"Exactamundo."

"But how is telling Steve that the Goatman's a serial killer gonna help? That won't fool him for long."

"You're right, but if I came out and told him the truth now, he'd blow me off like he always does. Remember, he hasn't seen the Goatman scratching at his window or the marks carved in the trees."

"True."

"The first thing to do is prove to him Mr. Hutchinson is a killer—which he is. The whole supernatural demon thing will come later. Baby steps, Paul."

"Ummm, okay."

"You think that's a mistake?"

"I dunno. He's your brother, so I guess you know what's best. I just don't like the idea of lying to him."

"Me neither, but if that's what it takes to get him on board, then oh well. And there's someone else I need to talk to."

"Who?"

"Kevin."

Paul grimaced. "That may be tough. He's pretty pissed off about the whole thing. Remember, he doesn't know you like I do. He's sure you were jerking him around since the day you two met, trying to get him to like you just so you could prank him."

"That's crazy! I'd never do anything that messed up. Kevin's one of the coolest guys I know."

"You may want to practice some of that sucking up 'cause it's going to take *a lot* of it to get him to buy into everything you told me."

"Will you help? Convince him, that is?"

The sound of gunfire erupted from the television as Marshall Dillon unloaded his Colt into some would-be bank robber.

"I'll try, but it's pretty much up to you. He thinks I was too soft on you, so he probably won't pay a lot of attention to what I have to say. We'll be lucky if we don't get the door slammed in our faces."

"I have to try anyway. I think we're going to need him before this whole thing is over. Besides, he deserves to know the truth. Let's head over to his house. It's at least worth a shot."

We were almost out of his house when Paul stopped. "Hold it. Don't move. I have an idea."

Paul disappeared back into his family room and reappeared a minute later.

"What was that all about?"

Paul slapped me on the back. "Don't worry about it, Scooby Doo. I got a plan that'll get us in the front door. The rest is up to you."

As luck would have it, Kevin answered after one knock. He glared at me before turning to Paul. "What's up with this?"

I interrupted before Paul could respond. "Kevin, I'm sorry. Sorry about jerking you around and messing with our friendship. It was very uncool."

Kevin did a great job ignoring me. He tilted his head in my direction as he spoke to Paul. "What's *he* doing here?"

"I invited him."

"Why would you bring a liar to my house? What, do you want to be lied to again?"

Kevin rolled his eyes as he looked at me. "What's it this time, liar? Did you spot Bigfoot in Paul's backyard, or maybe the Loch Ness Monster in his toilet?"

I smiled. "Toilet's too small for Nessy—everybody knows that. As for Bigfoot, I'm pretty sure he's nothing more than a myth."

"Lame." The word was loud and flat as it came out of Kevin's mouth. "Is that the best you got? I would have thought you could have come up with some better lies by now."

"Listen, what I said to you guys about the Goatman –"

"Was lame," Kevin exclaimed. "Just like it was lame to leave those clues around and start freaking us out. What kind of a loser does something like that anyway?"

"Let him finish!"

The strength in Paul's voice took Kevin back. "Why? What are you, on the liar's side all of a sudden?"

"I'm not on anybody's side. Just cool it and give him a chance is all."

Kevin crossed his arms. "Why should I give him another chance to play us both for chumps?"

Paul pulled a palm-sized object from his pocket and showed it to Kevin. "Because of this."

Kevin frowned as he took the item from Paul's hand. "Is this –"

"Yep. Basketball. Picked it up yesterday at Kmart. Figured since you got your Atari a couple weeks ago, you'd be ready for a new game by now. It really is cool; you can play against the computer or another person."

"What's the catch?" Kevin asked.

"Let Chris and me in, and give him a chance to explain. This is something you need to hear."

"Fine." Kevin clutched the cartridge and pushed the door open.

Paul's smooth move bought me some time to try and turn Kevin from the dark side of the Force. I had to make the next words out of my mouth count, so I took a deep breath and dove in. "So the Goatman's real. The reason I lied to you is because I had to protect you from him. Second, Mr. Hutchinson is the Goatman, and he threatened to kill anybody I told." I stopped to allow the revelation to sink in.

Paul and I watched as a sour smile grew on Kevin's face. The sound of him laughing in his throat wasn't a particularly good sign. "In your dreams! Did you really think that tired old gag was going to work on me again?"

Kevin turned to Paul. "You believe this jerk? He yanks our chains getting us to buy into this Goatman crap. Then he makes us look like fools when he says it was all a joke. *Now* he's trying to sucker us all over again. Have to hand it to you, Chris, you have big balls. No brains but a lot of balls."

"Be cool and give him a minute," Paul said.

"Wait, are you kidding me? Geez, Paul. I knew you were gullible but come *on*."

"Hear him out, or give me back the game. You can decide for yourself what you want to believe when he's done."

Kevin kept a tight grip on the cartridge. "Fine." He smirked as he looked at me. "Please don't pile it too deep. I'm not wearing boots."

I laid it all out like I did with Paul. Kevin's arms remained folded and his face frozen the entire time. After several minutes of ranting, I paused to catch my breath.

"Have to hand it to you, Chris, they could make a real blockbuster movie out of that BS. I mean, I'd pay to watch it. I can see it now. *The Goatman of Bowie*, starring the hundred-year-old fart whose lawn you mow. Man, that's got to be the best whopper yet."

Frustrated, I turned to Paul. "It's no use. He's not going to believe a word I say."

Kevin stepped between the two of us. "Don't try and get him on your side. Paul's with me on this. Unless you have some proof, I suggest you take a hike."

"I will have proof—after tomorrow."

"Like what?"

"I'm going to record Mr. Hutchinson. I'll get him to confess he's the Goatman, and then you'll have to believe me."

"Reeeaaaly?"

"Yes."

"And how do you plan to do that?"

"Don't worry about it. Just be ready to eat your words when you hear him admit to everything."

Kevin seemed surprised by my bold challenge. "Seriously, what are you going to do? Get your brother to pretend he's the Goatman and record a fake confession?"

"Please. If you think for a second that Steve would help me try and fool you guys, you're a real space cadet. If you don't believe me, come on over and watch as I go into his house. I'll play the tape back afterwards, and you can decide for yourselves."

Kevin eased up on his clever comebacks as he considered my offer. He hunched his shoulders. "Whatever. If you want to waste your time trying to get old Mr. Hutchinson to admit to being the Goatman, that's your problem. Who knows? It might actually be fun watching you crash and burn. Now if you'll excuse me, I have a game to play."

Chapter 23

The lawn took me a half hour longer to mow than usual, but I barely noticed. I weaved and wound through the grass as my mind wandered to after. My best bet would be to burn the script and wing it. The demon was bound to admit to something as long as he was sure I had no ulterior motives. He seemed to enjoy our conversations. Whether it was because he finally had someone to talk to after being cooped up in that dark, smoky house for so many years or because he liked toying with me the way a cat toys with a mouse, I couldn't say. It might have been a combination of both.

After turning the mower off, I pulled the microcassette recorder from my shorts pocket and, with sweaty hands, pushed record. I carefully tucked the machine back. It ran silent, but I could feel a slight vibration on my thigh that let me know it was working. "Okay, Dwyer, don't screw this one up."

Corabas wore a big grin when he answered the door. I used to think it was warm and friendly, but now I knew better. It was a crocodile smile. "Good afternoon, Master Dwyer. Please come in and cool off. We have much to discuss."

I took my usual seat.

Corabas produced a frosty bottle of Coke from the refrigerator and popped the top off before sliding it across the table to me. "I must admit, Chris, you are taking our arrangement far better than I anticipated. Perhaps you have been having second thoughts regarding the upsides to our deal? Or could it be you have resigned yourself to the role of tragic hero and opted to go gentle into that good night?"

I took a sip. He was being too vague. I was going to have to draw him out. "Two nights ago, the man you killed, who was he?"

Corabas took his seat opposite me. "Why do you pose such trivial questions, child? There are so many more meaningful, interesting things to discuss."

Still too subtle. Trying to be as casual as possible, I slid my right leg out from under the table to get a better recording. "Call it curiosity. I guess I just want to know how many people you've killed over the years, seeing as you're going to be moving in soon."

The demon's eyes shrunk to quarter inch slits. "That is an uncharacteristically ghastly question for you. Perhaps the assimilation is moving along faster than I anticipated. Tell me, have you experienced any atypical feelings or desires?"

"Atypical?"

"Unusual, child. Have you found yourself desiring a food you normally don't like or behaving in a way contrary to your nature?"

My thoughts immediately turned to my last conversation with Tracy, and a warmth spread through my cheeks.

His wild grin made me shudder. "I knew that would spark a memory or two! Good. I'm glad to see you are progressing."

The direct approach was getting me nowhere. There were questions I was sure he was eager to bite down on; I just had to use the right bait. He had circled back twice now to his pending control of my body. With that in mind, I cast long. "Will it hurt? The possession, I mean?"

"There it is. The real question you've been dying to ask but could not for fear of the answer. Take heart, child. I promise there will be no pain for you. You will simply fade to the background as my essence enters and assumes control of your mind and body. There you will linger for the rest of your days, until such time as I find another suitable host many decades from now."

"What happens to me then?"

"What, you mean when I abandon you?"

I didn't like his choice of words. They made me feel like an old toothbrush or pair of holey underwear. "Yes."

"You will die at that point. I've done it but few times; however, the vessel I depart has always perished."

I fell silent and thought about my fate. I would be a helpless passenger in a body controlled by a monster wearing my skin. At the end of the ride, I would be kicked to the curb to die alone.

Corabas laughed dryly. "But that is nothing you need to worry yourself about for a long, long time. As I've said before, you should make for an exceptionally strong vessel. The omens portend it. While we are one, you will never be sick a day in your life, and, in the unlikely event you are injured, you will heal quickly. How many people can make such a boast?"

"Few, I guess."

"Indeed. While you have my attention and good humor, are there any other inquiries you wish to make?"

"Are you going to kill again? Before October? Before Samhain?"

"As I said before, this body grows weary and needs sustenance more than a younger vessel. As such, yes. I will have to feed between now and then. How much I do not know. When the hunger calls upon me, I am bound to it and have little control—as you are aware. Why do you ask such a thing?"

It wasn't the best of confessions, but it would do. It would have to. Before I could whip up a good answer, he continued.

"I see. Your silence and pallor betray you."

Oh crap.

"If it will ease your malaise, until your time is at hand, I shall refrain from calling upon you when I am ready to dine. Know that I did this to familiarize you with the rapture of the hunt, but I can see that you are not yet strong enough for it. A pity. Soon enough though, you will yearn for the chase with an appetite the likes of which can only be sated with flesh, bone, blood and marrow."

I had no idea how to respond to that, so I said the first thing that came to mind. "Okay."

"Very well then. So, is there anything else you would ask of me before I send you on your way?"

I slowly shuffled to my feet. "No, I think I understand now."

Another raspy laugh. "You do not, but you will soon enough." Corabas rose and stared into my eyes. "Our dialogue today took a different turn, didn't it Master Dwyer?"

I had to play it cool. Having come this far and being this close to my getaway, now was not the time to spaz out. "I don't know. I guess."

"Ah, another ambiguous response from a normally articulate child. Tell me, Chris, have you confided in anyone regarding our bargain? I would hate to think you reneged on the promise you made. Remember, so many people are counting on you."

I fought the urge to bolt for the door. Such a move was guaranteed to arouse the demon's suspicions and could easily result in the discovery of the recorder. Usually I had trouble lying to adults, but this time I was Joe Cool. "Nope. I remembered what you said, and I know what would happen if I told."

"Good." Corabas took a step closer. I watched in horror as tiny rosebuds blossomed in his eyes. The blood quickly spread, gobbling up all the white in them until he was staring at me with a pair of swollen cherries. His freak show eyes pinned me to the wall. "Treachery and lies carry their own bouquets. Those with the talent—such as I—can sniff them out." He leaned in close and inhaled. "Once more, if you please. Which of your friends or family have you confided in? Be true in your response and give me a name. I may be merciful yet."

I'd been around Corabas long enough to know when he was lying. If I said someone's name now, that person would be dead by tomorrow. I shrugged and flashed a smooth smile. "There's no name to give. Your secret stays with me until the day you swoop in and take over." Steve *definitely* needed me as the lead in his next blockbuster.

He hovered inches from my face for several seconds, sniffing the air. Finally, he stepped back. "The redolence of fear is thick about you, child; however, the foulness of duplicity is absent. Lucky for you."

I had no idea what he was talking about. "If you say so."

"Remember, Chris, your acquiescence is the only reason those you love have been spared. I want you to pause for a moment to consider how simple a task it would be for me to dine upon sweet Katie's plump form, or the leaner meat of your two comrades."

Unspeakable images flooded my mind. "No. If you hurt any of them, I won't let you take me. I'll kill myself."

Laughter rumbled in Corabas's throat. "You're serious, aren't you?"

"I am," I whispered.

"It seems I have made the right choice. Here is a boy that possesses courage beyond his contemporaries."

Corabas backed off, closed his eyes, and breathed deeply. When he opened them again, they were the mix of brown and green I knew. "My apologies for the fright, Chris, but in my experience a good jolt to the senses can oftentimes help with the truth. That said, you should pay heed to the words spoken. I do not make idle threats. You must be honest and forthright with me, child, and I with you. Agreed?"

I nodded.

"Wonderful! Now it would probably be best if you were off. We will continue to meet until the time of the black moon. When summer ends and the grass goes dormant, I will solicit your assistance for some equally innocuous task. This will allow me to keep tabs on you without suspicion. As long as you do what I say, I guarantee no harm shall come to your family or friends. You have the word of Corabas."

I wanted nothing more than to get the hell out of that place. "I understand."

"Good man."

I was back home and in my garage before the sweat-covered recorder came out. A sigh of relief slipped out when I saw the wheels of the micro-cassette still turning. I hit stop and rewind as I entered the house and ran up to my bedroom. When I opened the door, the anxious faces of Steve, Kevin, and Paul awaited.

"So," my brother said, "did it work? Did you get him on tape?"

"Think so. The recorder was working the whole time."

"Sweet!" Paul hooted. "Let's hear it!"

I noticed Paul holding a walkie-talkie in one hand and a pair of binoculars in the other. "What the heck were you doing?"

"Recon," he said with a smile.

"Your friends showed up after you left to mow," Steve said. "I put two and two together and figured you were gonna try and get your confession, so I decided to post a watch—just in case you ran into any trouble. If you weren't out of there in fifteen minutes, the cavalry was showing up."

I grinned. "Who is the cavalry?"

"That would be the three of us. We'd pay Mr. Hutchinson a visit and start making a big scene if we needed to."

The plan sounded unusually reckless for my brother. "And what if he pulled all of you inside and decided to have an early dinner?"

"Eh," Steve smiled, "taking out one pain-in-the-butt fifteen-year-old is one thing. Abducting four kids in broad daylight would bring too much heat down on anybody. Kevin and I waited up here while Paul gave us the play-by-play. As soon as you surfaced, he hightailed it back."

"That's right," Paul added. "Had you timed from the second you went in. Two more minutes and we were coming after you."

I glanced over at Kevin, who hadn't said a word. "All of you?"

His crooked smile and hunched shoulders signaled we were on our way to being friends again.

Steve's eyes fell to the recorder. "So?"

I sat cross legged, placed it in front of me, and hit play. Silence descended on the room as everyone huddled around.

The playback commenced with the metallic moan of a screen door opening followed by three knocks. Mr. Hutchinson answered with a muffled greeting.

"That's him," I whispered.

Steve was quick to shush me.

An exchange of muted voices could be heard as Corabas and I started talking.

"Yeesh! I can't hear a thing," Kevin exclaimed.

I looked at my brother. His scowl was currently directed at the cassette, but I guessed it wouldn't be for long.

"Just give it a sec," I said. "The recorder was under the table at this point; it should get better soon."

As if on cue, the sound cleared up. It was far from perfect, but at least we could make out some of what was being said.

"*Call it—mumble mumble –. I guess I just—mumble mumble mumble—killed—mumble mumble mumble mumble—soon.*"

The rest was a snatch of a word or two here and there mixed with indecipherable mumbling.

I broke into a cold sweat and crouched closer to the speaker. I checked the volume; it was already cranked up to maximum. Stupid microcassette. Damn thing was worthless unless you shoved it up in someone's face to interview them.

"Did he just say fumble like a dumbbell?" Kevin asked.

"I'm pretty sure he said rumble in the jungle." Paul said.

"Shut up and listen!" I barked.

"*You'll most—mumble—die at—mumble. I've—mumble —*"

I stopped the tape. "There! You heard it! He said die." I was desperate. The recording was a flat out bust, but I needed something to keep them believing in me.

Steve shoved his thumb and index finger behind his glasses and rubbed his eyes. "I'm having trouble making anything out on this. Maybe we can figure a better way to record what –"

"No! Wait!" I hit play again.

There was creepy laughter for a few seconds followed by more muddled conversation. Steve put his hand over mine and squeezed to stop the player. "It's a dud, little brother. It's not your fault. That's just the way it goes sometimes."

"But he said it! He admitted to everything! To killing people. To what it would feel like to take my…"

In my anger I almost forgot Steve didn't know what the Goatman truly was.

My brother was quick on the uptake. "To take your what?"

Kevin and Paul exchanged a startled glance and then looked to me.

No time to think; I had to roll with it. "My life. He threatened that if I told anyone he would kill me. Gut me like a fish. That's what he said."

Steve's words were slow and deliberate. "Chris, look at me."

I did as instructed.

"I went along with this because you seemed really depressed and weirder than usual. I believed you let your imagination get the better of you, and I'd have to talk you back down to Planet Earth like I always do. But if you're serious this time, if you can look me in the eyes and swear to God you're telling the truth, do it, because this isn't funny anymore."

Even though I was technically lying, I justified it because in an odd way Corabas *was* killing me. True, my body wouldn't be harmed, but I'd be a prisoner in it until the day I died. "Mr. Hutchinson threatened to kill me, Steve. He threatened to kill me, Kevin, Paul, you…even Katie."

Steve stared at me long after I finished talking as if trying to decide whether to believe me. Finally, he spoke. "Then I guess it's settled. We have to call the cops. This has gone too far. No one is going to threaten my friends or family and get away with it. Just remember, if I find you've been lying to me, I *will* kick the shit out of you."

It felt good being backed up by my big bro, even if it was based on a white lie. Unfortunately, his plan to call in the cops would hose up everything. There had to be a way to get the proof I needed, the proof to convince my brother and friends that Mr. Hutchinson was actually a demon fresh out of Hell. The answer came to me in sudden, bloody detail.

The hunt. It was just two nights ago, and there was a headless body buried somewhere close by. "Wait! What if I told you I knew where he stashed one of his victims?"

"How the hell could you know that?" Steve asked.

"He told me—just now," I lied.

"Where?" Paul and Kevin asked in unison.

I closed my eyes and visualized the murder. Faded white goals sat on a blanket of turf. "He killed someone by a soccer field. Not too far from here."

"What makes you think it's close?" Steve asked.

"Call it a gut feeling."

Chapter 24

The yellowed map my dad got from the Shell station had seen better days, but it was the only one of Bowie I could find buried in the stash of road atlases he kept in his home office. I unfolded it and laid it out on the bedroom floor. Steve had called Perry in to lend a hand, believing the more eyes, the better. My friends and I weren't convinced of the wisdom of such a move. When Steve finished bringing Perry up to speed on Mr. Hutchinson's murderous tendencies, Perry nearly split his Levi's laughing. It took him a good minute to calm down before we could continue.

"So," I took a pencil and drew a large circle encompassing all of our houses and the bike trail, "here are all the places we know the Goatman has claimed."

"Wait. What?" Perry interrupted.

I continued. "Mr. Hutchinson—aka the Goatman—likes to mark his hunting grounds with a symbol he carves into trees."

I drew the sign of the horned god on a corner of the map. "The first place we saw one was on the bike trail near where they found the mutilated dogs. Since then we've spotted them in all of our yards."

"That's a bit of bad luck, isn't it?" Perry asked. "I mean, what are the chances of all of us being marked for death by the Goatman—or old man Hutchinson as we called him up until a few minutes ago? Reeaal bummer." Perry made little effort to hide the sarcasm.

"It's true," I said.

"*Gee*, Chris, so what are you trying to say? Are we next on his list or something?"

Perry wouldn't believe Mr. Hutchinson was the Goatman until he saw him waving around a bloodied ax and screaming, "I love to chop people up!" at the top of his lungs. Knowing he was a lost cause, I continued. "I'm not sure if we're next, but we're definitely in danger. If you look–"

"Okay, if that's the case," Perry teased, "if I carve that weird moon thingy on Phil Gerbetson's house, will it go after him too? The jerk owes me ten bucks, and I'm pretty sure I'm never gonna see that again."

"This is serious!" Paul barked. "If you're going to keep acting like a buttwad, you can just go home!"

"Easy, you little bed-wetter," Perry said. "I'm just trying to make sense of Chris's story. The logic is hard to follow is all. Are we really supposed to believe the Goatman is creeping around our backyards carving his initials in the trees? It seems a bit cheesy to me, especially since they already arrested that Drake kid for the murders."

"There are more bodies," I said. "And if you give me a few minutes, I think we can figure out where to find one."

Perry looked at his younger brother. "You better hope Chris is right; otherwise, you know where you'll be spending the night."

"Tuba case," Paul mumbled.

"All right, guys, give Chris a chance," Steve said while tapping the map with his index finger. "Go ahead, bro."

"Like I was saying, these are the areas we know the Goatman has been. The closest soccer fields are going to be Kenilworth, Buckingham, Somerset, and White Marsh."

"Didn't they close Somerset?" Kevin asked.

Before I could answer, Steve broke in. "No. The school itself is shut down, but the fields are still in use."

"It's not Somerset or Buckingham; I've played on both those." I closed my eyes. "This one was pretty close to the woods. He came out of them and surprised his victim." I breathed in and remembered. "The field was just mowed and had that fresh cut grass smell. It was over in a matter of seconds. One slash to the throat to stun him and start him bleeding. Then another to finish him off. Bye-bye head." I shuddered as a twisted blend of horror and delight washed over me. When I opened my eyes, everyone was staring at me. My left hand was stretched out with my fist closed like I was clasping something, maybe an imaginary head.

"Oookay," Perry drawled. "That was super creepy. You got all that from the old man?"

"Yep."

"Was the field on top of a hill?" Steve asked.

"No, I'm pretty sure it was surrounded by level ground."

"Then it's not Kenilworth either," Steve said. "Looks like you found your park. So, who's up for a ride to White Marsh?"

The summer sun beat down hard as we pedaled north on Stonybrook. I couldn't help but think of the cool, blue waters of Belair Bath and Tennis as I crawled up the long hill leading to the entrance to the bike trail. One by one, we swooped under its shaded threshold. I should have felt anxious. Instead, an odd excitement overcame me. It wasn't the sick type I heard some people got from seeing messed up things like dead bodies. This came from knowing that I was finally not alone. My brother and friends believed in me—even if it was only based on the half-truth I'd given them. A half-truth was better than nothing and a good start.

We weaved our way along the winding asphalt trail with Steve in the lead. Perry was next, followed by me and then Paul and Kevin. Soon we reached a split in the trail. Steve shouted, "Bear right!"

Less than ten minutes after that, the trail opened up to a larger paved road, and the forest gave way to fields of green grass. A lonesome colonial sat behind a wall of overgrown laurels to our left. Its rickety tin roof and worn brick walls looked like they had seen a hundred years of sun, rain, and snow.

"That place is definitely haunted!" Perry shouted.

I looked at his smiling face. "What makes you say that?"

"Anything that old has to have *some* ghosts in it. It's just a fact."

I often found myself amazed at Perry's ability to speak on almost any subject with complete confidence. To be honest, I was a little jealous of it. For most of my life, I've been a little scared to share my thoughts or opinions for fear of being laughed at. Perry definitely didn't have that problem.

Below and to our right, a series of emerald fields dotted the landscape. The one farthest away as bordered by thick woods on two sides with large white goal posts on either end. I hit the brakes. The rest of the group stopped alongside me.

"What is it?" Steve asked.

I pointed to the field as my stomach began churning. "That's it, down there. That's where it happened."

We went off-road, bouncing and rolling down a series of grassy hills until we leveled off and arrived at the scene of the slaughter. Everyone launched off their bikes and into the woods as if they knew where they were going. I chuckled despite my growing nausea. They were so eager to find the body, yet none of them asked me where to start. Typical. I tried to block out their stomping feet and chatter so I could concentrate. Closing my eyes, I went back in time to that horrible night. My belly moaned as an image came into view. It was night, and the man was cleaning up the field and humming that silly song as he passed a bench. I opened my eyes and found my mark. Walking toward the bench, I glanced to the wall of oak and sumac running parallel. I broke right and started looking for anything unusual. Moments later, I stumbled on a clump of weeds that had been crushed flat. Something large had marched through here not too long ago. I looked over to my friends. The closest was a dozen yards away. Turning back, I dove into the heart of the forest.

I couldn't say with a hundred percent certainty there was even a body to be found. It was a gamble, a calculated risk, but it made sense that Corabas would dump the corpse close by. The forest was thick, and no homes were nearby. It seemed the perfect place for him to hide the evidence of his crime.

As the trees gobbled up all of the sunlight, the shrubs, ferns, and brambles thinned. Aside from a few stunted poplars and the rotting remains of fallen oaks and maples, there was little else to see. I heard footsteps.

"Did you find anything?"

"No, Paul, not yet."

"Perry is already bitching to Steve that this is a waste of time. He thinks you're cuckoo for Cocoa Puffs. Can you believe it? We've only been looking for a couple of minutes."

It didn't surprise me. It was just a matter of time before my checkered past came back to haunt me. I probably didn't have more than another ten minutes until I was the only one left in the woods. Kevin and Paul might hang out longer than Steve and Perry, but their patience would quickly wear thin. "I'm going to go a little further in. Why don't you check this area out for me?"

Paul nodded. "Cool."

The more I drifted away from the group, the quieter it got. After a few minutes of walking, I heard the gentle roll of water from a nearby stream. I made my way toward the noise, keeping an eye out for footprints, broken branches, or drag marks along the way. Eventually, I came on a bluff overlooking a small brook. I didn't see a point in going any farther. If Corabas went this far, the body could be buried almost anywhere in the woods.

Kneeling, I grabbed a quarter-sized piece of sandstone. I aimed to launch the thing into the river but stopped when I saw a tiny rust-colored splotch on its smooth surface. Moistening a finger with spit, I rubbed at the stain. It vanished. I glanced at my finger and noticed a reddish tint to it. Looking around my feet at the leaf covered ground, I spotted a bunch of tiny black drops hidden in the mix of brown and yellow foliage. It looked like someone had taken a brush and shook it, leaving a fine splatter of paint on the earth. Except it wasn't paint; it was blood. I was sure of it. But was it human or from some other unlucky creature? I stood and hopped off the bluff to the bank of the stream four feet below.

Footsteps and talking came from above. It wouldn't be long before Steve and Perry showed up and busted my chops for sending them on a wild goose chase. I stared at the clay wall of the tiny cliff and considered plastering my back against it so they couldn't see me. Yes, it was a childish move and would only delay the inevitable, but I didn't think I had the heart to face one more failure today. Before I had a chance to act, something caught my eye. I approached the wall and placed my hand in one of two handprints that was squished into it. From the ends of each of my fingertips, the impressions extended another three inches. Whoever made them must have been huge. I noticed small triangular indentations at the end of each finger pushed deep into the soft earth.

For reasons I couldn't explain, I started peeling layers of clay away from the section of earth between the impressions. Steve was shouting my name, and he didn't sound happy. After digging out a few inches, I felt something hard. My heart kicked into overdrive as I gouged clumps of muck and grime out from around the object's edges until a pattern emerged. *Oh shit.* I stumbled back and, tripping over my own feet, fell butt-first into the cool waters of the stream.

"What the heck are you doing down there?"

Steve stood at the top of the bluff. I opened my mouth to speak, but could only gasp and point to my gruesome discovery.

My brother jumped down. "What's wrong, Chris? What's going on?"

Before I could find my voice, the rest of our party arrived, dropping one at a time to join us.

As soon as Perry saw me, he started in. "Bah-ha-ha-ha! How's the water? Do you –"

"Shut up!" Steve hollered. "Guys, look at what he's pointing at."

In a more subdued voice, Perry asked, "What is it?"

"Is it another one of those symbols?" Paul asked.

Steve approached the cliff wall. Kevin filed in behind him and peered over his shoulder. "It looks kind of like a –"

"Foot," Steve said. "It's a foot."

The two detectives slowly backed away from their find.

"You mean it's a shoe, right?" Perry asked.

"No." Steve turned to us as he pointed at the object buried in the clay wall. "That is a fucking foot over there. I saw part of it in the shoe…and

I'm willing to bet a whole body is attached." My brother looked at me and smiled. "Guess you were right for once, dorkus."

The unlikely compliment kick-started my vocal cords. I lowered my hand and smiled back. "Told ya."

Perry walked over to the foot and poked it with his finger. "What we're saying here is, the Goatman killed this dude, chopped his head off, dug a hole into the side of this bank, and stuffed the body into it?"

A murmur of *yeahs* and *guess sos* bubbled up.

"Okay, cool. So, what do we do now?"

Silence descended.

"Seeeriously?" Perry stretched the first half of the word out as long as he could. "None of you knuckleheads have a clue what to do next?"

"I think it's obvious," Steve said. "We call the police and tell them we know who the Goatman is." He motioned to the foot. "Between the body and what Chris knows, they should be able to lock up Mr. Hutchinson for a long, long time."

"I like it," Perry said. "We'll be heroes, get our names in the paper. I wonder if there's a reward for –"

"You can't!" I blurted.

Perry and Steve turned to me. Where Perry's face showed frustration, Steve's showed concern.

It was now alarmingly clear I hadn't thought everything through. In my defense, I was only fifteen and cursed to surrender control of my one and only body to a demon. "We need more evidence. I have to sneak into Cora—I mean—Mr. Hutchinson's house to get enough proof, so they can lock him up for good."

In an uncharacteristic show of affection, Steve put his hand on my shoulder. "There's no way I'm letting you go back into a house with that man again. It's over, Chris. This is way too serious and dangerous. Besides, I'd have no one to torture if you were killed."

Perry agreed. "Time for the cops, definitely. Think about it, dude. You'll be the kid that caught the Goatman. You'll be famous—we all will. Hell, I bet we make the front page of *The Bowie Blade*."

Arresting Mr. Hutchinson would do nothing for my cause. The black moon would come in October, and Corabas would assume control of my body. I finally had my brother and friends believing Mr. Hutchinson was the Goatman, but that would be meaningless unless I could convince Steve and Perry of his supernatural origins. But how? With no admission and no additional proof to offer, that would be nearly impossible.

Steve gave me a gentle shake and then let his hand drop. "C'mon, guys. Let's go home and spill the beans. There'll be hell to pay with our parents, but we'll still be heroes in the end."

Perry fell in behind him. "Damn, forgot about that part. Oh well."

I pushed Perry aside and grabbed Steve's arm. "No, you can't; you don't understand! I-I haven't told you everything!"

"What, are there *more* bodies?" Perry asked.

I glanced at Kevin and Paul. They looked almost as desperate as I felt.

Kevin sighed and said, "You should tell them."

"Yeah," Paul mumbled.

"Tell us what?" Perry exclaimed.

I knew telling them would do no good. The story was just too fantastic. Getting them to believe our neighbor was a serial killer was one thing, but having them buy into the idea of him being an immortal soul-sucking demon was something else entirely. The key was convincing Steve. If I could do that, Perry might follow his lead.

"I can't," I said to my two best friends. "They need to see it."

"See what?" Steve asked.

I pointed to the clay-caked shoe. "The body. You have to see the body."

Steve leaned down within a few inches of my face. "Say what?"

"We have to dig it up, so you can see for yourself."

"See what for myself?"

Paul piped in. "The Goatman, he's not a normal person."

Perry looked at his kid brother. "What's that supposed to mean? You spazzes better start making sense real quick. If this is some kind of lame-ass prank, Steve and I are gonna beat the crap out of each of you."

I looked Steve in the eye. "It took a little convincing, but in the end you believed me when I said Mr. Hutchinson was the Goatman. Now that we've come this far and found the body, I'm asking you to trust me again when I say we have to dig it up."

"Chris, it's not that I don't believe you. It's just—digging up a dead body is a whole 'nother level of trouble. We'd be disturbing a crime scene. It's illegal."

"I know, and all I can say is that you'll understand as soon as you see it. There's more going on here than meets the eye. More lives are on the line, and the only way for us to save them is for you to believe what I'm going to share with you. That all starts with us looking at the body."

"You're saying more people could die?"

"I'm saying more people *will* die—even if we call the police."

It was the truth. As long as Corabas was free to possess different people through the generations, he could slaughter to his heart's content.

"And by digging up the body we could somehow help these people? We'd be saving lives?" Steve asked.

"Yes."

The bubbling of the brook and singing of nearby cicadas grew loud as silence fell on our group. If I couldn't convince my brother, I was doomed. I was pushing the limits of our relationship and wouldn't have blamed him if he called me a freak and headed for home.

Steve spoke. "I guess we should start digging."

"Wait," Perry broke in, "we're seriously doing this?"

Steve stooped to pick up a large, thin piece of slate. "My little bro says more lives are on the line and that we might be able to help. He's gotten us to where we are, so we might as well see this thing through to the end as far as I'm concerned." He shoved the side of the rock into the moist clay and started digging.

Perry shook his head thirty long seconds before grabbing a rusty soup can from beside the stream. "Jesus, Steve," he said as he sunk the tin into the soft earth, "at the rate you're going, we'll be here until school starts."

We took turns digging around the feet, switching between Steve and Perry, and Kevin, Paul, and myself. Over the course of the next thirty minutes, we had to endure Perry's constant threats of an imminent beat down in the event we were jerking him around. By the time we finally cleared out enough clay to reach the corpse's waistline, we had to take a break out of pure exhaustion.

I peeked in the tunnel. It smelled like our garbage can after being baked in the sun for a while, but the stink wasn't as bad as I thought it would be. "Do you think we're in far enough to pull it out?"

Steve wiped a stream of sweat from his forehead, smearing it with clay. "Don't know. We could give it a shot. Perry and I can get on both sides, grab the body by its belt, and give a tug. You guys get around the feet and pull at the same time."

We moved to our assigned positions and took hold.

"Okay!" Perry shouted. "We're gonna do this on three. Plant your legs good, and get ready to push off. One! Two! Three!"

The body gave an inch before the clay sucked it back in. Paul slipped and went down.

Perry howled. "Man! That was the weakest thing I've ever seen!"

Embarrassed, Paul got up and brushed the mud from his butt. "Shut up, zit face! You didn't do any better than the rest of us."

"You kidding?" Perry said. "I was the only one trying! My side was starting to come out until the rest of you wimps gave up."

"All right, all right," Steve cut in. "Let's give it another shot. I think we loosened it up. One more hard tug, and we should be able to get it out."

We took our places and waited for Perry's countdown. On three, we pulled. The body held fast for a few seconds before giving a little. Then, with a loud, soggy *slurp,* the headless corpse flopped down smack dab between the five of us. Chaos followed.

Perry flinched. "That is siiiccck!"

"Gaaahhhhh!" Kevin shouted as he back-stepped to get some distance from the corpse.

"Son of a bitch," Steve muttered.

Paul probably would have said something if he wasn't too busy dry heaving. I found myself fighting the urge to join him.

The fact that the mud-covered corpse was headless was no surprise to us, but the condition of the body turned us into babbling monkeys. The shredded muscle and skin around the man's neck made it look like his head had been twisted off with a giant corkscrew. As if that wasn't bad enough, the body was gutted from chest to stomach, exposing insides that bore a startling resemblance to Mom's meat lasagna. Around the gaping wounds claw marks were gouged deep into the victim's body.

Perry walked around the remains, closely examining them. "This is like something straight out of *Jaws*! Dude, what the hell did this?"

After taking a few seconds to mellow, Steve spoke. "What are we looking at here, Chris? Is this some kind of animal attack?"

I thought about the question and answered as truthfully as I could. "Yes and no."

Perry made a fist and slammed it into his open hand. "You better come clean now! This has gone from cool to seriously messed up. What's the deal?"

Steve moved in for a closer look at the body. "These look like claw marks, huge ones."

"There aren't bears near that size around here," Perry said.

"This person was killed by the Goatman," I said. "It killed him, ripped him apart, and then ate his guts."

All eyes turned to me. Steve was the first to speak. "You're saying Mr. Hutchinson is some kind of monster and that he did this?"

"Exactly."

"Okay, I think it's time for you to come clean and tell us everything."

"You're right. But first, we need to shove that body back in its hole. If Corabas finds out he's been dug up, he'll know I'm responsible."

"Who the hell is Corabas?" Perry asked.

"I'll explain everything as we work."

It took twice as long to bury the dead man as it had to dig him out, which turned out to be a good thing because it took nearly that much time to bring Perry and Steve up to speed. Paul and Kevin chimed in every now and then to elaborate on certain events such as the late night visits Corabas paid to both of them. It was Perry's idea to brush away our footprints from the muddy banks of the stream using pine branches. Unless someone was actually looking for the corpse, there was a good chance they'd walk right by the makeshift gravesite. By the time we were finished, the sun was casting hazy, late afternoon beams of light between the oaks.

"You do realize how incredibly insane your story sounds?" Steve asked.

I grimaced. "Yep."

"You believe him though, right?" Paul asked.

Steve looked to Perry. His friend hunched his shoulders and cocked his head.

Steve huffed and said, "That story is just too damn weird—even for you. It must be true."

The urge to hug my brother was almost overpowering, but I managed to suppress it. I smiled instead. "It's about damn time."

Paul and Kevin high-fived each other.

"Not sure exactly what the two of you are so psyched about," Perry said. "Now what the hell do we do? We have the Goatman going around ripping people's heads off, and it turns out the guy lives just down the street from us. On top of that inconvenience, unless we try and stop him, he's gonna turn your little brother into a mini-Goatman come Halloween. Am I missing anything?"

Paul raised his hand. "Don't forget, he threatened to kill all of us if Chris told on him."

"There's that too," Perry said.

Steve shot me an *I know you're up to something* look. "I have a feeling my little brother has thought of that and worked out a plan. Am I right?"

184

I was always the dreamer, the crazy kid brother who, though enter-taining at times, was mostly a pain in the butt as far as everyone was concerned. This was different. My big brother believed in me, and for the first time in my life everyone was looking to me for direction. I didn't hesitate.

"We're going to need help, and I know just the guys for the job."

Chapter 25

The Johnson brothers needed less convincing than I thought they would. Both were quick to say they always thought something wasn't quite right with Mr. Hutchinson. With Brian and Mark on board, I had all the help I needed. The plan was worked out over the course of the next two days, and now it was go time. Steve's reputation as the neighborhood's Spielberg served as my inspiration in crafting our daring stunt. With backup from Perry, the two of them would make a perfect distraction. Brian and Mark would be our eyes and ears, and Kevin our free safety—a critical role. That left me and my right hand man Paul to bring the goods home. Easy-peasy.

I was positive Corabas had smelled us out the night of our stakeout, and I sure as heck wasn't letting that happen again. To evade his kid-sniffing nose, Paul and I waited at the corner of Belair and Spindle downhill and downwind from the Goatman's residence.

Brian started the play-by-play with a broadcast over the walkie-talkie. "Breaker, breaker, Perry and Steve have the old man, and they're heading over to your house, Chris. Mark will let you know when they're inside, and the coast is clear."

Steve had taken my idea of interviewing Mr. Hutchinson for a fake school project on the history of Bowie and ran with it. In just a couple of hours, he compiled a list of interview questions intended to take at least thirty minutes to get through. That would be more than enough time to break into the demon's house, find the book, copy the necessary spells, and scram. If Perry managed to disable the lock on the demon's door while Steve had him distracted, sneaking inside would prove no problem.

Mark's voice broke over the radio. "Your brothers and the creepy old devil man just went inside. You guys are good to go. I suggest you split, like now!"

We ran the entire way to the Goatman's house. Three lung-bursting minutes later, Paul and I stood panting on his front porch. I reached a hand out and put it on the front doorknob. "You ready?"

Between breaths Paul whispered, "Uh-huh."

I twisted the knob and the door gave. Perry had done his job. Nothing like a little Silly Putty to save the day. You could bounce it, copy comics onto it, and wedge it into your neighbor's door locks if you wanted to break into their home.

The inside of the house held the familiar oatmeal scent of the demon's pipe smoke. Before we entered, I pulled out two pairs of kitchen gloves that I had tucked in my waistband. "Here, put these on before you touch anything."

Paul smirked. "Why? You think he's gonna dust for prints or something? He doesn't even know we're here."

"No. But I *do* think he might be able to sniff us out if we put our hands all over everything."

I shoved the gloves into his chest. "Hurry up. We're wasting time."

With a minor amount of grumbling, Paul complied.

We went straight to the room where Corabas kept his book and other hidden treasures. As anticipated, the knob turned with ease. Corabas had no need to lock his valuables away because he had no fear of intruders. After all, anyone crazy enough to break into the Goatman's lair would probably find him or herself soon enough missing a head.

The room was shrouded in smoke curling upwards from a fancy pair of brass burners opposite us.

"Whew!" Paul waved a hand in front of his face. "Smells kind of like church but ten times stronger."

From the worn carpet below us to the ceiling eight feet above, shelves of books covered all four walls. In the far left corner sat an upholstered chair in front of a large roll-top desk. On it a stained glass lamp stood close to an open book. Blue dragonflies and green beetles glowed as they hovered above its yellowed pages.

I pulled out the folded tracing paper and pencil I had in my back pocket and approached the desk.

Paul slipped into the room behind me and tiptoed over a creaky wooden floor to stand beside me.

"Do me a favor, Paul. Step back to where you just were."

Once more, the floor moaned.

The Levitt houses that made up most of Bowie were all built on concrete slabs. The floors were then usually covered with laminate or shag carpeting. I looked to my friend. "How many homes around here have you been in that have wooden floors?"

"None."

"Same here." I pointed to a corner of the carpet. "Flip that carpet back."

My friend did as I asked.

The words slipped from my mouth. "Well, what do ya know."

Paul flinched backward. "*Whoa.*"

The outline of a trapdoor was cut into the oak floor. A small grip was hand-carved at one end.

"This is different," I said. "Corabas must have had this room and whatever's below added on after he moved in."

"Why would he do that?"

We stared at the door for several seconds before I spoke up. "To hide something."

"So," Paul moved toward it and reached out, "do we open it?"

I wanted to tell him no, that we didn't have time. But I also knew we'd never get this chance again. If some dark secret down there could help us defeat the demon, maybe it was worth exploring. Plus, this was probably the closest I would get to a true dungeon crawl. "Sure."

Paul grabbed the handle and gave it a tug. Nothing. He gave it a stronger pull, and the oak panel creaked open an inch. Paul reached down with his other hand and, using his legs, stood while yanking upward.

With a loud creak, the door swung open on hidden interior hinges. Out of the hole in the floor rose a sickly-sweet odor, infecting the room and overpowering the incense.

"Holy moly," I muttered as I tucked my nose into the crook of my arm.

"That smells like barf and burnt hair," Paul hissed.

I edged over to the opening and saw stairs.

Between gags Paul choked out, "You're not thinking about going down there, are you?"

I didn't want to. It was obvious from the stench that some form of death waited in the darkness. But considering that Corabas didn't believe the book was important enough to hide, yet he did whatever was below, I figured it must be important. "Maybe a few steps—just to take a peek."

Paul shook his head and pointed back to the book. "C'mon, Chris, let's focus on what we came for. We don't have time for jerking around."

Ignoring my friend, I pinched my nose and descended the wooden steps. Fumbling in the increasing gloom, I felt a switch on the wall. I took a few slow, deep breaths to keep from hyperventilating and then flipped it. A pale light flickered on and then another as a series of fluorescent bulbs sputtered to life. Beneath their sickly glow, a scene unfolded that could have been torn straight out of one of my *D and D* adventures. The metal pots sat a foot apart in rows of six and stretched back in perfect lines that were also six deep. They were a foot-and-a-half in diameter, and all were filled to the brim with a nose-melting brew. I inched closer to one and peeked in.

It looked like a bowl of greasy black pudding, but it sure as hell didn't smell like pudding. I glanced in the one next to it and saw the same thing but with an added ingredient. The tip of a bone jutted out of the wicked stew. It was large and long—too long to be from any animal you'd eat for dinner. Then it hit me. These were *ngangas*, the cauldrons used in Palo Mayombe to gather power and cast spells. This was the heart of the demon's power. It must have been what allowed him to stay in the mortal world for so long and to use the spell book.

I considered kicking the cauldrons over and emptying their contents, but aside from the fact that I didn't believe my stomach could handle doing something so epically gross, I wasn't sure what the result would be. Would it weaken Corabas? Possibly. Would it destroy him or banish him back to Hell? I didn't think so.

Paul's voice came from above. "*Psst*! What did you find?"

"Nothing much." I wasn't sure why I lied to him. Maybe because an accurate description would have taken too long, or maybe I was worried he would suggest the same crazy course of action I thought of moments earlier and I'd be tempted to do it. Before I did something I'd likely regret, I started back up the stairs.

"Paul, shut the trapdoor, and pull the carpet back over it while I look at the book."

Calling upon my fuzzy memory of the afternoon the old geezer put the whammy on me, I flipped to the beginning of the book. Soon I found what was looking for. I pointed a gloved finger to the page. "This is it, the spell Corabas used on me."

Paul leaned over my shoulder. "Does it say anything about how to reverse it?"

The words were English, but the writing style seemed ancient. "No. I mean, I don't think so."

I resumed my search, paging through spells on love, luck, protection, and more sinister forms of witchcraft. Finally, I came on something. "Here, the ritual of unbinding and exorcism. This has got to be it." I placed the tracing paper over the spell and started copying the words. It said something about blood, *ngangas*, and years of life, but I was too busy tracing and didn't have the time to read or try to make sense of the words. That would have to come later. Paul hovered over my shoulder, breathing way too loud until Mark's voice on the walkie-talkie called him away.

Finished with the tracing, I looked to see if any other spells could be of assistance. In my rush, I almost missed what I was looking for.

"Wait," I mumbled as I flipped back a few pages.

"Banishing Lukankazi's Children," I whispered. I had seen that name before while doing research at the library and was pretty sure it meant something like the devil. Freeing myself from Corabas's clutches was priority number one, but in the long run we would still have to deal with a pissed off demon. Finding out how to send him back to Hell after the exorcism was the only way to make sure the Goatman no longer haunted Bowie. I started copying.

Paul's head popped over my shoulder. "We have to wrap it up. Mark said Perry told him Steve only has a couple questions left, and the old man is starting to get cranky."

"Okay, just give me a sec." I was almost done when the last sentence of the spell grabbed my attention. "Paul, what do you make of this? It says, 'Beware of the tethers, they must be severed in entirety, lest the power someday return. The name and sign of the spirit must be destroyed wherever it resides.'"

"Don't know, dude. Look, just copy everything you can, and let's split. Our time is up."

He wasn't paying attention. I didn't blame him, but the warning was stuck in my mind. Something Corabas said to me long ago was starting to make sense. I closed my eyes and repeated the phrase. "The mark serves as an anchor binding me to the land and the land to me."

"What?" Paul asked.

The day was proving to be full of surprises. I looked to my friend. "These spells aren't enough, Paul."

"What do you mean? What are you saying?"

Paul was on the verge of freaking out, but there was no time to explain the situation to him. Closing my eyes again, I walked to the center of the room.

"Chris, we should –"

"Ssshh!" I put my hands out and walked around the room, stretching my fingertips in search of something I knew must be tucked away in some corner of the demon's private library. The connection between us was growing stronger. A day was coming when I might no longer be able to shield my thoughts from him, but for now I believed I was still safe. Otherwise, I sure as heck wouldn't be in his house. But if there was some connection, no matter how tiny, it might guide me now. Spines. My fingers were touching one of the bookshelves. My eyes remained shut as I felt along a row, letting my hands glide over the ends of all different kinds of books, old and new, thick and thin. After a few seconds of touching and probing, they hovered over the worn edges of one of the skinnier ones. I opened my eyes and pulled the book from the shelf.

"Chris."

"I know, Paul, I know. This is important though."

A voice blared on the radio again and Paul disappeared. He was back a few seconds later. "That was Mark. He said that Mr. Hutchinson just left your house and is on his way back."

I broke open the book. "I just need a minute—two tops. Tell Brian to send in the staller."

"The *staller*. Forgot about him. Hold on."

As Paul relayed the instructions back to Mark, I flipped through the pages. To my surprise it was filled with pictures and maps of the surrounding area, most of them very old. I stopped on a page with a hand-drawn map. None of the geography looked familiar, but I knew it was relevant. Speckled throughout the drawing were a dozen or so stars. I took out my last sheet of paper, placed it over the map, and quickly traced the borders, major geographic features, and stars.

Paul was back. "Okay, Kevin has been deployed. That should give you an extra minute, but then we *gotta* go."

I finished copying just as Brian's voice blared, "The diversion is done, Paul! You guys need to haul your asses out of there pronto!"

We took a few seconds to ensure everything was back in order before scrambling to the front door. The row of pink azaleas bordering the front porch gave us cover as we hunched down and scurried to the left side of the house.

"Wait," Paul whispered as he tugged on my shirt. He hustled back to the door as fast as his hunched body would allow. Opening it a crack, he pulled the glob of Silly Putty out of the lock.

With the last piece of evidence retrieved, we scampered around the house. From there we wormed our way from one backyard to another until we arrived at the opposite end of Spindle. We took the long way back to my house, walking down Stonybrook, turning up Belair, and then back onto my street in a huge loop. The route took us twenty minutes to finish, but we both felt the farther we were away from Corabas and his kid-smelling sniffer, the better.

I had crossed the point of no return and brought my friends and brother along for the ride.

Chapter 26

Back in the safety of my room, Paul and I took turns telling our story to the crew. When I described what I saw in the basement, Paul started giving me the stink eye.

After I finished, he piped in, "Guess you forgot to tell me there was anything in the basement."

"Yeah, sorry about that. It's just we were kind of in a rush."

Mark's head started shaking as soon as I got to the part on the *ngangas*. "You're saying the old man's basement is filled with cauldrons that have bones and blood, and junk like that in them?"

"That's right," I said.

Brian rolled his eyes. "Man, white people."

"So," I said turning to Kevin, "I have to know, what was this distraction that saved our butts?"

He snickered. "I got stuck in that old elm tree in Mr. Green's yard."

It was common knowledge in our group that Kevin was a mutant—part monkey and part human. He could climb pretty much anything and had scaled the tree in question thousands of times. "Say what?"

"Yeah," Kevin continued, "I was all, Mr. Hutchinson, can you help me pwetty pwease? I'm stuck. The old man tried to talk me down, but I moved real slow. By the time I crawled off the last branch, he looked ticked. He's normally all smiles and, 'How are you doing, son?' But not this time."

"Anyway," Steve said, "what did you copy?"

I pulled the tracing paper from my back pocket and handed it to my brother. "I didn't get a chance to read the spells that carefully. I was too busy trying to copy them without making a mistake or missing something."

Steve started reading. "The ritual of unbinding and exorcism. The top has a list of ingredients spelled out. Salt, lemon, soil from hallowed ground, a crow's skull, a hair from the claimed one, and the blood of the trade."

"The blood of the what?" Perry asked.

"Ssshh," Steve said. "It goes on to say for each year the claimed one has walked the earth, a year will be taken from the blood of the trade. Blood is the price that must be paid."

"Damn," Mark muttered, "I *do not* like the sound of that."

"What the hell does it mean?" Brian asked.

Whether because of all of the research I had done on Palo Mayombe or my unnaturally close connection to Corabas, the answer came to me swiftly. The flare of my eyes must have given me away.

Steve glared at me. "Chris, do you know what this means?"

A queasiness spread in my gut as I looked at my friends, knowing what would be required of all of them. I couldn't speak.

"C'mon, little bro, out with it. What is the blood of the trade?"

It was no use lying or faking ignorance. I couldn't change the facts. After letting out a long sigh, I spoke. "I read about this type of thing when I was doing research at the library. Basically, you can't get something for nothing. To free me from being possessed, an offering of blood—the blood of the trade—must be made."

"Riiight, but what *is* that?" Steve pressed.

My gaze fell to the floor. I lost the courage to look my friends in the eye. "I'm pretty sure it means a year of life will be taken from the person that offers their blood for each year that I've lived."

"See," Mark blurted, "I *knew* that whole blood thing was bad. You're saying that one of us has to give up fifteen years of their life so you don't get possessed?"

My guilt doubled and I fell silent, ashamed of the danger I had forced on my friends.

"Wait, hold on," Steve said. "Does it actually say the blood all has to be from the same person?"

"Well, no."

Steve thrust his hands on his hips. "The way I see it, there's the six of us. If we all added some blood for the spell that would only be about two and a half years off each of our lives."

There weren't enough bonus points in the world to give Steve for what he was trying to do, but it didn't lessen my guilt. "I guess. I mean it makes sense to me, but I haven't seen anything in my research on it."

Perry smirked. "Yeah, but if we do, does that mean he could possess *us* then?"

Steve shook his head. "I don't think that's the way it works."

"Two and a half years isn't so bad," Paul said.

"Paul, no." I looked at him with a defeated smile. "I can't let any of you give up some of your life for me. There's no way. It's just too much, too much to ask."

Before anyone else could object or agree, Steve said, "You're missing the point, Chris. We're way past whether we want to give up some of our life. Look, we all know now Mr. Hutchinson is the Goatman. When he takes you over, how long do you think the rest of us are gonna last? I'm pretty sure he's guessed Perry and I are onto him. I got a feeling he wasn't buying into the whole school interview thing. He gave us this really weird stare just before he left."

"Yeah he did!" Perry scowled. "His eyebrows bent up and down kind of like Spock's." He attempted to copy the Vulcan's famous look.

Steve nodded. "As for Paul and Kevin, they're your best friends and know you the best. If I was the Goatman, they would be my first victims." Steve looked at Mark and Brian. "You two are the only ones that probably aren't on the Goatman's radar yet."

The Johnson brothers exchanged glances. Mark spoke up first. "The way we figure it, we're all in this together. If we have a chance to stop the Goatman, we have to try. Brian and I are in."

"Eh," Perry said, "what's the difference between going at seventy-six or seventy-eight? You're an old fart either way."

And with Perry's words of wisdom, the decision was made. Through the years much of my memory has faded. Names have been lost. Christmases and birthdays blend and blur. First steps and little leagues have grown hazy in my mind. But to this very day, I easily recall the precise moment my brother and friends offered to sacrifice years off their lives for me. I remember the Star Wars T-shirt Perry wore and the smell of the blonde brownies Mom was baking in the kitchen. I remember the glint of Kevin's braces as he smiled and the sound of our neighbor's mastiff barking as if approving the collective decision.

"It's settled then," Steve said. "We have the blood of the trade." He looked back down at my tracing. "It says the altar used for this sacrifice has to include the bones and blood of one of the recently departed." Steve glanced at me. "So, what do you suppose that means? What kind of altar is made of blood and bones?"

"They're talking about the *nganga*; it's the source of the magic used in Palo Mayombe."

"You mean like the things you found in Hutchinson's basement?" Steve asked.

"Exactly. We need to make one to get the power to cast the spell. Fortunately, we know just where to find the ingredients."

Perry groaned. "Wonderful. I'm sure Headless Harry smells real ripe right about now."

"What else does it say?" Paul asked.

"There's a phrase we have to recite at the same time we pour the ingredients into the altar. It says, 'A year for a year, the bound one is freed with the sacrifice offered. The bargain made is now unmade.' That's it. There's nothing more."

"I think that's enough," Mark said.

Steve shuffled the tracing paper to look at the second sheet I had copied. "What's this?"

"It's another spell. One I think will come in handy. It's not enough we break the possession spell put on me. We need to send the Goatman back to Hell, or he'll just find some other vessel."

Steve read. "This one looks pretty basic. We'll need the *nganga*, a few simple household ingredients, and the true name of the demon."

"Corabas. His name is Corabas," I replied.

Steve put the tracing paper down. "Are you sure that's his real name and not some nickname or something?"

"I'm sure. He's not a big fan of the Goatman or other names people have given him over the years. He got a real kick out of introducing himself as Corabas. Even though I couldn't find any mention of him during my research, I'd bet my life it's his real name."

"You are betting your life, dude." Brian said.

Nodding, Steve returned to the paper. "It says all we have to do is add the ingredients to the *nganga*, call the demon's name, and order him to return to Hell. That's easy enough I—wait." Steve brought the paper close to his face and began mouthing the words from a portion of the spell over and over.

"What now?" Perry asked.

Steve's eyes stayed glued to the sheet. "It also says, 'The unholy can only be banished from the place from whence it was birthed upon the mortal world.'"

Everyone groaned.

Kevin's impression of Howard Cosell was lousy, but his timing was spot-on. "And that, my friends, is how the cookie crumbles."

"What's *whence* mean?" Mark asked.

"It means we're screwed," Perry said.

I raised a hand. "Hold on. Corabas told me the story of how he was first summoned by the witch. He mentioned a river."

"Did he name it or say where it was?" Steve asked.

"No, I don't think so. He did mention something about the Ogle Family though. Dang, what was it he said?" I stood and started pacing the room, hoping it would help kick-start my memory. "The witch in his story had a baby and wanted to get revenge against its father. I think he was actually one of the Ogles. When Corabas was first summoned, he said he would do whatever she asked but for a price. He demanded the life of the witch's baby in return for his service. She agreed and threw the child in a nearby river as a sacrifice. As soon as she did it, she regretted it. She jumped in after the baby, and they both drowned in the river. That's how he ended up being able to stay. There was no one to send him back to Hell."

I looked at Perry and Steve. "Does that help?"

They looked at each other and smiled like they were in on some joke together. Perry spoke first. "You thinkin' what I'm thinkin'?"

"Sounds like Crybaby Bridge," Steve said.

Perry nodded.

"What about it?" I asked.

Brian pointed at Steve and then Perry. "Yeah, it all fits! The baby and the woman both drowning and the crying. The details are a little different, but so what. How many bridges can there be in Bowie that are haunted by crying babies?"

"But I thought that story was a bunch of BS made up just to scare kids," I said.

Brian shook his head. "No, man. That story is for real. Two of my friends from school heard it themselves. At first they thought it was a cat or a bird wailing away, but the more they listened, the more they were sure. It was a little baby crying in the middle of nowhere late at night. They got so freaked out they lost a hubcap peeling out of that place."

Perry's head bobbed up and down. "My sisters Lynn and Leigh cruised over the bridge late one night with the windows down and said they heard the *exact* same thing. Said they're never going back to that place, even in daylight."

Something about the comparison was eating at me. "But the stuff with Corabas happened over a hundred years ago. That bridge would probably be long gone by now. Even if it's still around, I bet you couldn't drive a car over it."

"It is long gone, little bro. They built a replacement bridge about sixty years ago in the exact same spot though. I learned that last year when we went on a field trip to see Bowie's historic landmarks. Crybaby Bridge is also known as Governor's Bridge. It was built for Samuel Ogle back in the 1700s, so he could make trips from his home to Annapolis."

The puzzle pieces were coming together. The connection between Crybaby Bridge and the Ogles was too big to ignore and deserved further investigation.

"Maybe we should do a little recon," I said. "Find out if there are any clues at the bridge that will help us figure out whether we have the right place."

"Agreed," Steve said. "We shouldn't leave this to chance; we need to make sure we have the exact spot so the spell will work. I think Chris and I should go. I know the history of the bridge better than anybody, and Chris knows Corabas."

Steve turned toward the Johnson brothers. "Think you guys can gather up the ingredients for the spells? Most of them should be easy to get."

Big grins broke out on their faces as Mark said, "You know it."

Steve looked to Perry. Before he could get a word out, Perry stopped him.

"Don't say it! Don't even say it! Why do you always stick me with the suck jobs?"

Paul spoke up. "What are you talking about?"

"Think about it, numb nuts." Perry shoved a thumb in Steve's direction. "Captain Kangaroo here wants us to play cleanup for him. Isn't that right, Captain?"

Steve responded with a not-so-innocent smile. "Hey, we need someone to do it, and you're the most capable. You're the strongest and don't mind getting your hands dirty. Plus, you'd have Kevin and Paul to help you out."

"Wait, what?" Kevin asked.

Paul persisted. "What's he talking about?"

"Gravedigger duty!" Perry barked. "Who do you think is gonna shovel out the body and get the blood and bones for the altar?"

"Hold on," Steve said. "There's more here at the bottom of the paper, something about tethers."

"I was waiting for you to get to that," I said. "Corabas said something about anchors that connect him with the land. That's what I think the spell is referencing. We've seen them in our backyards and on the bike trail."

"You're talking about the carvings, right?" Steve asked.

"Look at the last sheet," I said, pointing at his hands.

Steve studied the drawing. We watched him frown as his head moved slowly from left to right. After a minute of intense examination, he laid the paper down for all to see. "It's a map as far as I can tell, but none of it looks familiar. What's the connection with the symbols?"

The group gathered around to make their own guesses.

Kevin's talent for solving riddles and puzzles had saved his butt countless times during our *D and D* adventures. He was the first to take a stab at it. "The stars, those are where the carvings are located."

"That's my guess," I said.

Mark placed a finger on a dark area of the map. "So, this is a river." He slid it to a cluster of cloud-like formations. "And these are forests, right?"

I nodded.

"Doesn't look like any place I know," Brian said.

"Hold up." Paul got up and went over to Steve's desk. He grabbed the gas station map of Bowie and unfolded it next to my drawing.

"How is that going to help?" Perry asked. "Chris's map is nothing but forests and farmland. None of that looks anything like Bowie."

"No," Paul replied, "but maybe this was Bowie before it became Bowie. You know, before everything here was built up."

"That's what I was thinking," I said. "But if that's the case, how can we use the map to find the anchors? All the forests have been cut down and the farmland paved over."

"One thing hasn't changed," Mark said, looking from my drawing to the map.

"What's that?" asked Perry.

"The river," Mark said. "It's the same river on both maps."

"That's the Patuxent!" Steve took the tracing paper and placed it on top of the map. "The scales are a little off, but we should be able to get approximate locations of the anchors from Chris's map. So, now that we know where they are, what do we do with them?"

The question had been buzzing around my brain from the moment I traced the map. I always arrived at the same conclusion. "We burn them. Burn them all."

Chapter 27

"You think it will work?"

I looked at Kevin as we rode our bikes through the tree tunnel. "Huh?"

"The plan. Do you think it will work?"

Something was wrong. I was having trouble focusing, getting my bearings. It was a warm summer morning, and from the gear we wore, it was clear the two of us were heading to the pool. But I couldn't remember anything prior to this moment. Had Kevin come to my house to get me, or had I gone to his?

"Hello." Kevin took his right hand off his handlebar and waved it in my face. "Earth to Chris, come in Chris."

Confused, all I could do was give a weak smile. "Oh, sorry."

"No problem. Anyway, do you think our plan will work?"

Something was different about him. Kevin was pretending to be laid back and cool, but there was a weird urgency in his voice. I decided it would be a good idea to play dumb. "What plan?"

Kevin skidded to a stop. I stopped beside him.

He frowned at me. "What, are you serious? The *plan*. You know, the one all of us have been working on. *That* plan."

I noticed another odd thing about the way he talked. By now he should have zinged me for forgetting about the plan, but there was no typical —*You serious, doofus?* or *Kidding me, spaz?* His sarcastic sense of humor was absent. I shook my head and kept a blank expression. "Dude, I don't know what you're talking about."

Kevin fell silent and stared at me. His frown slowly transformed into a cold, calculating smile. Mocking laughter followed. "What gave it away?"

"What gave what away?"

"You really are quite astute, Chris."

Astute. Now I knew I wasn't talking to Kevin.

"I have to admit, I derived some measure of amusement from your antics, but I fear you and you friends may be hatching some ill-advised scheme. You've been poking around my house, haven't you?"

This was a dream. Corabas was in my head trying to get me to spill the beans. But if that was the case, he couldn't read my mind—yet. He could only sneak into it and try and trick me into giving something away. "No, I wasn't at your house."

For some reason the demon decided to keep Kevin's face, even after I sniffed him out. His smile turned into a sneer. "No use denying it, boy. I could smell you there polluting my beautiful azaleas with your stench. What were you doing? Spying on me again?"

Good, he didn't know Paul and I had made it into the house. Time to throw him a bone, make him think he busted me. "I guess," I whispered.

He shook his head. "Tut, tut, tut. I thought we had a clear understanding of your predicament. It appears we're going to have to make an example of one of your friends."

"No, please! I promise—no more snooping!"

"Ah, but you promised that last time too. You swore not to do anything foolish, and in return, I agreed to spare the lives of your friends and family. Now the questions are, why didn't you take me at my word and why should I take you at yours? It seems some manner of punishment is required." Corabas looked at his hands. "Perchance this one could provide sufficient motivation to gain your compliance. What do you think, Chris? He would make a tasty snack, wouldn't he?"

"No."

"Okay then. How about your other friend or maybe your brother? Yes, he's a little older, has a little more meat on his bones. What about him?"

"Please, I'll behave. There'll be no more sneaking or anything like that. I promise to go willingly when my time comes. All I ask is you leave my family and friends alone."

Corabas's appearance as Kevin was seriously creeping me out. He studied me for several seconds before letting out a long sigh. "As satisfying as it would be to slaughter one of your comrades, the resulting attention could make things uncomfortable for a while. Still…the status quo isn't acceptable either. I believe we'll need to put a leash on you, my curious little friend."

A sudden tapping echoed through the tree tunnel.

Corabas put a hand to his ear. "Do you hear it? Someone's knocking."

It repeated. *Tap, tap, tap.*

Corabas's smile grew wider, showing two rows of razor-sharp teeth. "You may want to get that, son. It's not polite to keep company waiting." He got off his bike and started toward me. "But before you run off, I do have one question. If I took a little taste of you in here, do you think that would hurt you out there?"

I tried to dismount from my bike, but tripped over it and fell.

Corabas approached. His voice grew thick and labored as a blood lust slowly consumed him. "Just a mouthful is all I need. A couple fingers or an eyeball. Ohhhh, I do enjoy those—so tender."

I tried to stand, but my legs had turned to rubber. The tapping grew louder.

He loomed over me. A stream of drool dripped from his foaming mouth onto my leg. "It's snack time, Chris. Think I'll start at the top and work my way down." He lunged.

My legs kicked out straight as I jerked awake with a, "Gah!" As I lay catching my breath, I looked to my right. As usual, Steve was sound asleep in his bed. Ever since I could remember, my brother possessed the uncanny ability to sleep through anything from window-rattling thunderstorms to the cries of our teething baby sister. As a matter of fact, the only thing I ever noticed that could actually wake him was the sound of his own snoring, which was loud enough to wake the dead.

Tap, tap, tap. That was real, and it came from the window. I inched my way to the end of my bed for a peek, knowing deep down the evil origin of the sound. With the new moon, a pitch black world greeted me. Despite the dark, the glow of our streetlight outlined the silhouette of the beast perched outside on our porch roof. Too scared to get any closer, I strained my eyes for a better look. He was holding something small in his hands and waving it in front of the window. Tiny arms and legs flopped as he taunted me. Holy crap, was he holding a baby? No, not a baby. A doll. Why was the Goatman holding a doll? I dared to move closer. It had blonde hair and wore a pink and white dress. Even in the gloom, I could tell the toy had seen better days. When it finally hit me, I froze. *Baby Jackie.* "Jesus."

My body jolted to life like I'd been struck by lightning. Springing to my feet, I blundered out into the hall and made a beeline for Katie's room. *Please, God, not Katie.* I pushed open her door and immediately noticed the window was open—it was never open in the summer. I looked to her bed and felt a surge of relief. She was there. Moving close to her side, I kneeled as my heart dropped out of my throat back to where it belonged. I leaned in close enough to smell the stale apple juice on her breath. Relieved, I moved in to kiss her cheek and noticed a tiny dot on her forehead. At the risk of waking her, I touched it. I drew my finger back and glanced at the red smear. Blood. I looked back at my sleeping sister. She was fine. The blood must have been from Corabas, but why?

I shut the window and locked it. There could be no more mistakes. Never in a thousand lifetimes would I forgive myself if something bad happened to her. I leaned down and gave her a peck on the head. "Love you, stinky."

Back in my room, sleeping beauty was still catatonic.

Though Corabas had departed, I stayed awake for the next several hours half-expecting him to return. Eventually, I drifted off to sleep.

Chapter 28

Over a breakfast of Cheerios, I briefed Rip Van Winkle on what he had missed. At first Steve was steamed that I hadn't woken him.

"What do you think?" I asked him.

He scowled at me but didn't miss a beat. "Stick to the game plan. We just have to be more careful. No more snooping around Corabas's house under any circumstances. Got it?"

"Yep."

We heard the lazy plod of footsteps as someone descended the stairs. Moments later Katie entered the kitchen. She yawned and rubbed the sleep out her eyes as she sat beside me.

"Morning, Stinky."

Katie would typically respond to such a greeting with a jab to my shoulder, but this time she just ignored me.

"Are you hungry?" Steve asked. "Dad's at work and Mom's running errands. I can get you some Fruit Loops or Cocoa Pebbles if you want."

Katie nodded and said, "Cocoa Pebbles" on the tail end of a yawn.

Steve got up to get her breakfast.

"You sleep all right?" I asked her.

She stared straight ahead with a dazed look. "Yeah."

"Listen, Katie," Steve said as he emptied way too much cereal in a bowl, "Chris and I are heading out in a little bit and will be gone for a few hours, but Tracy is coming over to babysit. Won't that be cool?"

"Where are you guys going?"

Katie always spazzed out when she knew Tracy was coming over. She loved her and considered her the big sister she never had, so Steve and

I were confused by her lack of enthusiasm. Before Steve could answer, I blurted, "We're gonna go hang out with Perry and Paul for a while."

I looked at Steve, hoping he understood what I was doing. Katie could know absolutely nothing. Sharing our covert ops with her would be risking her life.

"Why can't I go?"

Steve put the bowl in front of Katie. "Seriously? Tracy is coming over to spend like the whole morning with you. You can play *Candy Land*, dress up, or do whatever you want."

She looked at the bowl but made no move to eat. "I know. I like Tracy, but you guys never spend time with me anymore. I want to go with you."

"Well, you can't," Steve said. "But next time for sure."

"Why not now?"

I groaned. Most of the time Katie was low maintenance, but sometimes she fell into a pouty, woe-is-me mood that could last all day. "Because we're doing grownup things," I snapped.

Katie's eyes locked onto mine. "What *kind* of grownup things?"

Something about her stare bothered me. "Just things little girls would find boring. You know, like video games, maybe jump some ramps—that kind of stuff."

Her unblinking eyes stayed fixed on me. "Oh."

"Katie," Steve interjected, "eat up before it gets soggy."

Katie finally took a bite of her breakfast, and her face lit up like the Fourth of July. "Wow! Cocoa Pebbles! They're my favorite!"

My sister shoveled down spoonful after spoonful of the chocolatey cereal as squeals of delight escaped her stuffed mouth. Steve and I exchanged glances while looking on in disgust. Something was definitely going on with our sister.

My brother cut her off after her third bowl. He made sure she changed and brushed her teeth while I got our bikes out and filled a couple of canteens in preparation for a long ride. Tracy arrived a few minutes after that, and we were on our way. As we headed out the door, Katie shouted, "Steve, keep Chris on a short leash! He likes to get into trouble!"

A gray sky loomed overhead as we rode to Governor's Bridge Road. The bridge was on the other side of town, but for riders like us that was no biggie. With Steve in the lead and me right behind, we weaved our way through the K and H Sections of Bowie until the houses thinned out. After we crossed Route 3, they all but disappeared, replaced by thick forests of white oak and sugar maple. I itched with a mild case of claustrophobia as the woods seemed to close in on us. When we arrived at our destination, we pulled off onto a sandy patch of dirt to the right side of the steel-trussed bridge and stopped under an old sweetgum. In the shade of the tree, we spent a minute catching our breath and draining most of our canteens.

Steve looked up at a mass of gray clouds. "I'm not liking that."

Since we left our house, I couldn't get Katie out of my mind. I had to know if Steve was thinking what I was thinking. "Okay, am I the only one scared of our six-year-old sister?"

"Yeah, that was freaky. I don't think I'll ever eat Cocoa Pebbles again. What was the whole, 'Keep him on a tight leash,' thing about?"

"Corabas mentioned something about that in my dream. He said he was going to put a leash on me."

"Wonderful. So what, did he do some kind of hocus-pocus mind control on Katie?"

"Don't know. That looked to be more than just mind control. It was almost like she was someone else."

"Someone with a serious appetite."

"Exactly. It's as if there's a different person in there. The way she talked and looked at us—it's so not Katie."

Steve put a hand on my shoulder. "For now it doesn't matter. Whatever is going on with her, she can't know what we're up to. We'll spread the word when we get back and have all follow-up meetings at the Perrets'."

"What about Katie? Do you think she'll be all right when all of this is over? Is there something we should be doing now to help her?"

Steve took a long swig from his canteen before answering. "I think we need to focus on Corabas. We get rid of him, and all of this should go away—I hope. If we get sidetracked with Katie, we risk screwing up everything."

I knew he was right, but I still felt guilty over leaving our kid sister at the mercy of the Goatman.

Up above, cicadas called to one another from the trees rooted along the Patuxent. A cool breeze kicked up, causing their lush branches to sway and rustle. The river ran slow and silent, save for some bubbling here and there along its banks. From the moment we arrived, I felt an energy pulsing through me. It was stronger in some areas than others and was pulling at me, tugging me north along the western bank of the river.

"C'mon," Steve said. "Let's get going before the storm rolls in. I'll take the left side, you take the —"

"No, let me take the left."

"Oookay. After we're done on this side, we'll cross and scope out the other. From what I can remember, they built this bridge on the exact same site as the old one, so hopefully we're not too far off from the spot where Corabas was summoned. I'm just not sure exactly what it is we're looking for. Maybe keep an eye out for any of those tree markings you and your friends were talking about."

"Got it."

A throbbing sensation spread in my body, rippling from my head to my toes. I was walking toward a narrow dirt trail running parallel to the river. The sluggish, muddy water of the Patuxent reminded me of the pea soup my dad made, minus the chunks of ham. Turning my eyes from its slow currents to the overgrown path in front of me, I stepped over half-rotted branches and past thorny bushes as the pulsing sensation grew, guiding me deeper down the trail and away from the trash-filled fishing spots used by the locals. There—up ahead and to my left. I veered off the path and pushed through a tangle of hazel alder into a clearing thirty feet across and half as long. The energy was more intense here, coursing through me in powerful, constant waves. Dead center in the hollow, a patch of bare earth formed an almost perfect circle about five feet across. I knew what I was looking at the moment I saw it. "Steve!"

I walked forward and knelt just outside the circle. Putting my hands on the ground, I felt a surge of energy rush through my fingertips and into my body. The hairs on my arms were standing at full attention.

With the grace of a hippo, Steve stumbled his way through the swampy vegetation behind me. "Where the heck are you?"

"Just follow my voice! It sounds like you're pretty close."

I glided my hand over the dirt. As soon as it left the circle, the pulsing sensation lessened.

"Wow! I'd say it looks like you found what we were looking for." Steve wiped beads of sweat from his forehead as he approached and dropped down beside me. "This is great; I figured we'd be here for an hour or two easy. How did you find it so fast?"

I kept both hands hovering just above the ground, moving them in circular motions. "Guess you could call it a gut feeling."

"What the heck are you doing now?"

"There's some kind of weird energy coming from the circle. I can feel it."

Steve copied my hand movements. "I got nothing. You sure about this?"

"Absolutely. It's the reason I found this place to begin with—I felt it."

"That's...strange."

"*Very* strange. Ever since Corabas put the whammy on me, things have been different, and they're getting worse."

"What do you mean?"

"Take the body we found. I didn't know about it because Corabas told me. I knew because I was there—sort of."

"Sort of?"

"It was like he pulled me into his head and made me watch while he hunted the poor schmuck."

"Sounds creepy."

"That's only part of it. When he calls on me, I kind of do a Vulcan mind meld with him. I experience everything he does. I see what he sees, smell what he smells…I even taste what he tastes."

Steve said nothing. From the way his he looked at the ground, I could tell he knew the horrible deed I was referring to.

Despite the warmth of the day, I shuddered.

He put an arm around my shoulder. "Sorry, bro. I had no idea."

I closed my eyes and forced the dark memories from my mind. Steve stayed silent as I spoke. "Anyway, I think this is kind of like that. We're linked somehow, and that's how I was able to find this place." I opened my eyes. "And there's more."

"What are you talking about?"

"Hold on." I stood and walked over to a nearby fallen oak. Planting my right foot on the trunk of the rotting tree, I grabbed one of its branches and pushed down. It snapped off with a loud crack. "This should do just fine."

I went back, knelt down beside my brother, and stabbed at the soil with the jagged end of the stick. Moments later, a pile of dirt and clay lay next to a small hole. Not having the faintest clue what I would find, I reached in the cool, damp earth and grabbed a fistful of it. I began sifting. When all the dirt had slipped through my fingers, a tiny, rust-colored object remained.

"What is it?" Steve asked. "Looks like a small twig."

I wiped the muck off my discovery as best as I could. "Nope. It's too hard. I think maybe it's a nail."

"Let me see."

I handed it to Steve. He spit on it and cleared the remaining gunk away. "You're right. It looks old though." He put it between his thumb and index finger and held it up between us. "See the squared head on it? This was hammered by hand, like they used to do in the olden days."

"There's more of them." I pointed to the lifeless patch of ground. "They're spread out in a circle all around the brown spot."

"Why? What do they do?"

"I think the nails served like a sort of jail cell protecting the witch from Corabas."

"How could you possibly know that? Did he tell you?"

"It's like I said. With our connection growing stronger each day, it's something I can sense. These nails trapped Corabas. I guess when the witch drowned herself, their power disappeared. I bet if we cast the spell from inside this circle, the nails would keep Corabas out just like they contained him. That would give us enough time to break the possession spell *and* banish him without worrying about being torn to shreds."

"Hope you're right on that. Still, I don't like the idea of nothing but a handful of rusty old nails standing between us and Corabas."

Before I could respond, a bolt of lightning ripped through the sky, followed by an ear-splitting crack.

"Fudge me!" I shouted.

Above us, swirling clouds were threatening to unleash a downpour the likes of which Noah had never seen.

Steve jerked a thumb over his shoulder. "We need to split before we end up having to swim home."

We flew through town as the wind picked up, and it started to sprinkle. A couple of minutes from Spindle, Steve eased up until he rode beside me.

"I'm going over to Perry's," he shouted over a wicked gust. "I'll ask him to keep the nails and share the skinny on our sister. I'll let Mark and Brian know too. You just take care of Kevin."

I nodded and pedaled away as Steve broke right onto Stonybrook. A few soggy minutes later, I arrived at Kevin's only to discover he was with Perry and Paul over at their house. With nothing left to do, I headed home. As I pulled into the driveway, I spotted the figure of a little girl staring down at me from my bedroom window.

Chapter 29

The storm surged for the remainder of the day and into the early evening, grounding Steve and me. After quizzing us on our travels, Katie got bored and raided the pantry, gorging herself on Devil Dogs and Ring Dings. Next, she popped the heads off all of her dolls and proceeded to draw the most horrific scenes of carnage and ritual sacrifice on the inside of her closet walls. Steve and I did our best to cover up the freak show that was our sister, but it was exhausting. The highlight of the day came when Steve caught Katie halfway through a can of Dad's beer. Fortunately, my brother managed to dispose of it with no one the wiser. It was a trick I guessed he had some prior experience with. We said a silent prayer of thanks when she was finally put to bed.

Not long after that, Steve and I found ourselves fading. Between our riverside adventure and chasing Katie around, we were totally wiped. Knowing we had another full day ahead of us, we decided to turn in earlier than usual.

I heard the sounds as I lay in bed on the edge of sleep. A metallic *ping* was followed by a long, low creak. My eyes popped open as I wondered whether the noise came from my dreams or the waking world. Looking to my far right, I noticed the bedroom door Steve had closed and locked was now ajar. The dark side of my imagination slithered out, urging me to look where I dared not. It was no use resisting. I always ended up surrendering to it. I shifted my gaze to the foot of the bed. There, just above my toes, a pair of silvery eyes shined back at me. *Katie.*

She whispered with a gravelly voice empty of childish charm. "Helllooo, brother. Hope I didn't disturb you. You looked to be having a nice sleep."

I tried to keep my cool. "What are you doing in here? Haven't you been a big enough pain today?"

"Sorry. I'm still getting used to things up here. It's very nice. Lots of good food, sweet and tasty! Of course, there's no comparison to dining on something fresh off the bone, but a promise is a promise, and I said I would be a good little girl. But it is sooo hard."

Whoa boy. "Who'd you promise?"

Katie stood up but stayed where she was. "You know who. He asked me to keep an eye on you, make sure you behave until it's your time. You have been behaving, haven't you?"

Having my possessed sister interrogate me in the middle of the night should have freaked me out, but I wasn't the same person I'd been just two weeks ago. The nearer we approached Halloween and the coming of the black moon, the stronger my connection to Corabas. This resulted in some of his more dominant personality traits rubbing off on me. In many cases, such as talking to Tracy or facing a demonic interrogation, it came in handy. I was getting bolder, more confident, and—interestingly enough—less afraid of what was to come.

"I'm behaving," I answered. "Tell me, what do you get out of all of this aside from some Ring Dings and half a can of beer?"

"That's just the beginning. Once Corabas is free of his old vessel, he promised to give me this little one. Isn't that wonderful?"

That piece of crap.

"Oops! Come to think of it, I'm pretty sure he told me not to tell you that. Oh well, not like it's going to matter soon enough, is it?"

Whatever was in control of my little sister was trying to rile me up and definitely wasn't playing with a full deck. "What's your name?"

"Katie, silly!"

"You can come off it, dude. It's just you and me here—unless you count Steve. But he's sound asleep and clueless."

The demon's shining eyes narrowed. "Is he?"

"Absolutely. Despite what Corabas might think, the three of us are the only ones that have a clue about what's going on. You can take that back to the old man next time you see him."

"I might, but not yet. It's too early to be sure."

"So, back to my question. Who the heck are you?"

Dimples formed on Katie's apple cheeks as an evil little smile budded. She motioned for me to approach with her index finger.

I pushed myself up onto my knees and inched forward. "Okay."

The demon leaned in and whispered in my ear with great delight, "I am Raga, the hungry. But you should just call me Katie. That would be for the best until your time is at hand."

"Well, Raga, now that we know who you are and what you're here to do, how about you cut me some slack, and let me get some sleep? It's not like I'm going anywhere tonight."

"Are you sure? How do I know you're not planning to slip out and cause trouble? I think I'll just stay here."

"So, you plan to stand over my bed watching me while I sleep?"

Raga nodded.

"Yeah, that ain't gonna happen. You need to get out of my room, like now."

"Or what?"

I would like to think the idea that came next was entirely my own, the genius of my young, creative mind. But truth be told, ever since the bargain with Corabas, strange, often dark thoughts and ideas had begun seeping into my brain. "Tell you what, Raga. Here is what's gonna happen. Tomorrow I'm going to pay a visit to Corabas and say one of two things. I'm either going to ask him to have you back off because you are sooo good at your job that I can't even take a dump without you watching, or I'm going to make a couple wisecracks about how easy it's been to fool you and leave you in the dust. You dig?"

"What?"

Apparently, Raga did not dig.

"You heard me. I can tell your boss how great a job you've been doing spying on me or let him think that you're a big boob who can't do anything right. So, what's it gonna be?"

Raga scratched her head. "A big boob?"

I smiled and laid back in bed. "If that's the way you want it, you got it. Goodnight!"

"No, wait!" Raga was clearly confused. "Corabas cannot think I have failed him. If he does, he will send me back."

I sat up. "Well, if that's the case, you may want to start listening to what I have to say."

"Go on."

"I know I only have a little bit of time left, but in that time, I don't need you leaning over my shoulder all day long and watching me while I sleep. It's creepy. So, here's the deal. You're going to back off, and I'm going to tell Corabas what an amazing job you're doing."

She fell silent, clearly unsure how to respond.

I continued. "I just want a little privacy to spend the last moments of my life in peace with my family and friends. Surely you can understand that."

"I don't know. If Corabas suspects –"

"Or I can tell him how much of a dummy you are, and that you are doing nothing but screwing up his plans."

"No!"

"Ssshh! Keep it down."

"My apologies," Raga said in a hushed tone. "That is not necessary. We have an agreement, Chris Dwyer. I will allow you *some* space to say your farewells and put things in order, but that is all. In exchange, you will tell Corabas how merciless and ferocious I am. Agreed?"

For all of Raga's spookiness, she didn't appear to have a whole lot going on upstairs. With a little bit of luck, I could use that to my advantage. "It's a deal. Now hit the road, so I can get some rest."

Chapter 30

The next morning Steve and I got up early to head to the Perrets'. Before we could make it out the front door, our mom shouted, "Boys, why don't you take your sister with you? She was quite upset yesterday after the two of you left! Tracy said she went on and on about how she never gets to spend time with you anymore!"

While we were being guilt-tripped into taking our possessed sister with us, I noticed Raga descending the stairs. As the demon passed by, she flashed me an open-mouthed wink and made a beeline for the kitchen. Steve and I heard her talking to Mom but couldn't make out what she was saying.

"Never mind what I said, boys!" Mom shouted. "Your sister wants to stay here and help me make some congo bars, so go ahead and have fun, but remember to be back before dinner! We're having crabs tonight!"

Once we got outside and away from prying ears, Steve turned to me. "What was that about?"

I mimicked Raga's cheesy wink and said, "I'll tell you on the way."

By the time we got to the Perrets', the whole gang was already there. Mark and Brian looked rested and ready to kick butt. Perry, Paul, and Kevin were a slightly different story. Paul and Kevin were stone-faced, but Perry had a mean case of the stink eye, and was aiming directly at Steve and me.

If my brother saw the glare, he ignored it. "All right," Steve said, "how did it go yesterday?"

Brian was first to chime in. "We got it all!" He grabbed a nearby duffle bag and emptied its contents on the bedroom floor. A couple of lemons rolled out and settled in the blue shag carpeting. Close by was a box of kosher salt, a Ziploc containing some dirt, and another plastic baggie with something small, black, and covered in feathers.

"Oh yeah." Mark stepped in front of me and cupped my head in his hands.

"Hey, what's the deal?"

"Shut up," he said as he pulled my head down, exposing my scalp.

I felt his fingertips parting my hair. Before I could challenge his invasion of my personal space, I felt a slight tug.

"Got it!" Mark shouted as he held his plucked prize in front of everyone. "Check it out. The hair of the claimed one."

"You only needed one," I said, rubbing my head.

Mark handed the strands to his brother. "Better safe than sorry—in case we lose a couple."

"Uh-huh."

Brian stowed them in another plastic baggie. "And that is that. All the ingredients—minus the blood. The biggest pain was waiting to get that crow that was cawing near the church behind our house. Must have taken a couple hours before we were able to pick it off with the Daisy."

Steve looked to Perry. "How about you?"

"Oh, us? It went great. Right guys?" Sarcasm dripped from Perry's mouth as his gaze drifted to Paul and then Kevin. "Thanks for leaving me with Heckle and Jeckle. They were a *huge* help digging out the body."

Everyone knew Perry's crew got the short end of the stick when it came to the assignments. Just the thought of chopping up a body made me want to hurl.

"It worked though, right?" Steve pressed.

"Sure," Perry huffed, "the foot's in the backyard."

Steve frowned. "The foot?"

Perry pointed to his bedroom window. "Like I said, the foot is in the back. I wrapped it in a trash bag and threw it in a hole I dug out behind our shed. It should be safe there."

"You cut the foot off?" Steve asked.

"I sure as heck wasn't going to dig up the whole thing just to get a handful of slimy old bones. You never said what part of the body was needed, so we figured a foot would do just as well as anything else. Besides," Perry poked Steve's chest, "you weren't the one stuck with that crap job. I'd like to see you do better."

"I don't know; he might have done a little better," Kevin muttered.

Perry's head whipped back to Kevin and Paul. "What was that?"

Kevin hunched his shoulders. "Don't get mad. It's just…you had a little trouble getting started. That's all."

"I didn't see you coming to help. You were too busy getting ready to barf, and so was your girlfriend there."

"No I wasn't!" Paul protested. "Kevin's right. You hacked at that thing for over an hour before you finally got it. You could have chewed it off in half the time. On second thought, maybe you should have tried that."

Brian laughed first and then Mark followed by the rest of us—minus Perry.

Steve broke up the party before his best friend got too pissed off. "All right. All right. The spell calls for bones and blood. I guess it doesn't matter what part of the body they came from. In this case, we have a foot. It's cool, Perry. Sorry I had to stick you with such a sucky job. All joking aside, I did it because I knew you could pull it off."

"Yeah, well, next time you need a grave robber, call someone else. That was the grossest thing I've ever done."

"What about the time you went to kiss Tricia Patterson, and she barfed on you because she had some beer?" Paul asked.

Perry considered the comparison. "Okay, it was the *second* grossest thing I've done."

"What about you guys?" Mark asked. "How'd it go at Crybaby Bridge?"

Steve and I took turns describing our trip. When we finished our recap, Steve added, "So, we now have all the ingredients for the spells, and we know where to go and what needs to be done. There's just one more thing we have to take care of."

The words dropped from Kevin's and Paul's lips simultaneously. "The anchors."

Steve pulled the Shell map from his pocket, carefully unfolded it, and placed it on the floor. Sometime in the past couple of days, he had copied the locations of the anchors onto it from the tracing paper. "The good news is we have over two and a half months until Halloween. The bad news is these things are spread out all over Bowie, and we only have their approximate locations."

"I should be able to help with that," I said. "I think if you can get us within a block or two of the markings, I might be able to sense them—kind of like what happened at the bridge."

"You sure about that?" Steve asked.

"Nope. But it's worth a try."

I picked out a star that was within a couple miles of our home. "Let's see if I can find this one. Two or three of us can head out and track it down. If we find the marking, we'll hack it off and then burn it."

I then pointed to the stars that looked to be the farthest out. "Next, if that works, we'll start from the outside and work our way in. We'll save the anchor at Corabas's house for last."

"What if Corabas finds out what we're up to?" Kevin asked.

"Yeah," Paul broke in, "what if he knows when we destroy the first anchor?"

I looked to the worried faces of my friends. "I don't know, guys, but I don't think we have a heck of a lot of choices. These things have to be gone before we try and send Corabas back or else the spell won't work. I'm sure of that. My gut tells me we can do this if we're careful. I don't believe Corabas can sense the anchors unless he's close to them—just like me. If we're smart and cautious, I bet we can get rid of all the without him noticing.

Silence descended on a room full of guys not known for keeping quiet.

After allowing time for any objections, my brother spoke. "Guess it's settled then. Chris and I will find the first anchor and destroy it. If we're successful, we'll keep removing them until only the one on Corabas's property remains."

Steve looked to Perry. "We need to keep the ingredients safe and sound in one place, and our house is now compromised. You and your brother have to protect this stuff at all costs. If we're missing just one part of a spell, we're hosed."

Paul sidled up next to his brother. "No problem. Perry's got lots of great hiding places he can use. He may even have one or two I haven't found yet."

Ignoring Paul's comments, Perry punched Steve lightly in the arm. "We got you covered. Just watch your back, Jack."

"What about your sister?" Brian asked. "Is she gonna be spying on us the whole time?"

"You can bet on that," I said. "I got her to ease up a bit, but the demon possessing her is completely nutso. While Steve and I are tracking down these anchors, we'll need your help—we'll need everyone's help— to keep Raga distracted. Lucky for us, the demon is easily sidetracked and loves nothing more than stuffing her face on pretty much anything she can get her hands on."

"Ohhh," Paul blurted, you mean just like Kevin."

"Easy, Bugs," Kevin said, smirking. "Think I got a carrot here to shut you up with."

Steve raised his hand. "Okay, guys, be cool. We have a lot to do over the next few days, and we can't afford to make any mistakes."

Steve was right. Just one slip up could cost my friends their lives and me my soul.

Chapter 31

It was still late morning when Steve and I headed out from the Perrets' house to test my theory, and an orange sun blazed above in a clear blue sky. The anchor we picked was one of the closer ones, and I hoped it might be easier to find given how close it was to Bowie's most well-known landmark. A quick bike ride up Tulip Grove Drive brought us to the rolling grounds of the Belair Mansion. The brick plantation house looked like something straight out of colonial Williamsburg. Looking up to the mansion's second story windows, I expected to see some ghost or specter staring back at me, maybe even pointing me in the direction of the demon's mark.

We cruised up the long driveway and hopped over the curb onto the manicured lawn before coming to a stop. The tug of the anchor was like an invisible fishing line slowly reeling me in.

"Anything?" Steve asked.

I pointed to a brick path that wound around to the rear grounds. "It's in the woods."

We rode behind the mansion and down a series of sloping hills until reaching a tiny cemetery surrounded by several lonesome tulip poplars.

"There," I said pointing to one of the trees. "That one has an anchor on it."

We dismounted and walked past the cemetery to the base of a gigantic poplar. If the two of us stood on opposite sides of the beast and reached around there still would have been a good half foot separating our fingertips. I planted a palm on the bark and let the throbbing energy guide me. Circling around it, I raised my hand until it settled on a scarred section of bark. I took a step back.

I heard Steve's voice from behind me. "Is that it? It's hard to tell."

The faint curves of the crescent moon were barely visible, but there was no mistaking it. The anchor could easily have been more than a hundred years old and was now almost totally swallowed up from decades of growth. It made sense, I suppose. After all, the mansion was originally built by the Ogles and served as the heart of their entire estate. This could have even been the first place Corabas decided to mark after he was summoned. "Yep. A pretty old one too."

"Well, that answers our first question. You can find the anchors. Now," Steve reached into his knapsack and pulled out a small hatchet, "onto the second one. Can we destroy it?"

Steve aimed the edge of the ax slightly above the marking. As he raised it, I asked, "Do you think we could get arrested for doing this?"

Steve paused and frowned. "Yeah, I suppose we could."

He brought the blade down before I had a chance to say another word. By the fourth *thunk*, he had hacked off all that remained of the shallow carving. We were careful to pick up every shaving.

"Here." Steve motioned for me to follow him to a grove of nearby evergreens.

Leaves and twigs crackled underfoot as we entered the relative privacy of the forest. Steve pulled a small silver canister from the same knapsack along with one of our dad's Bic lighters. "You break up the wood into smaller pieces while I get a fire going."

Careful not to lose any of the pieces in the process, I began to peel sections of the soft wood and bark. After a minute of shredding, I handed the burn pile to Steve.

He looked me in the eyes as he dropped the first piece of poplar into the blazing tin of Sterno. "Here goes nothing."

I'm not sure exactly what we expected to happen. Maybe an explosion of hellfire or possibly a gust of wind carrying with it the shrieks and wails of the Goatman's past victims. Instead, we witnessed the painfully slow—and very anticlimactic—smoldering of freshly cut timber.

Halfway through the burn, Steve asked, "You think it's working?"

I stifled a yawn. "Don't know. Maybe."

For the next several minutes, we sat and silently watched as the last of the clippings turned to ash. Steve spoke again. "Guess that's that."

I stood up and stretched. "We'll see." I walked back to the wounded tree, closed my eyes, and touched it.

"So?" Steve pried. "Anything?"

"Ssshh. Let me concentrate." I calmed my mind, closed my eyes, and reached for the energy of the anchor. The wood felt cool and slightly damp, but that was all. There was no longer a heartbeat pulsing through my fingertips. The tether was cut, the anchor gone. "I think we did it."

Steve's voice rolled down the surrounding hills and echoed off the houses in the far distance. "Right on, little bro!"

I opened my eyes and turned to him. "This one wasn't too bad, but not counting the four anchors on Spindle and Stonybrook, we still have over a dozen more spread out all over Bowie that need to be taken care of."

"Baby steps, brother," Steve said. "We'll take them out one at a time."

For the next eleven days, my brother and I saw more of Bowie than we had in our entire lives. From Race Track Road on the north side of town all the way down to Allen's Pond and other points south, we spent almost every waking hour scouting out and trashing anchors. On a good day we could hit two of them, but those were few and far between given the distance separating them.

Fortunately, Raga's behavior had settled down to just slightly psychotic. That was due in large part to a conversation I had with Corabas following the destruction of the first anchor. My Oscar-worthy performance included a detailed description of the ruthless and unrelenting job Raga was doing spying on me. If the obvious delight Corabas took from my bitching was any sign of how pleased he was, Raga would be sitting pretty with him for some time. The junior demon was so happy with my complaints that she left Steve and me almost entirely on our own. Her obsession with all things fried, filling-stuffed, and covered in chocolate also proved an excellent distraction. If by some miracle we ended up surviving this, little sis was going to have to start Weight Watchers.

Chapter 32

I was dreaming about Christmas and snow when everything shifted. It was worse this time, much stronger than when I first felt it. All of my senses ratcheted up to ten, but my thoughts were a jumbled mess, blurred by a hunger that drove me into the night. In near-darkness I crossed a set of railroad tracks and silently crept up an embankment. New smells were there to greet me. Beneath the musty stink of soil and rotting wood, French fries, cheesesteaks, and vanilla soft serve floated on the warm summer air. I knew in an instant where I was. J-Mart had been a favorite of Steve's and mine ever since I could remember. The Italian hoagies always rocked, but my all-time favorite was a sugar cone of vanilla dipped in butterscotch hard shell topping. Such things meant nothing to me now. Peering out of the woods, I watched the fat lady lock the eatery's front door. She was alone. My stomach growled, and my whole body trembled as a wave of hunger pangs washed over me. Never in my short life had I felt anything like this.

I knew what was going to happen. Horror and revulsion haunted my dream, but their strength was less, replaced with a dark excitement. It boiled up in me as the thought of a fresh kill pushed everything else out of my mind. Even when I saw the woman's face and recognized her as Mrs. Lovelace—Kyle Lovelace's mother from my sixth-grade class—I didn't stop. I felt my teeth clamp down on her soft neck and tasted the coppery tang of warm blood gushing down my throat.

As I feasted on her flesh, the fire within me dwindled, and my mind cleared. I jerked awake and immediately realized someone was watching me.

"Having a late night snack?"

It took my brain a moment to catch up. The images of Mrs. Lovelace's screaming face were fresh in my mind as I looked to the foot of my bed. Raga's shining eyes hovered in the darkness.

"What did I tell you about watching people while they sleep?"

Raga put her an index finger over her mouth. "Mmm, it was creepy?"

"Yes, very. We had an agreement, no more night visits. Remember?"

Raga ignored the question. "You were feeding, weren't you? I could tell from the sounds you made."

The thought of Raga watching me while I was pulled into one of Corabas's late-night binges creeped me out and shamed me. "I was sleeping; Corabas was the one who was feeding."

Raga wasn't falling for it. "Uh-huh, must have been some sleep from the sound of things."

As sorry as I felt about the woman's death, the terrible truth was I wasn't really that upset. The first time Corabas summoned me to the hunt I was freaked out, totally traumatized. Now, as the date of my impending possession drew closer, I seemed to be growing used to the bloodshed and numb to the suffering of others. Though it was warm under my sheets, I shivered. "What about you, Raga? Do you enjoy dining on the residents of Bowie as much as your boss?"

Raga grunted. "No. It's too much hard work."

"Then why stay here? Why possess Katie?"

Raga took a seat on the edge of the bed. "Obviously, you've never been to Hell."

"That would be a no."

"It's not a pleasant place. Here is much easier. Here I can do whatever I want. I can eat what I want and drink what I want. Gluttony is one of my favorite sins."

No kidding. "You plan on turning my kid sister into the Goodyear Blimp? Is that it? Maybe have her die of a heart attack by the time she's thirty?"

Raga shrugged. "I don't know what this blimp is you speak of. I'm just enjoying being topside. Corabas is the planner. He's been at this for a long time and knows what he's doing."

"Tell me something I don't know."

"The second plane of Hell is not as cold as you might think."

"Come again?"

"The second plane of Hell is not as cold as you might think. That is not common knowledge."

"Uh-huh." The silliness of our conversation was starting to chafe my ass. "Raga, why exactly are you here?"

"Corabas summoned me to watch you when –"

"No. I mean, why are you in my bedroom again?"

"I am a light sleeper. Your grunts and slurping woke me. I thought you might have some ice cream or other delightful treats to share."

The sense of guilt returned. "Well, the shows over, so don't let the door hit your butt on the way out."

Raga cocked her head but didn't move.

"That means get out."

"Then why not just say get out?"

A heavy sigh escaped me. "I just did. Get out."

Finally, the demon took the hint. Raga stood and went to the door. Before exiting she said, "You are sounding more like him every day. It won't be long now."

Shortly after the demon left, I shut my eyes. The face of Mrs. Lovelace was there to meet me, but it quickly faded as I fell asleep.

By the time I woke up, Steve was already out of bed and the mid-morning sun was streaming in through my window. Slipping out from under the covers, I stretched and wiped the sleep from my eyes. As I staggered to the door, I heard voices carrying up to my room from downstairs. I walked into the front hall and noticed Steve at the top of the stairs listening with great interest. He put a finger to his lips when he saw me. With the stealth of a jungle cat, I crept next to him and leaned over the wrought iron bannister to catch some of the conversation.

"At the risk of being repetitive, I would like to thank you once more for loaning me Chris this summer. He has my lawn looking shipshape and undoubtedly saved me from a heart attack."

Corabas had decided to pay a visit. It shouldn't have surprised me. I bailed after mowing his lawn the last time and hadn't seen him face-to-face in more than a week now. Deep down, a part of me knew this meeting was inevitable and unavoidable. That said, I guess it was better to meet the old fart on friendly ground. Besides, I had a thing or two I had been itching to ask him.

"Is there a chance I could thank him in person?" Corabas asked Mom. "If he's awake, that is."

Before Mom could answer, I shouted from the top of the stairs, "Morning!" I motioned for Steve to say where he was as I started my heavy-footed descent.

I found them sipping coffee at the kitchen table. "Chris, Mr. Hutchinson came over to say how wonderful a job you did mowing his lawn this summer. Isn't that nice of him?"

I stifled a yawn. "Sure is. He's a heck of a guy."

My response came out more smart-alecky than intended. Mom's stony frown let me know an immediate course correction was needed in order to avoid her swift wrath. "I mean, it was really great of him to give me a chance and trust me to do a good job. Sorry, I'm still waking up."

Corabas laughed. "That's okay, son. Guess I caught you fighting off Mr. Sandman." He turned to my mom, whose mood had thawed a little. "Would you mind if I talked a little business with the boy? I have a couple other projects I'd like to see if he is interested in, but I don't want him to feel obligated because of his parents—if you know what I mean."

"Of course. I'll be upstairs folding laundry if you need me."

I did a quick scan of the kitchen and dining room and didn't notice Raga anywhere. "Mom, where's Katie?"

"She's next door at the Chambers' playing with Lynn. It's just you and your comatose brother. Apparently, ten hours of sleep isn't enough for him."

The warm smile on Corabas's face soured into a smirk as soon as my mom left the room. He motioned to the chair she had just occupied. As I dropped into the seat, he leaned over and spoke in a hushed tone. "Looks like you slept well. Must have been the midnight snack we had."

"*She* was Kyle's mom. *She* was a nice lady."

"Perhaps so, but *she* was delicious and just what the doctor ordered. You can try denying it all you want, but I know you relished it. It can't be helped; it's what we are."

"It's what *you* are."

"Let me ask you something, Chris. If you so despise my…tastes, why do you partake of the hunt?"

I knew I should have been scared of him, but for some reason I wasn't. He was so arrogant, so sure of himself. I wanted to punch him in his dumb old face. "You know why. You used your mojo on me and pulled me into it. It was something you promised not to do again, but you did anyway."

The smirk on Corabas's face grew. "And you believe that?"

He was toying with me, but I couldn't figure out why. "What do you mean? Why wouldn't I? What other reason is there?"

His eyes fell to the tablecloth. He traced its floral patterns with his finger. "I think you know, but you're too scared to accept it."

I could feel my cheeks warm. "Too scared of what? What do I *possibly* have to be frightened of anymore? Summer is almost over, and soon after you'll be taking up residence. Then that will be that. Game over."

Corabas's head rocked from side to side. "Oh, Chris, my child. Don't you understand? I didn't call you to the hunt. You sensed it and came of your own accord—to feed."

The moment he said the words, I knew they were true. Still, I couldn't bear to accept it. I shot to my feet. "That's bullshit! I'm not like you! You made me do it! You –"

The demon put a finger to his lips and then pointed to the seat I vacated.

Mom called out from upstairs. "Is everything okay down there? Chris, are you behaving? I thought I heard shouting."

"It's okay." I said, plopping back down. We're okay."

"He's just a little excited." Corabas added. "I have a new project for him with a rather generous pay day at the end."

"That's marvelous. Chris, please behave for Mr. Hutchinson, and try not to get too hyper. Remember, your bother is still sleeping."

"Yes, Mom."

"At the risk of pointing out the obvious," Corabas continued, "you will soon come to realize that with each passing day, you are more as I."

"I know," I said in a dull, defeated voice.

"I don't like to see you distraught, child. It is not good for your health; hence, it is not good for me. I sense your affliction may stem from some outlandish, irrational belief in the possibility of salvation. If such is the case, I hope these words will help you gain a better understanding and appreciation of your current predicament and help you come to terms with your fate. Chris," Corabas leaned over the table, closing the distance between us to a few inches, "on Samhain, during the time of the black moon, the possession will be final. But long before this happens, I will be in full control of both your mind and body. The contract has been drawn in blood, the die cast. Samhain is nothing but a formality at this point. Even now, I can almost read your thoughts. That is how I know you harbor some slim hope. I can feel it, you see. It flutters around your brain like a butterfly struggling in vain against a mighty gale."

As much as I wanted to believe this was another trick, some mind game to keep me quiet and in my place, I knew it wasn't. With each passing day his presence grew stronger, spreading in me like a cancer.

"I also know you have struck some type of bargain with Raga, though the details elude me."

Time was running out. Within the next few days, Corabas would have total access to my thoughts, and the jig would be up. I needed to stall, keep him guessing until we had time to act. Figuring a half-truth would work better than a total lie—especially if he had a foot in the doorway to my mind—I said, "It's true. I guess there's no use hiding it. I told Raga that if she eased up on the whole guard dog thing, I would talk her up with you, say how amazing and merciless a job she was doing keeping an eye on me."

Corabas chuckled. "I recall the performance. It was very convincing. So, what have you been up to with your bartered freedom? Scheming on some doomed plot to save yourself?"

"No," I lied, focusing my thoughts on all of the annoying, over-the-top spying techniques used by Raga in the hopes Corabas would sense some of my frustration. "The clown was watching me sleep at night and freaking out every time I went to see my friends. It was disturbing and attracted the attention of both of my parents. There were even a couple times I had to stop Raga from trying to hurt them."

"Really?"

I gambled that my exaggeration would get his attention. The last thing Corabas needed was some loose cannon screwing up his perfectly laid plans. An injured adult might get the authorities involved. "Yep. Where did you find that bozo anyway?"

Corabas's words were pinched. "Good help is hard to find in Hell. Raga had one simple task to follow: watch you and make sure you didn't cause any trouble."

"Well, when she isn't drinking my dad's beer or planning to decapitate my mom, she's doing a heck of a job with that."

Corabas held me in a cold, silent stare for what felt like hours. "It was never my intention for Raga to cause harm to you or your family. The issue will be dealt with posthaste. Just remember, child, soon there will be no secrets between us. If I find you have been false with me, the punishment will be severe."

What could be more severe than what he already had planned for me? The saying *In for a penny, in for a pound* entered my mind as I met his gaze. "I understand."

After Corabas left, I went back up to the bedroom and caught Steve with his ear to the floor vent. He had heard everything. We agreed tomorrow would have to be D-Day and that it would be best if he headed out alone to set everything in motion while I waited for Raga's return and kept her occupied.

When she got back from her playdate, the demon said little, but it was obvious from the get-go that Corabas had an opportunity to read her the riot act. Raga's behavior quickly graduated from annoying to downright unbearable. The highlight was when she stood outside the bathroom door while I took a whiz. Steve and I had to wait until she went to bed before we could devise an escape plan for the following morning. What we came up with was simple in design but touched by genius.

Chapter 33

By the time Raga walked downstairs for breakfast, I was in the dining room already polishing off the remains of milk-soaked Cheerios from my bowl. I looked up at her and smiled. "Morning, *Katie.*"

She peeked into the adjoining kitchen and then into the family room before asking, "We are alone?"

"Mom and Dad are at work. Steve is sleeping."

Ignoring the assortment of Frankenberry, Lucky Charms, and Captain Crunch stacked side by side on the kitchen counter, Raga went straight to the pantry. After banging and clunking around, she returned to the table and unloaded her breakfast. Witnessing her gobbling down two Hostess fruit pies in four bites was bad enough, but when she started dipping dill pickles into a tin of deviled ham, I nearly gagged.

In only slightly exaggerated disgust, I grabbed my bowl and went to the kitchen. After taking a minute to load the trap, I reappeared with a tiny plastic cup in hand.

As expected, Raga's eyes zeroed in on the purplish liquid it contained. Globs of deviled ham spewed from her mouth as she spoke. "What's that?"

"Oh this?" I downed the concentrated mixture of grape Kool-Aid in a single shot. With no sugar added and only a little bit of water, the bitter mixture almost caused me to choke, but somehow I managed. Wheezing in some air, I said, "It's a little treat I'm giving myself seeing as I don't have much longer. It's usually for adults, but I know you won't tell."

"Why is it for adults?"

"You remember the beer that Steve took from you?"

"Yes. It was delicious and filled me with warmth."

"This does kind of the same thing. It's a little stronger, and it takes some getting used to. You're too little to try it though."

Raga swallowed the food in her mouth with a loud gulp. "I want some. What is it called?"

Time to reel her in. "Robitussen." I crinkled my nose. "I don't know. This stuff packs a wallop. If Mom and Dad found out I gave it to you, I –"

"Soon enough Corabas will be in control, so why do you care?" Raga stood and approached with a hungry look in her eyes. "Give me some now!"

I raised both hands. "Okay, okay. Be cool." I fought to keep from smirking as I went back into the kitchen and twisted open the bottle of cough syrup. "This is potent," I said while pouring an inch of the medicine into an orange juice glass, "so you should only have a little."

Raga snatched the glass and swallowed the contents. Her face puckered but quickly smoothed back out. "The taste is foul, but I can tell it is a strong drink. You say this is like beer?"

"It's actually stronger."

Raga shoved the glass in front of me. "More."

"I don't think you should –"

"More!"

"All right, keep your shirt on." I poured a slightly smaller serving. "This is it though. We don't want you getting sick."

Raga emptied the second glass. This time there was no face. "I will tell you if I desire more after I finish my breakfast."

The demon returned to her feast of pies, pickles, and seasoned ham spread while I went into the family room, turned on the television, and waited.

Twenty minutes later, Raga stumbled in and said in a thick voice, "What are you doing?"

I pointed to an episode of *The Six Million Dollar Man*. "Just watching TV. I was planning on relaxing today. Might even take a nap later because I didn't sleep well last night. You don't have to worry about me,

Raga. We both know it's just a matter of time before Corabas is in complete control, and there's nothing I can do about it."

Raga's eyes flared open for a split second before constricting. "That is true," she slurred. "You are doomed and have nowhere to run to."

I put a finger to my nose and then pointed it to her. "Like you said. Think I'll just take it easy on this warm, comfy couch."

I shimmied my butt and shoulders back into the corner of the sofa. Once settled, I stretched both arms and released a drawn-out yawn.

Raga stood in the doorway considering her options. From the gentle sway of her body, I could tell the medicine was fast at work. After a few seconds of drugged indecision, she muttered something about me being doomed again and slowly zigzagged her way to the opposite end of the couch.

I fell silent and faked interest in the show while watching from the corner of my eye as her tiny head began nodding. Twice I started inching my way out of my seat only to freeze in place as she snorted awake. Before attempting a third escape, I endured five minutes of open-mouthed snoring to make sure the coast was clear.

When I finally made it upstairs, Steve was fully clothed and lying in bed reading. "What took you so long? It's almost eleven."

I shut the door behind me. "It wasn't my fault. Looney Tunes had to finish her morning pig out before she passed out on the couch."

"So, she's asleep?"

"Out like a light!"

We wasted no time ditching Raga. There would be hell to pay if our parents found out we left Katie alone, but that was the least of our worries given the situation. By the time we got to the Perrets' house, the rest of the gang was there waiting on us. We went over the plan one last time to make sure everyone knew their role inside and out. When our rehearsal was over, Steve looked to Perry. "Have the ingredients?"

Perry slid a hand under his bed and retrieved a large paper bag. "It's all here—except for the foot. That's still buried out back. Hang loose while I go get it."

Steve and I did a thorough inventory while we waited, checking twice to make sure the necessary ingredients were accounted for.

"Looks like we're good to go," he said. "We'll use the beach bucket Chris and I brought to hold everything in when we cast the spells." A grin broke on his face as he turned to me. "Never thought I'd be saying that."

The door swung open with such force all of us jumped in our seats. Perry stood at the threshold, his head bobbing. He shoved a thumb over his shoulder. "It's gone."

"What's gone?" Steve asked.

Perry continued his bobblehead impersonation. "The foot. Gone. Someone dug it up and took it."

He backstepped into the hall and pointed down the stairs. "Go see for yourselves. We're screwed, totally screwed."

We bolted out of the room and into the backyard in a free-for-all, arriving at the hole in a matter of seconds.

Perry pointed to an empty crater. "I checked it last night before going to bed, and everything was cool. Someone must have dug it up during the night."

A pile of dirt and clay lay next to the hole. Paul leaned over and placed a hand on the edge of the pit. "These are claw marks. An animal must have dug it up." Paul glanced at Perry. "You don't think…"

Perry cupped his hands over his face and mumbled, "Ahhh, shit!"

"What?" I asked. "What is it?"

"Frigging Chompers!" Perry shouted. "Has to be."

Chompers was a scraggly old bulldog that wandered around Stonybrook helping himself to anything remotely chewable to include footballs, Frisbees, baseballs, sneakers, and the occasional badminton racket. When he wasn't busy stealing things, he was gnawing on fences, knocking over trashcans, and making a general nuisance of himself. I'd witnessed the carnage countless times. He was the four legged gremlin of Stonybrook.

"You think a dog dug up the foot?" I asked.

Paul sighed and shook his head. "Like Perry said, has to be him."

Steve groaned. "Well, unless one of you happens to have a spare foot lying around, we got to get that thing back—quick like. Who owns Chompers?"-

The Perret brothers exchanged a look of dread before Perry spoke up. "You're not going to like it."

"C'mon," Steve snapped, "we're wasting time."

"The Drakes," Paul answered. "The dog belongs to the Drakes. He's probably in their backyard now munching his way through a foot sandwich."

Brian stifled a giggle, drawing glares from Steve and Perry. "Sorry, just had this crazy picture in my head."

This was going to be dicey. The two remaining Drake brothers, Daryl and Emmitt, were twice as mean as Russell. But now that their youngest brother was in jail for a string of murders he didn't commit, the other two were bound to be even worse than usual. If we ran into either of them, there was no telling what they would do.

Perry turned to leave. "Let's snap to it, ladies. We need to get that foot before there's nothing left of it but a toe."

Steve pointed to Paul, Kevin, and me. "You three hang back. I don't want any of you going in the Drake's backyard. This could get dangerous."

The Drakes lived two houses down from the Perrets'. Their tired old colonial sat on a quarter acre of the sorriest piece of land the entire S-Section had to offer. The front lawn was nothing but a pile of dirt, yellow grass, and chickweed. A wildly overgrown pear tree stood dead center, partially blocking a garbage littered porch. No cars sat in the cracked driveway, but it wouldn't have surprised me to see a dingy pickup truck with *Sanford and Son* painted on the side parked there. The four older kids circled around back first. My friends and I followed about twenty feet behind them.

The backyard made the front look like the Taj Mahal. Heaps of wet, moldy leaves piled up against the fences of the neighboring properties. The rest of the yard was mostly dirt save for a ten by twenty patch of earth that looked like it might have been a vegetable garden in some long forgotten past. Now dozens of chest-high stalks of pokeweed sprouted from the soil almost as if planted on purpose. Strands of their poisonous purple berries dangled in every direction as a tribute to the only type of life that could survive in such a toxic environment.

A half-rotted clapboard dog house sat in the middle of the yard under the shade of a stunted oak. We could see a bulldog's squished face within the rundown structure. The animal's square head rocked left to right as it eagerly licked the foot tucked between its front paws. A black leather collar was bound around the creature's neck, tethering it to a chain that ran ten feet to an unearthed corkscrew stake.

"That's just *nasty*," Kevin said.

"I knew it," Paul whispered.

We watched the older boys spread out and hunch low to the ground as they stalked their foot-munching target. When they were within half a dozen yards, the dog started growling. Aside from being a major nuisance and plague on the neighborhood, Chompers was thought by most to be a cowardly creature, liable to run away at the slightest sign of aggression. Watching the dog now, I reconsidered that assumption.

"Think he'll bite one of them?" Kevin asked.

Paul was quick to respond. "Nah, he's all bark. Just watch."

When the boys got within three feet of him, Chompers grabbed the foot in his mouth and ran directly between Perry and Mark. Both of them dove for the dog and missed, landing hard on the dirt.

Despite the seriousness of the situation, the three of us couldn't stifle our laughter.

"Get him!" Brian shouted as Chompers galloped around the far side of the house with the stake in tow.

My group circled back around the front of the house hoping to cut the dog off, but we just ended up running into the older boys.

"Where'd that little foot-eating fucker go?" Brian asked.

"We didn't see him," I said.

"We'll split up," Steve said. "Perry and Brian will patrol down the street side of the houses, and Mark and I will work our way through the backyards in the same direction."

"What about us?" Kevin asked.

"The three of you head back up Stonybrook; see if the dog went that way. There's less ground to cover, so you shouldn't have to split up. If you find the fleabag, shout as loud as you can."

It wasn't the best of plans, but desperate times called for desperate measures. The older boys split, leaving us to fend for ourselves. We agreed that the likelihood of Chompers doubling back in the direction of the Perrets' house was remote, but we had our orders. Combing through the yards of all the houses upstream from the Drakes, we looked under every car, shed, and tree we came across. After thirty minutes of searching, we ended up back in Paul's yard. We were hot, tired, and had no more feet than when we started.

Paul disappeared in his house only to return a minute later with ice-cold orange Fantas. As we sipped on the sweet, bubbly drinks, he muttered, "I think I got a plan. Keep your eyes peeled, but don't go wandering off. I'll be back in a jiff." With those mysterious words, Paul went back inside.

Kevin and I were in no rush to move. We did as instructed, finishing our sodas under the shade of a large pine tree while listening to the swishing of needles in the summer breeze. Soon another sound rose on its relaxing currents. We heard it at the same time. A faint jingling was coming from the neighbor's yard.

Kevin frowned. "You hear that?"

I nodded.

We crept toward the fence that separated the yards and saw Chompers on the far side. The canine lurched forward and was immediately yanked back as the chain link fence rattled.

"Look," Kevin said as he pointed.

I followed his finger to a section of fence a few feet away from the dog where a tiny piece of metal shimmered in the bright summer sun.

The corkscrew stake was caught firmly in its mesh webbing. Every time Chompers tried to pull himself free, the stake wound tighter.

Why Kevin felt the need to whisper I'll never know. "We got him."

We climbed over the five-foot fence and made our way to the trapped dog. He managed a formidable growl despite having a rotten foot in his mouth.

"How the hell do we get that thing out?" I asked.

Kevin reached out a hand but yanked it back when the dog lunged at him in vain. "Shit! Where the hell is Paul anyway?" he shouted.

We were so preoccupied with Chompers that we failed to notice the shadow creeping up on us from behind until it was almost too late. It was the dog that alerted us. His ferocious growls suddenly turned into a series of high-pitched yips.

Thinking it was Paul, Kevin swung around to give him a piece of his mind. "It's about ti—whoa!"

The *whoa* caught my attention. I turned and hopped backwards just as something large whizzed by my ribcage. "Gah!"

Her pancaked hair was silhouetted by the afternoon sun. Wild, bloodshot eyes glowed with rage. "You will not make a fool of me again, Chris Dwyer! I won't be sent back! I *like* it here!"

Chapter 34

Raga swung hard with the croquet mallet, narrowly missing my foot.

I put my hands in front of me and backed off, moving closer to the whimpering dog. "Are you nuts? If you kill me, Corabas is sure to send you back!"

The demon girl hefted the mallet back up. "Not kill, just break. A foot, a leg—it doesn't matter as long as you can't move. Then I will drag you back to my master, so he can see your treachery."

"Oh my God!" Kevin howled. "Your sister is cra-a-zy!"

Raga's gaze shifted to Kevin. "You, though, you I can kill!" She swung, missing Kevin's head by a hair as he ducked at the last second.

The smile dropped from his face as my friend realized just how close his head had come to being a croquet ball.

I shouted, "Hey!" to him and pointed to Paul's house. Once I knew he understood, I took off, cutting around Raga and making a run for the door. At the same time, Kevin broke into a sprint and circled around the demon from the other side. Raga was close behind us with the mallet raised. In retrospect, the image of my Oshkosh-clad sister chasing two boys while holding a large wooden hammer in her hands and screaming at the top of her lungs would probably have appeared comical to the casual observer. But I can say with the utmost certainty that at the time Kevin and I were dangerously close to staining our underwear.

We were over the fence and halfway to the back door when I went down, tripped up by the mallet Raga had thrown at my legs. Kevin stopped and came back to help, but by then the demon had recovered her weapon and was on me. She raised it as a ghoulish grin sprouted on

247

her face. "Smashy time! I'll start with the left knee and then get the right one. Corabas will be so proud!"

With a hollow *thunk* Raga's head lurched to the side. She dropped to the ground like a sack of potatoes, leaving Paul standing behind her with a thick piece of oak in his hands.

Doing his best impression of Chico Rodriguez, Kevin shouted, "Loooking good, Paul!"

I got to my feet and cautiously approached Raga. She was out cold but breathing. "Dude! You knocked out my sister!"

Paul dropped the piece of firewood and shrugged. "Sorry. Didn't know what else to do."

Kevin slapped Paul on the shoulder. "Sorry nothing! She was going break Chris's legs and kill me. You're the man!"

From around the side of the yard, the older kids came running.

"We heard screaming," Steve said.

"Daaammmn, Steve!" Mark pointed at Katie's collapsed body. "Is that your sister?"

"She attacked us," I said. "Paul was able to sneak up behind her. He saved our butts."

Paul showed his toothy grin and took a bow.

Steve's face twisted into a frown, making him look much older than he was. "We should tie her up before she wakes. She'll be dangerous until we can get rid of Corabas. When we send him back to Hell, she'll come around to her old self. At least I hope she will."

"There's some rope in the shed," Perry said. "We could put her in there and come get her on the way back. Only my dad goes in, and he won't be home till late."

The four older kids went about binding my possessed sister while the rest of us returned to Chompers and the severed foot.

As we headed back to where the dog was stuck, I glanced over at Paul. "Where the hell were you this whole time?"

He produced a ball of tin foil from his pocket and unfolded it in front of us. "Getting this without getting caught."

Kevin and I looked into his hand and smiled at one another.

"Not bad," I said.

"Genius," Kevin added.

When we got just outside of biting range, Paul knelt down and tossed his two stolen hamburger patties in front of Chompers. We watched as the dog inched forward. After sniffing around the closest one for a few seconds, Chompers dropped the mutilated foot and woofed down the beef in two bites.

"Quick!' Paul shouted, "Someone get it!"

Kevin and I glanced at each other. Neither of us wanted to touch the slimy, rotted zombie foot, but we knew we wouldn't get the chance again. As Kevin looked around for something to pick it up with, I went for it. While Chompers tore into the second piece of hamburger, I nabbed the foot between thumb and index finger and gave it a quick flick out of the dog's range. Unfortunately, Kevin was standing directly opposite me, and my spastic toss landed it smack dab in the middle of his face. "Sorry, sorry, sorry!"

"Ugh! Chris, you dipstick!" Kevin yelled.

Paul burst out laughing.

Kevin came at me. For a couple of seconds, I was sure he was going to clobber me. Instead, he grabbed the front of my limited edition *Kiss* T-shirt and wiped his face with it. When he was done cleaning, he glared at me and Paul. "I'm going in to wash my face off!"

Holding the tin foil in my hand, I held my breath and carefully wrapped up what remained of the rotten foot while Paul released a very happy, very full bulldog from his chain link prison. We met up back at the shed as the older boys finished tying up my sister.

Steve looked at his watch. "It's already after one. We need to get moving."

The group fell quiet. With the distraction of Chompers dealt with, we all knew it was time to prepare for the real challenge.

Perry spoke up. "So, who's gonna stay behind to deliver the message?"

"What message?" I asked.

Steve pulled a folded piece of notepaper from his pocket and handed it to me. "This message. It's the only way to guarantee Corabas takes the bait."

I unfolded it and read aloud, "Salt, lemon, soil from hallowed ground, a crow's skull, a hair from the claimed one, and blood of the trade. I have everything I need to break the spell. It's time for us to renegotiate our deal. Meet me at Crybaby Bridge at sunset."

I looked at Steve. "Why sunset?"

Steve shrugged. "Why not? It sounds cool—kind of like what they say in the movies sometimes."

"I guess so. But telling him we know how to undo the possession spell—isn't that a little risky?"

"This whole thing is risky for all of us, but we need to get Corabas to Crybaby Bridge. If we can't lure him there, he'll be free to go on killing people until he can find another vessel. None of us will be safe. We came up with the note idea yesterday when you were on lockdown. All of us feel this is our best shot, but I need to know if you're okay with it. It's important that we're all together on this."

"But who's gonna get stuck delivering the message?"

"It needs to be someone who's really fast on their bike," Steve answered. "They'll have to remove the last anchor, deliver the note, and make it to the bridge before Corabas can. If he gets the message too soon and shows up before the last one of us arrives, it will get real messy."

Brian's words were soft but steady. "Mark. It should be Mark." He looked at his older brother. "He's crazy fast on his bike—faster than any of us."

There were no objections. Everyone knew Brian spoke the truth.

"I'll do it," Mark said. He opened a hand and motioned for the note.

Steve handed it to him. "You have fresh batteries in your walkie-talkie?"

"Sure do."

"Here," Perry said, handing Mark his hatchet. "You'll need this."

Steve continued. "Set up a lookout post, so you can see the front of the old man's house. Make *sure* he doesn't see you; otherwise, we're sunk.

Start reporting in every hour until we give you the signal. Then make quick work of the anchor, and slip the note under his door. When you're finished with that, haul ass here as fast as you can. Remember to collect all of the wood shavings, so we can burn them here. Got it?"

Mark nodded. "You know it!"

Perry looked as serious as the grave when he said, "Be careful."

The rest of us mumbled words of good fortune to Mark as he headed around front to get his bike. He turned around before he was out of sight and shared his trademark grin. "Be seeing you fools soon!"

Chapter 35

We had just arrived at the bridge and were unloading our gear when Mark's static-infused voice came over the walkie-talkie. "I'm in position. The Goat's driveway is empty, so I guess he's out chewing on some grass. I'll report back when he shows up. Over."

Steve acknowledged the transmission and rested the radio against a nearby maple. "Paul, keep close to this, and let us know if Mark says anything."

After I showed everyone the place where Corabas was summoned, the older kids broke off and started separating and organizing the ingredients for the spells. While they focused on that, I closed my eyes and opened my mind to the heartbeat resting in the ground. I placed a hand on the dirt and let the energy course through me in waves.

"What are you doing?"

I opened my eyes and looked to Kevin. "Just making sure we're operational."

Paul popped his head up over Kevin's shoulder. "And?"

I smiled. "All systems are go."

"Okay, everybody, might as well get this over with!" Steve declared as he pulled his pocketknife out. "We can add Mark's blood when he gets here."

The group gathered around the circle of earth where the witch first brought the demon into the world. Following Steve's lead, we all dropped to our knees. He produced a collapsible plastic cup from his pocket, flicked it open, and placed it in front of him. "We'll fill this. Then, when it's time, I'll say the words and pour the blood of the trade in the *nganga*— or Katie's beach bucket as it's better known. Once the first spell is done,

I'll empty it out—except for the foot—and add the ingredients for the second spell. Then it's bye-bye Corabas."

Steve took a deep breath and placed the knife in the palm of his hand. Silence descended as we watched my brother's self-mutilation with a mix of curiosity and dread. He wrapped his fingers around the blade and grimaced while swiping down. Squeezing his fist over the container, Steve let a steady stream of scarlet droplets fall. After ten seconds of bloodletting, he loosened his clenched fist allowing the trickle to ease up and finally stop. Having no cloth or towel, he wiped the knife clean on his sock and went to hand it to Perry.

"No thanks." Perry pulled a large buck knife from a sheath he had tucked into his waistband. "I'll use my own."

"Why'd you bring that?" Steve asked.

Perry looked at my brother like he had grown a third eye in the middle of his forehead. "You serious?" He started waving the eight-inch blade around as he spoke. "If things go as planned, soon we're gonna have a pissed off Goatman running around here. I don't know about you, but I'd like to have a little more protection with me than a few rusty old nails buried in the ground."

Steve opened his mouth to speak, but no words came out. His eyes narrowed as he turned to the rest of us. "How about it? Anybody else bring along a little *extra* protection?"

Brian emptied his pockets and three pointed pieces of metal dropped to the ground.

Paul stooped to examine the contraband. "What are those?"

"Throwing stars. I know they won't kill the Goatman, but they might slow him down long enough."

"Long enough for what?" Paul pressed.

Brian smiled. "For me to get the hell out of here."

Nervous laughter simmered through the group.

"Anyone else?" Steve asked.

Kevin reached into the small of his back and pulled out his BB Gun.

Perry huffed and said, "All you're gonna do with that is piss the Goatman off. I bet that thing can't even break the skin."

"It sure can." Kevin protested. "I shot my cousin with it once by accident. They had to take her to the hospital to get the BB out. I was grounded for like three weeks."

I'd heard the same story from him at least three times, but with each telling the length of the punishment had grown. I'm also pretty sure the cousin was a boy the last time he told it.

Perry rolled his eyes. "Whatever."

Steve looked to Paul and me. "Your turns."

I started to profess our innocence but caught myself when Paul reached a hand down the front of his shorts. For the life of me, I don't know how he managed to fit the thing in there.

"Holy crap! Is that a Jart?" Steve asked.

Paul let the foot-long lawn dart drop to the earth where its pointed metal tip buried itself. "It's all I could find."

Perry fell to the ground howling.

My mouth dropped open. "How long have you had that thing?"

"I grabbed it earlier when I got the hamburgers."

"Well, I guess it sure would hurt someone if it landed on them."

Another round of laughter escaped Perry as he rolled around hamming it up.

Steve picked the Jart up. "Tell you what, Paul. Let's save this as a last resort. We don't need someone getting excited and launching this sucker straight up in the air." He tossed the lethal toy next to the *nganga*.

"No, wait!" Perry raised a hand as he stumbled to his feet. He pretended to wipe a tear from his eye. "Let's get the target ring from the Jart set, and see if we can get the Goatman to step in it. That way if Paul hits him, he gets a point."

Paul's face went from pink to beet red. "Yeah? Well at least I didn't cry like a baby when we watched *Snoopy Come Home*."

The smile dropped from Perry's face. "I wasn't crying! Besides, you know I always wanted a dog!"

It struck me like a thunderbolt as I watched them bicker and joke. They were clueless—all of them. I was the only one that witnessed what Corabas could do, how he could tear apart a man with nothing but his bare hands and then feast on his flesh. The taste of Mrs. Lovelace's blood was still fresh in my mind. To them this wasn't real. It was just some crazy summer adventure that I'd dragged them into. True, Paul and Kevin saw the Goatman outside of their windows and most of the crew saw the torn remains of one of his victims, but it still wasn't *real* to them. The danger wasn't sinking in.

"Shut up!" I shouted at the top of my lungs. "Shut up all of you!"

Perry and Paul fell silent and all eyes turned to me.

"Don't you get it? Corabas is coming for us—for *all* of us—today! He's coming and he's going to rip you apart to get to me! He'll make me watch as he tears your heads off one by one!"

Steve put a hand on my shoulder. "Easy, bro. They were just letting off some –"

I swatted it away. "I don't care what they're doing! It doesn't matter. In a few hours you'll all be dead and I'll—I'll be alone with *him*."

A wave of guilt and despair washed over me as I came to realize what I'd done. They were all going to die because of me. I couldn't look at them anymore. Brushing past my brother, I stumbled into the woods and away from the group. "I need to be alone."

No one tried to stop me and no one followed me. I wandered for several minutes before stopping near a huge oak. Confident that I was out of earshot, I rested an arm against the tree and buried my head in it, letting muffled sobs escape. Everything I'd said was true, and it was all my fault. Turns out I wasn't the hero after all. I was a coward, a bawling child so scared of being alone that I was willing to sacrifice the lives of my friends and brother. It was unforgivable. Maybe it wasn't too late for me to go back and beg the demon's forgiveness.

"Don't worry, bro. We'll fight him together."

I jerked to attention at the sound of Paul's voice. Wiping the tears away from eyes, I said, "How can you be so sure? You haven't seen what I've seen, what *he* can do. None of you have."

"You're right; we haven't. But you have. You have and yet you still played it cool and managed to convince us all the Goatman was real. After that you came up with a plan to beat the dickhead. That was all you, amigo."

"But aren't you scared?"

Paul squeezed my arm. "Yeah, but we've come this far, and there's no going back. Everything you said back there was right—except for the whole we're all gonna die thing. None of us have seen what you have, but I still have to believe that there's hope, that we have a chance."

"Why? Why do you believe we have a chance?"

Paul smiled. "Because I believe in you."

"Also, Paul and I have a plan," Kevin blurted as he clambered through the underwood to join us. "He's gonna shove that lawn dart right up the Goatman's ass while I shoot both of his eyes out."

"Thanks, guys. If things don't –"

Perry's voice blared through woods, "Get your butts back to camp! We have contact! I repeat, we have contact!"

The three of us took off and made it back just in time to hear Mark's static-filled voice over the walkie-talkie. "Breaker, breaker, this is the Mailman. Be advised, the Goat is in the barn. I repeat, the Goat is in the barn. Over."

Steve picked up the radio. "Got it, Mailman. You may chop the wood and deliver the package when you are ready. Over."

"Copy that, Magic Man. Will proceed. Over."

"Magic Man?" Perry asked, grimacing. "Since when did you guys work out code names?"

Steve grinned. "We didn't. Mark's just having some fun, I guess."

It was five long minutes before Mark called back. This time the words came out fast, broken up by heavy breathing between sentences. "Okay, the wood is chopped and package delivered. I repeat, the package has been delivered. The Mailman is getting his butt back to the post office."

Steve keyed the radio, but Brian leaned in before he could speak. "Don't slow down for anything, Mark."

"Is that Brother Bear? C'mon now, we don't use names on the radio. Never know who's listening. Anyway, it's all cool. I fixed the Goat's tractor before delivering the package. We have plenty of time."

Brian looked at Perry and Steve. "What does that mean?"

"Flat tire maybe?" Steve guessed.

"If that's the case," Perry said, "Mark is good. He'll make it here long before Corabas can put on a spare and catch up."

I got up and moved toward Steve and Brian to better hear Mark's play-by-play. Halfway there a rage overcame me with such force I staggered to one knee. My hands clenched into fists and my whole body shook. Words came out of my mouth, but they weren't mine. With a pitch and power beyond my capability, I shouted, "Those little shits! I'll rip their fucking heads off!"

I looked around to everyone's shocked faces. The next words were my own. "He's coming."

Chapter 36

"Are you sure?" Steve asked.

"I felt his anger. He's pissed. I mean really, really pissed. I never felt such hate before—even when he was hunting. Then it was the hunger driving him on, making him kill. Now," I glanced at Steve, "he just wants to tear us apart."

The news brought an eerie quiet to the group. Death was approaching, and all we had were some nails, a BB gun, a couple of knives, a few throwing stars, and a Jart to defend ourselves with.

Once more, Steve took the reins and tried to steer us back on course. "Okay, the first spell is ready to go now that we have the blood of the trade. We still have a little time to –"

"No," I said. "There's no time; he's coming *now*."

"But Mark said he jacked up the old man's car," Perry said. "How can he be on his way?"

"Because he's not driving. He's running."

"Ha!" Perry said. "On foot it will take him hours to get here."

"It won't. He's changed into the Goatman, and he's running at full speed."

"How fast is he?" Brian asked. "Like, is he faster than someone on a bike?"

For a moment I had forgotten Mark was out there and that the Goatman's sights were currently locked on him. "I don't know. He's fast, but even with the sun getting low, he'll have to stick to the bushes and backyards or risk being discovered. If Mark puts the pedal to the metal, I think he can make it." It was a total guess, but it felt like the right thing to say.

Steve grabbed my arm and turned me to face him. "Chris, can you connect with him again? You know, get in his head?"

"I don't want to. It's too –"

"Stop for a minute, little bro, and think about the jam we're in. We're flying blind here. If you can pay his mind a visit, we'd know how soon to expect him. But more important than that, we could figure out if he's catching up to Mark."

For as far back as I could remember, my brother had a way with words that made him difficult to resist. Sometimes it could prove very annoying. "I guess if we can help Mark, it's worth a try. I'll do it."

I closed my eyes and focused on the image that first angered Corabas. The flat tire quickly came into view, and a terrible urge to maim and murder followed. Soon I found myself looking through the eyes of the demon. "He stopped in a backyard. His head is up, and he's sniffing the air." Corabas caught a curious blend of sweat, hot dogs, and Fruit Stripe Gum on the air. *So, that's what Mark smells like.* "He's back on the move. Holy crap! He just jumped like ten feet to clear a fence."

I broke the connection for a split second and grabbed Steve's shirt. "He's fast! Get on the radio, and tell Mark not to stop for anything! No traffic signs, no lights, cars, nothing. If he's gonna make it, he needs to *haul ass.*"

Perry grabbed the radio. "Hey, Mark, are you listening?"

"Go ahead, Big P."

"The Goat is out of the barn and not on the tractor."

Mark took a couple of seconds to respond. "Say what?"

Perry cleared his throat. "The Goat isn't taking the tractor. He's left the farm—I mean, barn—and he's…" Perry paused and scowled at Steve. "Ah, fuck this! Listen, Mark, the Goatman is tracking you. He's already on your tail and closing in fast. You have to be like Evel Knievel and fly back here. Take every shortcut, and ease up on the brakes when you're going down Kenhill. Don't stop for anything. Got it?"

"Got it. I'll be like greased lightning, Big P."

With the demon's own eyes, I watched Corabas dive through bushes, leap over fences and sheds, and scale huge maples to use as springboards to other trees. Every so often I caught a glimpse of something familiar. "That was city hall; I'm sure of it! He just passed city hall!"

"Good, Chris," Steve said. "Keep with it."

After several more minutes of climbing and running, Corabas quickened his pace as the scent of his prey grew stronger. "He's getting closer!"

Perry got back on the walkie-talkie. "Where are you at?"

"Got a little slowed down on Collington, but I'm doing good now."

"You need to pick it up! The Goatman is closing in on you!"

"Copy that, Big P!"

Steve motioned for us to join him. "Let's get in the protective ring while we wait."

I could hear my brother, but my other senses stayed with Corabas. There were more backyards and woods. Though the route was filled with obstacles, Corabas moved like Spiderman, jumping and weaving his way through what looked like the H Section with ease. He was almost here.

Heavy breathing came over the radio before Mark huffed out, "Okay, crossing over to the beginning of Governor's Bridge Road. Shouldn't be long now."

I watched the forest part before Corabas. About a quarter mile off, I saw a boy furiously pedaling on a bike. "I can see him! I mean, Corabas can. Tell Mark to speed it up! Now!"

"Move it, Mark!" Perry barked on the radio. "The Goatman is on your ass. Give it all you got!"

More heavy breathing preceded one word. "Okay."

Perry stood and turned to leave. "One of us should go out to help him."

Steve grabbed his arm and held fast. "We can't risk it, Perry. Mark has to come to us. He has to make it into the circle. You going out there would just mess things up."

Brian picked up his throwing stars. "Stay out of my way, guys. As soon as I see that old goat, he's gonna get a stomach full of these."

"He's gonna get Mark!" I shouted. "No!" I repeated the word over and over, shaking my head. "No, no, no, I can't watch! I can't see it happen!"

"Move it!" Perry screamed into the radio.

Mark wheezed out two words from lungs that were running on empty. "I'm trying!"

Refusing to be a part of it—to participate in the butchering of my friend—I pulled out of Corabas's mind.

Brian whispered, "Mark?"

Seven seconds of silence followed. I know because I started counting when I bailed from the demon's head.

The metallic *clank* of a bike dropping to the ground broke the tense silence. Mark rounded the bend in the road at full sprint. His eyes flared wide and his mouth locked open in a silent scream. From behind him came a bone-rattling howl. He was about fifty yards out when the Goatman appeared.

Paul and Kevin were the only ones besides me to have seen the demon in all of his glory, but even we were stunned at the sight of the beast barreling toward us. His fur-covered, heavily muscled frame stretched eight feet long as he thundered down Governor's Bridge Road at full gallop. His eyes were embers glowing with hellish rage. Thick black smoke billowed from his mouth as if he was a locomotive racing at top speed.

Perry was the only one able to verbalize the fear we all felt. "Jesus."

We froze in terror and watched as the beast quickly closed the gap. At forty yards out from the circle, it was clear Mark wasn't going to make it. We were going to see him ripped to shreds right in front of us.

To my left came a *pop*. I turned and saw Kevin pulling the slide back on his BB gun. He took aim once more and pulled the trigger. Corabas didn't even flinch, didn't slow down. Kevin had either missed his mark or the pellets were having no effect on the demon. On my opposite side, a spinning silver star whizzed to the far right of Corabas.

Thirty yards away now.

Kevin continued shooting as Brian flung another star. This time it fell short, bouncing along the ground before coming to a rest.

The Goatman stretched a gnarled hand out toward Mark but flinched when something wacked him in the face.

"Damn! Got him with the handle!" Perry shouted.

Corabas quickly recovered from the failed knife attack. He grabbed Mark's shoulder, whipping him around and flinging him to the ground.

Mark raised his hands and screamed as the demon went in for the kill.

Something made a wet *thump*.

The demon paused and looked down to the lawn dart embedded in his foot. He let out a blood-curdling shriek.

We all turned to Paul. His hand was still extended in what had turned out to be the mother of all tosses. He dropped it, glanced at us, and flashed his devilish smile.

"Right on, bro!" Perry yelled.

In the chaos that followed, Mark scrambled to his feet and ran into the circle, greeting Brian and Paul with simultaneous high fives.

The demon yanked the Jart out of his foot and tossed it aside. He looked at us with smoldering eyes, snarled, and then charged.

Out of instinct we got to our knees and huddled, inching as close to one another as possible. I closed my eyes and tried to block out my concerns regarding the potency of our nail-powered shield. As if in response, a pulse of energy flowed up and outwards from the ground. It was quickly followed by the stench of burned flesh and fur and a high-pitched yelp. I looked up to see smoke rising from the Goatman's singed hand. Apparently, the barrier was working just fine.

"Hurry," Steve said. He handed his pocketknife and the cup of blood to Mark and made a cutting motion across his palm.

Mark pressed the edge of the knife against his soft flesh to keep it from shaking in his hand and sliced, running the blade deep. He cursed and dropped it as blood ran in a steady stream.

Paul put a hand to his mouth. "Oh shit!"

"Kevin!" Steve shouted. "Give me your sock, quick!"

Kevin slipped off one of his Nikes, removed a tube sock, and tossed it to Steve.

"Here." Steve wound the cloth around Mark's gashed flesh. "Keep pressure on this, and you'll be fine. That was my fault. Should have helped you with the cut."

"That magic trick of yours won't protect you for long. Soon enough I will be feasting on all of you!" Corabas bellowed.

Mark managed a weak smile as he held the makeshift bandage tight. "Think you got enough of my blood?"

With a shaking hand, Steve took the cup and held it over the *nganga*. He inhaled and then spoke in a loud, steady voice. "A year for a year, the bound one is freed with the sacrifice offered. The bargain made is now unmade!" He poured.

I held my breath as the blood spilled over our noxious stew, waiting for some sign of spiritual liberation. I felt the weight of everyone's eyes on me. Even Corabas stopped his assault. I tensed in anticipation.

"Anything?" Steve asked.

I realized my eyes were shut. I opened them and looked to my brother. "Nothing."

"What the hell?" Perry spouted. "We did everything right! We had all the ingredients, and you quoted the spell word-for-word. Didn't you?"

Before Steve could respond, laughter oozed out of the demon. "Thought you could trick Lukankazi, did you? Fools. So naïve, yet so typical for your generation. You believe you are above the rules. You look for shortcuts where there are none." More laughter followed. "Tell you what, give me the child now, and you may live—all of you. Just push him through the ring, and I will leave. Such a generous offer won't be made again."

I watched Steve as he reread the spell and examined the contents of the *nganga*. "I know I said the words right," he said, scowling. "We had all the ingredients too, right down to the hairs on your head."

"What do we do now?" Brian asked.

"If he stays still long enough, I might be able to shoot him in the eye," Kevin said.

While my friends debated our limited options, I watched Steve's mouth purse as he whispered, "Shortcut."

Rarely does a day go by I don't ask myself what I would have done in that moment if I had known what my brother was about to do. Would I have tried to stop him? Would I have stepped out of the circle and offered myself up to Corabas? I guess none of that matters now. At the time it all happened so fast.

The strangest smile crept across Steve's face and froze there. "That's it." He pulled out his pocketknife and flipped it open. He repeated the spell with no pause, no moment of self-doubt, and then let the knife slip through his hand once more.

I was able to get one word out before his blood—and only his blood—dropped into the container. "No!"

Even in the fading light, I saw the change. Steve's face turned gray and a darkness settled beneath both of his eyes, but the worst part was the sound that slipped from his mouth. The sigh was barely a whisper, but I will never forget it, for it carried away fifteen years of my brother's life.

A tightness spread through every muscle in my body. I strained against an invisible force that drew me closer to the demon. Corabas wailed as he reached for me, but the same power that pulled at my body kept his at bay. I wheezed as all of the air was sucked from my lungs. The world turned gray while little flashes of light danced all around me; I was on the verge of passing out.

Suddenly the building tension snapped like a rubber band stretched too far, and I flew forward, face-planting in the dirt. I lay there for several seconds catching my breath before pushing myself up and spitting a wad of grass from my mouth. Looking to my friends, I said, "It's over. The connection is gone. I'm free."

Corabas ripped up a small tree and shrieked as he flung it over our heads.

Steve looked at me with a tired face. "We have to send him back." He quickly emptied the *nganga* and then added the second mixture of salt, rust, and blessed earth.

"Corabas!" Steve shouted. "We command you to return to Hell!"

A stench of ozone pierced the atmosphere.

Perry waved a hand in front of his face. "Whew!"

Kevin pinched his nose. "Man, it smells like the devil farted!"

The grass beneath the demon browned and died, mixing with the earth to form a black pool of decaying matter. Corabas started to sink.

Mocking laughter preceded his final words. "I am a part of this land, little ones. You think you have stopped me, but I assure you the bonds that connect me to this world—to this place—cannot be so easily undone." Before the muck consumed him, Corabas looked at me with his terrible red eyes and delivered a final warning. "My roots run deep, child, and your cut is too shallow."

Then he was gone.

Chapter 37

An anonymous call was made to the police the next day. The voice on the line said the old man living at 2808 Spindle Lane had died. They also mentioned a hidden basement that should be inspected.

We watched the first police cruiser show up. A little over five minutes later a dozen more swooped in, lining both sides of our usually quiet street. Neighbors came out and stared as gloved officers formed a bizarre kind of bucket brigade, passing along cauldron after cauldron that ended up being loaded in the back of an evidence van. After examining their contents, police were able to identify ten victims—including the ones Russell Drake was accused of murdering. The dipstick was released from jail only to end up back in six months later for selling PCP to an undercover cop.

By the end of the week, they were referring to good ole Mr. Hutchinson as the Butcher of Bowie. For the next month, we couldn't turn on a TV without seeing Corabas's mug plastered on it. Not that it mattered. Even the long arm of the law couldn't get him now, at least not without a pair of oven mitts.

Katie returned to her normal, nagging self after the demon's departure. Fortunately for us, she remembered nothing from her time as Raga. She did, however, develop a rather unusual taste for a six-year-old; deviled ham sandwiches were now on her menu.

Unfortunately, there was one casualty. Baby Jackie was forever lost. I have a sneaky suspicion she met her end at the bottom of one of the Goatman's *ngangas*, but we could never prove it. Mom and Dad were quick on the uptake though, and found the same doll at Toys "R" Us.

With some dirt here and a scratch there, I think we did a darn fine job resurrecting Baby Jackie. As far as I know, Katie never found out.

Within a couple of days of the Showdown at Crybaby Bridge—as we began referring to it—Steve was back to his old self. At least that's what everyone else said. To me, he looked a little older from that day on. There were no wrinkles on his face or white streaks in his hair. Still, every time I looked at him I could see the added years in his eyes…

One good thing that came out of our adventure– aside from me not losing control of my body to a murderous demon—was my renewed tightness Steve. The wall between us, built out of self-doubt and anxiety and plastered together with a steaming pile of resentment, was gone. True, Steve had his friends and I had mine, and we still argued once in a while. But the weeks of silent treatment and spontaneous bareknuckle brawling were gone. Instead, Steve was there to listen to my bitching, dish out a little frank advice, and, on rare occasions, take me down a few pegs when I was acting a little too high and mighty for my own good.

As for the rest of the gang, we spent many more summers together getting into all sorts of trouble around the neighborhood. Fortunately, none of our subsequent adventures involved demonic eighty-year-old neighbors, mallet-wielding kid sisters, or foot-chewing bulldogs.

As it turned out, Bowie had other secrets to share.

About the Author

Raised in Bowie, Maryland, Mark Reefe moved his homestead to the beautiful Shenandoah Valley some years back, where he now resides with his lovely wife, two boys, and two devilish dogs. After a quarter century in federal law enforcement catching drug smugglers, money launderers, and fugitives, he decided to scratch the itch tickling him and start writing. Many of his works blend his experiences along the southern border with supernatural elements in haunting tales that have received numerous accolades. Most recently, his fondness for the urban legends of his old stomping grounds spurred him to write *Spindle Lane*, a darkly nostalgic story of childhood friends facing off against none other than the Goatman of Bowie.

When he's not writing, Mark enjoys woodworking, camping, breaking small appliances when they don't appear to work, apologizing to his wife for breaking the previously mentioned appliances, and bourbon (not necessarily in that order).

Apprentice
House Press
Loyola University Maryland

Apprentice House is the country's only campus-based, student-staffed book publishing company. Directed by professors and industry professionals, it is a nonprofit activity of the Communication Department at Loyola University Maryland.

Using state-of-the-art technology and an experiential learning model of education, Apprentice House publishes books in untraditional ways. This dual responsibility as publishers and educators creates an unprecedented collaborative environment among faculty and students, while teaching tomorrow's editors, designers, and marketers.

Outside of class, progress on book projects is carried forth by the AH Book Publishing Club, a co-curricular campus organization supported by Loyola University Maryland's Office of Student Activities.

Eclectic and provocative, Apprentice House titles intend to entertain as well as spark dialogue on a variety of topics. Financial contributions to sustain the press's work are welcomed. Contributions are tax deductible to the fullest extent allowed by the IRS.

To learn more about Apprentice House books or to obtain submission guidelines, please visit www.apprenticehouse.com.

Apprentice House Press
Communication Department
Loyola University Maryland
4501 N. Charles Street
Baltimore, MD 21210
Ph: 410-617-5265
info@apprenticehouse.com
www.apprenticehouse.com

CPSIA information can be obtained
at www.ICGtesting.com
Printed in the USA
LVHW081936160920
666201LV00018B/388